TO REFORGE A DESTINY

BOOK 2 OF THE RED WOOD SERIES

CLAIRE BUTLER

Page Turner Publishing

Cover by 100covers

Editing by Emily Marquart

CONTENTS

For a certain piscean, because some things are worth protecting.

CONTENT WARNING

Please note: This book contains explicit content and elements that may be triggering to some. It includes explicit sexual scenes, mature language, sexual assault and violence. It is not intended for anyone under the age of 16.

CHAPTER ONE

C itric stood on the parapet as dawning light began to peek over the horizon of the Southern castle. Looking out over the city, he took in every empty street, every thatched-roof house, before moving his gaze beyond the city walls out across the land and further, to the tree line of the Red Wood.

The woodland looked tranquil as it rose out of the morning mist, like a beautiful sleeping beast.

But it was not sleeping.

No, it was wide awake like it hadn't been in centuries. The wood stared back at him, its senses heightened in anticipation, just like the dozens of men from the other camps in the Red Wood who stood waiting beneath its canopy. They had gathered at his written instruction and now stood waiting for his signal to confirm that their ancestral lands had finally been reclaimed.

Citric inhaled a long breath of cool morning air and committed this heartbeat in time to memory. He had lived his whole life for this moment. As a boy, he had seen it in his dreams so many times. His parents had spoken of it as if it were a prophecy. His grandparents had foretold that one day it would come true. The stories had been passed down by his people for generations as they waited, hidden and patient, to take back what had been stolen from them. Most had died with the dream still in their hearts and hope on their lips, praying that it would be realized in their children's lifetime.

His people's existence and attempted annihilation had been burned from the pages of history, covered up by palatable lies, but now history would be re-written with the charred ashes of bloody truth. At the dawning of this auspicious day, the course of the future would change forever.

Retrieving an arrow from his quiver, Citric ran the fletching goose feathers through his calloused fingers. He wrapped a piece of soaked cloth around the arrowhead and struck a flint on the castle wall. Setting the arrowhead aflame, he knocked it into his longbow and raised it up to the cloudless sky. Citric watched as it flew over the city and past the outer castle wall, a soaring arc of hope and retribution in the dawning sky.

Brielle was born in the castle of the Southern Kingdom and had lived there her entire life. She had walked every hall, explored every chamber, and supervised the interior decorating of most rooms. But she had never in her life even thought of, let alone ventured to, the dungeon. She tried to steel her nerves as the King's Guard—now Citric's guards—escorted her down a narrow, stone staircase. Down, down, and around it went, descending into murky shadows and rotten air. She had thought fleeing her birthright to live as a traitor in the Red Wood amongst outlaws and rebels was the lowest she could fall.

She was wrong.

This was worse.

On the last step, the staircase opened into a dark room, dimly lit by two sconces. Directly ahead of her were three cells.

"Brielle!" Henri rushed to clutch the bars of the middle cell.

She could see Jameson behind him, furiously pacing.

"Henri." Brielle tried to go to him, but one of her escorts blocked her path.

"Remove your weapons."

Brielle blinked up at him, the picture of feminine innocence. "What weapons?"

They had already taken her crossbow and the dagger from her belt when they arrested her in the council chamber.

"Don't play games, girl."

"Girl?" Brielle spat the word at him like it was venom. "It's Your Highness, you—"

"Not anymore. Now, remove your weapons or we will remove them for you. Lady Evelyn warned us you were armed."

So Eve got to be called a lady while she was reduced to a girl. There was nothing ladylike about that wretched traitor. Brielle schooled her features into a coy smile.

"Oh, my boot." She daintily lifted her right foot. "I clear forgot it was there."

The guard bent down to retrieve the short, slim dagger tucked inside her boot. He passed it to his comrade, who was standing behind her, before fixing her with a hard stare.

"And the other one."

"What other one?"

The guard moved so fast she barely had time to put up a defense as his hands reached down the front of her bodice. She screamed as she tried to twist herself away to protect her modesty, but the guard behind her grasped her shoulders tight, keeping her firmly in place.

"Don't touch her, you bastards!" Henri yelled.

"All right, all right, stop!" Brielle shrieked.

The guard behind her released her shoulders, while the guard in front of her took a measured step back. Even then, he was still towering over her; a wall of muscle, a brute brick. She glared at him as she retrieved the dagger from her bodice and handed it over. He passed the weapon to his comrade and gestured for her to enter the first cell. Brielle's eyes slid to the second cell where Henri and Jameson were being held, before resting on the third cell where someone was curled up on a pile of straw against the wall.

Her gaze returned to the cell in front of her as she took slow steps toward it. The floor and walls were made of black stone, which seemed to be covered in a damp sheen of gray mildew. The cell itself was barely wide enough to lie down in. Someone had dumped a pile of straw in the corner, an attempt at bedding perhaps. A foul-smelling, soiled, crusted bucket sat in the opposite corner. Her short steps inevitably landed her inside the bars, and the guard made quick work of securing the door behind her. The sound of the lock clicking into place made her body shiver with panic.

"Are you all right? Are you hurt?" Henri asked as he stood at the bars which joined their cells.

She couldn't look at him, couldn't seem to tear her eyes away from her abysmal surroundings. She was in shock. Utter disbelief. Today was the day she was meant to become Queen of the Southern Kingdom or die trying. And she had failed at both. How had it come to this?

"Where is my wife?" Jameson called out, his voice strained as if he had been yelling for hours.

Brielle turned to see that the guards who had escorted her had already left, leaving behind one guard standing on either side of the staircase. *A bit of an overreaction,* she thought. They posed no threat from behind bars, especially without weapons.

"I demand to speak to Citric!" Jameson yelled.

The guards stared straight ahead as if they didn't have eyes or ears.

"Sienna is fine." Brielle tried to soothe him.

He turned on her, his face gaunt with anger and worry. "We left her with them!"

It was true. They had left his pregnant wife, Brielle's best friend, at Alkhiem, thinking she would be safe there. But now they knew they had left her with the enemy.

"They won't harm her," Brielle insisted.

At least she hoped they wouldn't.

Jameson hissed between his teeth and resumed pacing.

Brielle lifted her eyes to Henri, and at the sight of him, tears threatened to spill onto her cheeks. He looked like he had been to hell itself. Her voice was fragile as she asked, "What happened?"

Henri's features darkened. "Citric betrayed us."

"How?"

"When we found the private study, I went in alone to confront Nathaniel."

"Nathaniel?"

"The Butcher," Jameson explained with a heavy look.

Brielle's eyes widened as her mouth parted in shock. Henri averted his gaze, as if he was ashamed of the truth. Thoughts swirled around in her head making her dizzy. How long had Henri known that the Butcher was Nathaniel? Why had he never said anything? Had he really been prepared to kill his friend?

"When the warning bells sounded," Henri went on, "Citric broke down the door and shot an arrow into his shoulder. I should have known then that something was wrong."

Indeed. Citric was an expert bowman. He did not miss.

"Within minutes the guards were upon us, but Nathaniel ordered them to stand down."

Brielle considered this for a moment before she concluded, "Citric spared Nathaniel's life because he knew that Nathaniel would surrender the King's Guard if your life was in immediate danger."

Henri furrowed his eyebrows. "How could he possibly know that?"

"Eve."

The girl had the eyes of a hawk. Always watching, observing every minute detail. Even though Henri and Nathaniel had only been at the Southern castle for a brief week over a year ago, she must have seen something to convince her of Nathaniel's loyalty to him. Henri shifted his weight between his feet as if the knowledge made him uncomfortable.

"After Nathaniel relinquished control of the King's Guard, Citric ordered our arrest," he continued.

"Why didn't you take control of the King's Guard?"

"Citric would have killed Nathaniel." His expression was grave, but his tone sounded like he regretted his choice.

Brielle exhaled a deep breath. "Where is Nathaniel now?"

Henri looked over to the third cell, where a body lay curled up against the wall.

Brielle's lips parted in surprise. "How is he still alive?"

"One of Citric's men came in and tended to his wound. He passed out from the pain or the blood loss, I'm not sure which."

Henri turned back to her and she could see the war of emotions on his face. Anger and hurt, fear and hope. She could only imagine what it would have been like for him to find out that his closest friend was the right hand of King Heroux, the man who had killed his father. And hers.

"What happened with Eve?" Henri asked.

"We were waiting in the stairwell when a servant girl walked in on us. She ran out into the courtyard and raised the alarm."

At the time, Brielle had thought it was bad luck, but now she knew better; it was carefully planned. Eve had been their sole eyes and ears at court. She would have known the movements of everyone, including the servant girl. She would have used that knowledge to ensure they would be discovered.

"We tried to run and barricade ourselves inside the council chamber, but the King's Guard saw us and ..." Brielle hesitated, recalling those frantic moments, the fear and panic. "We had to defend ourselves."

She did not say how a guard had almost crushed her windpipe with his bare hands, squeezing the very breath from her lungs. Nor did she confess to plunging a knife into his neck and watching the life drain from his eyes before his body slumped to her feet. But she knew Henri could see the bruises blooming on her neck and the blood splattered on her dress, her hands, her face. There were some things Brielle could not say out loud just yet, could not even admit to herself.

"When the warning bells stopped, Citric found us. He claimed that the Northern and Southern Kingdoms had once belonged to his people and that a great army had waged war against them. The conquerors slaughtered his people and claimed the land for themselves, then divided it into two kingdoms and wrote the Old Treaty. He said he was righting a wrong by reclaiming the land."

Henri's face was impassive as he listened to the story. He did not rage or condemn these preposterous claims. He seemed to accept them. Or worse—not care about them at all.

"Did you hear what I said?"

"I heard you."

"Then say something."

"What is there to say?"

"He is claiming that we are not the rightful heirs! It's a lie! He has been lying to us this whole time, pretending that he did not want to be a part of this campaign when really it was his plan the whole time to make himself king. We have been unwitting pawns in his game. Every word that he has ever said, everything that he has ever done, has been a lie."

Including what had happened between them. Brielle wondered if that had also been a part of his plan; to seduce her so that she would trust him. Or perhaps it had been a simple distraction, serving no purpose other than a moment's pleasure.

She wasn't sure which one was worse.

"The truth does not matter. He has won." Henri turned away from her and walked to stand at the back of the cell. His body slid down the wall to the ground in defeat.

Brielle watched him, outraged. He didn't care. Of course he didn't care. She shouldn't be surprised. King Heroux had stolen his kingdom from him and he didn't care. Now that it had been stolen again by Citric he still didn't care. He had not joined this campaign to reclaim his kingdom. He had joined to help her reclaim hers. And while he might be angry at Citric for betraying them, he did not feel the puncturing wound to his soul of losing his kingdom all over again. He felt nothing of the agony of what she was feeling right now.

Brielle wanted to scream at him, to tear her lungs out and shatter the world into a million pieces. She had risked everything for this, including her own life and the lives of those she cared about the most. She had suffered every humiliation, rose to every challenge, only to have her birthright stolen away from her. Again. By a man she trusted. By a man she had given herself to. By—a man.

There were no words for the tempest of emotions surging inside her right now. The betrayal cut to her very bones. She felt numb from disbelief, anger beyond rage, the deepest ocean of pain, and utter exhaustion. As if every ounce of emotional and physical strength had been drained from her, leaving behind an empty, worthless, storm-ravaged shell.

Brielle stared blankly at Henri, wishing he would say something, do something, feel something. But he didn't. Because he was not a king and she was not a queen. Because there was nothing left to say, and nothing left to do but wait.

The hours passed by slowly, but eventually the changing of the guard spelled the end of the day. No one had spoken a word in hours. Jameson had screamed himself hoarse, demanding to speak with Citric, his desperation for news of Sienna rising with every hour that passed. Now, though, he stalked the length of his cell in silence while Henri sat against the wall, his knees drawn up in front of him. Nathaniel had not stirred once. Brielle was beginning to wonder if he was still alive.

Over time, her thoughts had gone quiet, as if they too were exhausted. This morning they had flittered about like birds trapped in a cage, frantically trying to grasp onto slivers of hope for escape. Like perhaps the King's Guard would rebel against Citric once they learned their princess had been imprisoned. Citric's men would be no match for the King's Guard, despite half their numbers being sent away on a fool's errand of her creation. Citric would not be able to hold the castle with thirty men.

Yet she hadn't heard any sounds of rebellion. She had tried to convince herself that they must not know of her imprisonment, but she didn't believe her own lies. They knew, and they didn't care. It was near impossible to keep a secret at court. Word would have spread by now that the Butcher had been imprisoned, the traitors to the Crown had been captured, and the Southern Kingdom had been liberated from the tyrannical rule of King Heroux. Victory belonged to the notorious Vogel.

She wanted to laugh. It sounded fanciful. Like a story a bard would tell. Something so unbelievable that it could never have actually happened. And yet, here she was. Born a princess, forced to live as a fugitive, and now a prisoner.

In her own castle.

Brielle clenched her jaw until her teeth hurt. She looked over into the next cell to see that Jameson had finally stopped pacing. He was now standing in the middle of the cell, looking lost. It was like he would not allow himself to sit down for even a minute because that would be accepting the situation. Henri simply stared ahead into nothingness, more than willing to accept the situation.

She glared at him even as she rubbed a hand along her arms, trying to generate some heat. Brielle was thankful for the small measure of warmth the two sconces provided, but she knew all too well that as night fell, the temperature would descend into a bitter cold. She doubted they would be given blankets or bedding. Then again, she had been surprised when, about an hour ago, servants had delivered food and water under the watchful eye of the guards. It was basic: bread, cheese, and dried fruits. But even so, it was an unexpected mercy.

Brielle wondered how long they would remain down here, and what exactly Citric intended to do with them. When she voiced these thoughts out loud, Jameson had explained that this section of the dungeon was separate from the main dungeon because it was specially designed to hold temporary prisoners. Prisoners were brought to these cells to await trial, or to live out their last night before public execution. Neither thought was comforting, and Brielle did not speculate any more after that.

At the echo of boots coming down the stone staircase, everyone's heads snapped up. Jameson rushed to the bars, gripping them anxiously until his knuckles turned white. Henri and Brielle exchanged a wary look before pushing themselves to their feet. At the sight of Citric, Brielle's heart swelled with hate, so much so it made her nauseous. How dare he stand in front of them without a trace of remorse on his face, without a hint of guilt or regret in his eyes.

She was going to kill him. Slowly. And she would enjoy it.

"Celebrating, are we?" Brielle's tone was sickly sweet as she jerked her chin to the cup in Citric's hand.

"Where is Sienna?" Jameson demanded, but the sound was more like a croak. His throat was screamed raw.

"In Alkhiem, safe," Citric replied. "You have my word she will not be harmed."

"Your word means nothing anymore."

"My word means as much as it did yesterday. I told you I would help you reclaim these lands, restore the peace, and protect the people. I have kept my word."

"You failed to mention the part where you betray me and steal my kingdom," Brielle shot back.

"I cannot steal something that is not yours."

She clenched her fists, her eyes blazing.

Citric ignored her and turned to address Jameson. "Once I have secured the castle, I will send for your wife. Or ... " He cocked his head, as if he were considering something.

Jameson went deathly still.

"You can swear allegiance to me now and retrieve her yourself."

Jameson gripped the bars eagerly. "I will swear whatever you want. Just let me see my wife."

Citric flicked his gaze back to Brielle, and she tried not to wince at the sting of betrayal. Jameson had sworn an oath to her, to his queen, to protect her. Sienna had personally charged him with her safety. But he had also sworn a vow to his wife on their wedding day, and Brielle knew that nothing in this world would ever surpass that. Part of her was grateful for it, for knowing that Jameson would protect her friend at all costs, no matter what happened.

But his words still hurt. Citric gave a nod of acceptance before focusing his attention on Henri.

"I will make you the same offer. Swear allegiance to me and you will be set free. You may return to the Sodisce or go elsewhere. Wherever you choose."

Brielle held her breath. Henri didn't look at her, but she knew he could feel her eyes on him, watching him, waiting for his answer. It was all he had ever wanted: freedom. A life of anonymity, the life of a simple man. Would she be able to forgive him for abandoning her? For relinquishing his oath to protect her? She knew she shouldn't resent him for accepting such an offer, but she also knew that her heart would wither to ash if he did.

"Take it."

Nathaniel's strained words startled all of them. She had thought him dead, or at the very least unconscious. Henri shot his friend a murderous look, as if he might rebuke him for daring to speak to him.

Instead, he mastered himself and turned back to Citric, his voice tight. "What about Nathaniel? Will you make him the same offer?"

"No." Citric's features hardened. "If he lives from his wound, he will be executed for his crimes. The people demand justice. And so do I."

Something flickered across Henri's face before it turned to smooth stone. "And Brielle?"

"He should kill me."

She stalked closer to the bars as if she were a predator. She didn't care that her words were signing her own death warrant, that she was tempting the worst kind of fate. She was beyond fearing for her life. She had endured losing everything that had ever mattered to her—twice over. There was nothing more he could do to her, nothing more she could not bear, and nothing she was not willing to do in order to have a chance to rip his throat out.

"But we both know you won't do it," she purred as she fixed her eyes on him in blatant challenge.

He had said those words to her in the river that day when she had held his own blade to his throat. And he had been right. That girl would have never drawn the knife across his throat, or anyone else's. But she was no longer that girl. She had killed. She had watched men die right in front of her. Their blood was still caked on her skin. Citric's expression remained unmoved, but she knew that he recognized those words. Perhaps he was even thinking about what else had almost happened between them that day.

"I have no need to kill you," he said dismissively. "I could simply keep you locked up here forever as my prisoner."

A sly smile spread across his lips.

Brielle's cheeks flamed. "I am the rightful heir to the Southern Kingdom. A clear threat to your reign."

"You are no threat to me."

"My people will rise up against you in my name."

"I don't think so." Citric shifted his weight, his stance infuriatingly nonchalant. "The people want peace and prosperity and protection from injustice. I can give that to them."

She scoffed. "They will never accept you. You are not of noble blood. You are an outlaw. Even worse, you are a pagan."

Citric regarded her as if her words had no merit at all.

"You have no legitimate claim to the throne!" she insisted.

"I have the only legitimate claim. The land has and always will belong to my people. That is my claim."

She shook her head stubbornly. "They will never accept you."

"If she swears allegiance to you," Henri interjected, throwing her a stern look, "will you set her free?"

Brielle balked, incredulous. "I will never!"

"Brielle," Henri hissed in warning.

"I refuse to be banished from my own kingdom! Sent across the sea to become some merchant's wife. I would rather die."

"If she swears allegiance to me, she may live here at court." Citric directed his words to Henri.

They were negotiating her fate as if she were not standing right in front of them. As if she had no say in the matter. She might as well have been screaming into the wind. Citric slowly slid his eyes back to her. Once she had thought his eyes to be mesmerizing, like water trapped under ice. Now they just looked cruel.

"I will even allow you to keep your title as princess and marry a nobleman of your choosing. But you will be a princess in title only, and you will never be queen of these lands."

Brielle pressed her lips into a defiant line. So he wished to placate her with a false title and a noble husband while he stripped her of her true power. If he thought she was going to be grateful for his benevolence, he was sorely mistaken.

Reading the insolence on her face, Citric turned away from her and gestured to one of the guards to open the door of the middle cell. Jameson stepped back to give them room, his body tense as if he might spring free the moment the door opened.

"You will swear allegiance to me now and be on your way to your wife. If you ever try to come against me, I will kill you," Citric warned.

Jameson nodded in acceptance and threw a sidelong glance at Brielle as he stepped out of the cell. She dipped her chin in understanding and forgiveness.

Jameson dropped to a knee before Citric and bowed his head. "I swear on my faith and my honor and before the witnesses here today that I will be true and faithful to you as my king, pledging to you my undying loyalty, the strength of my sword, and the truth of my words, all the days of my life."

Jameson stood and Citric passed the cup to the guard before he unsheathed the dagger at his side. Brielle stilled, but Jameson didn't resist when Citric took hold of his hand and sliced open his right palm. Then he drew the blade across his own palm and clasped hands with Jameson in strength.

"My blood is now your blood, my life force your life force. You have chosen me, and I have chosen you as a blood brother. Wherever destiny takes us, we will be as one. Let the man who would break his oath to his blood brother be forever cursed."

Brielle watched, transfixed by the strange ritual. Usually oaths were sworn on a holy book or consecrated relic during an official court ceremony, but somehow what she had just witnessed felt infinitely more powerful.

It felt sacred.

Citric released Jameson's bloody hand and stalked past him to the third cell. "You will be executed in three days, if you live that long."

Nathaniel didn't respond.

Citric retrieved the cup from the guard and then turned back to Brielle and Henri. "You have three days to decide if you will swear the oath to me. If you do not, you can choose whether to remain my prisoner forever or share his fate."

Brielle stiffened. He was bluffing. He had to be. Mere hours ago he had been inside her and now he was threatening to end her. She could not believe that he would be capable of carrying out such a threat. But then she wouldn't have believed him capable of such betrayal.

The more she thought about it, the more the truth unraveled before her eyes. He had been planning this from the very first day they fled into the Red Wood. Citric's men had been watching them. They would have heard her lamenting and scheming for her kingdom. They would have followed them as they traveled along the edges of the wood to Clontarf. Maybe even followed them to the Sodisce to see who they were meeting with. In any case, they had been ready for them when they fled back into the Red Wood pursued by the King's Guard. They had escaped King Heroux's men only to run right into Citric's trap.

It was not like they had a choice in trusting them. It was either trust them or be slaughtered by the King's Guard. Still, Citric had played his role to perfection, not rushing his hand but waiting for the perfect opportunity to offer her the assistance of a mysterious wealthy benefactor. Someone who, she had later learned from Henri, he had placed at court a year earlier to be his spy. To establish herself in the heart of the court, Brielle's ladies' court, and gain valuable information to feed his rebel cause.

Eve had changed her face so often, she belonged on a stage. From the young impressionable lady at court eager to gain acceptance from her betters to the reckless rebel pining after the infamous outlaw, she had been a key player in this deception. Together they had fooled them with their playacting, pretending to be at odds with one another, even to the point of fighting each other to prove how little Citric wanted to be a part of her campaign. All so she would not see him as a threat or question his willingness to help her.

Clearly Citric had been playing this game for a long time, and Brielle had been too short-sighted, too desperate to see it. She had been wrong about him, so very wrong. The truth was, she did not know what he was capable of. It scared her to think there might be no lines he was not willing to cross.

Brielle watched as Citric approached her cell and held the cup out to her through the bars.

"Poison?" She arched a mocking eyebrow.

"Tea."

"Tea?"

Brielle's scornful expression slipped as she felt the blood drain from her face in realization. She had heard talk of girls drinking herbal tea to rid themselves of unwanted pregnancies.

"Oh," Henri growled knowingly, and her heart plummeted through the floor. "You are a rutting bastard."

❧⟡☙

Henri sat with his back against the wall, his legs drawn up in front of him, bloody knuckles draped over his knees. He had punched the stone wall in a blind fit of fury. He had most likely broken some knuckles, but he didn't care. The pain only fueled his rage. He wanted to murder someone. To tear someone apart limb from limb and then start all over again. His fury was a ravenous beast detained in iron chains, straining to be unleashed. Even after an hour's silence, he did not trust himself to speak. His blood was still boiling at the thought of it. The thought of them. The thought of Citric—

Henri pinched his eyes closed and clenched his jaw until he thought it might crack. He had feared it would happen. He had known what Citric was capable of. Henri was not a fool. He had seen the way Brielle's eyes followed him in a crowd, the subtle change in her behavior whenever he was around. He had noticed Citric's behavior too. The way he appeared largely indifferent to Brielle, with some fleeting moments of vague, fickle interest. As if she were easy prey and he preferred more challenging game.

Turned out Citric had been right. She had been incredibly easy. She had fallen into bed with him as easily as she had fallen for his betrayal. Henri had known it would happen if she spent the night alone with him, but he had failed to stop it. He had begged her to come with him and she had chosen not to. She had chosen Citric. Perhaps she had been hoping he would seduce her. Perhaps she had even initiated the seduction herself. The thought made him want to hurl his guts up.

"Henri."

Brielle's whisper chafed against his raw anger. She had quietly approached the bars connecting their cells and he hadn't even realized. He refused to look at her. He couldn't. She would never look the same again.

"Henri."

"I don't want to talk about it." His words sounded dangerous, even to his own ears.

"We have to talk about it," Brielle insisted. "We have three days to talk about it."

Right. She didn't want to talk about her utter stupidity in giving herself to that bastard. She wanted to talk about whether he would swear allegiance or not. After everything that had happened, after everything she had done, she still expected him to stand by her side all the way to the butcher's block. A martyr for her failed cause.

"It's over, Brielle." He bit out the words one by one.

"Could you come a little closer, perhaps?" she asked pointedly.

He reluctantly raised his eyes to her, and she tilted her head to insinuate her concern. The guards. She wanted him to come closer so that they could whisper to each other without being overheard. No doubt the guards would be reporting every word they said back to Citric. But the thought of being close to her, of scenting her skin and looking into her beautiful face, knowing that Citric's lips had kissed her lips, his hands had touched her skin, his tongue had tasted her—

"There's nothing to discuss," he snarled and turned away. "We swear allegiance or we die. You will still be a princess, and I will get to live my life in peace. End of story."

A heartbeat of silence passed. "Are you angry with me?"

For the love of fucking god.

He swallowed all the harsh words on his tongue like razor blades. If he opened his mouth, he would certainly say some things he could never take back. And even though she would deserve every word, he didn't want to hurt her. He didn't know why he still cared. She clearly didn't care about him.

"Because of what happened last night?" she asked carefully.

His eyes flashed at her in warning. "I don't want to talk about it."

"Good, because I'm not going to talk about it. In fact, it's none of your business. It has nothing to do with you. And you have absolutely no reason to be angry with me."

"No reason!" he roared.

"Yes," she replied firmly. "No reason. You are acting like I betrayed you. I didn't. I never could. Because I was never yours to begin with."

He felt like he'd been stabbed through the heart. The stinging truth of her words spread slowly through his mind like poison infecting a well. She was right. She had never been his. Maybe that was his fault. He should have told her how he felt about her.

Should have kissed her the dozens of times he'd wanted to but hadn't. Something always seemed to get in the way. An argument usually, like the one they were having right now. He was always falling short of her expectations, and she was always calling him to task over his decisions. But now it was the other way around. He was disappointed in hers.

Uncomfortable silence settled in the space between them until she finally gave up. Letting go of the bars with a huff, she wandered over to sit down next to the pile of straw in the corner of her cell. The empty cup sat beside her, the only remaining evidence of what had occurred last night. He could still feel the heat of her eyes on him before she laid down on the stone floor and curled up into herself for warmth. Sleep was a welcome thought. The very marrow in his bones was tired. But he knew he would get no sleep tonight. It was all he could do to keep his breathing steady and his fists from pounding the stone wall until he broke every bone in his hands.

CHAPTER TWO

B rielle felt wretched. Her sleep had been painfully uncomfortable thanks to the hard stone floor, the biting cold, her roiling emotions, and the combative thoughts that interrogated her mind for hours. From Citric's betrayal to Henri's self-righteous condemnation, her thoughts and emotions erupted. Without any windows, it was difficult to tell the hour, whether it was morning or still night. In any case, she was done trying to sleep. She hauled herself up into a seated position. Henri was still sitting with his back against the wall, eyes staring forward, as if he hadn't moved or slept at all.

Good.

She hoped he felt as miserable as she did.

He didn't speak to her, though she knew he was aware of her sitting up. She had no intention of speaking to him either. She had absolutely no interest in hearing more of his sanctimonious judgments. She would only be interested in a profound, groveling apology. Which, judging from the deafening silence, was not forthcoming.

Brielle sighed. She wondered if Citric would come today to see if they had made a decision. Or worse, if Henri would tell the guards to fetch Citric so that he could swear allegiance to him and be on his way. He probably wouldn't even say goodbye to her. The thought made her eyes sting with tears, but she quickly willed them away. If their friendship was so fragile that it could not survive her making choices he didn't agree with, then so be it.

The thought made her pause. She remembered that day in the woods when he was teaching her how to defend herself. She had challenged him about his choice to do nothing in the face of King Heroux's destruction. He had told her that she did not have to agree with his choices. She hadn't. And she'd kept trying to change his mind, to guilt him into wanting to become a king and reclaim his kingdom.

It was different, her mind protested. She had slept with Citric, made a selfish choice for one night of her life. Her actions hadn't hurt anyone. Henri had turned his back on his people, made a selfish choice to change the entire course of his life. His actions had had dire consequences for many. His choice had contributed to the deaths of hundreds. It was different. And yet it was the same. They had both seized a rare moment in time to make a choice that was purely their own. To taste the freedom of a life they had never known and may never know again. Perhaps they had both chosen wrong. There had been consequences. But maybe the choice itself was understandable.

Time passed before a servant girl appeared to deliver three plates of food, placing them down in front of each cell. Brielle was the first to retrieve hers. She bit into an apple despite the fact that she had no appetite. She was bored and it was something to do.

Henri eventually moved to retrieve his food and then returned to sit against the wall. They ate in silence until there was nothing left, but somehow, she still felt empty.

She would forgive him, she realized. When he swore allegiance to Citric and left her here to pursue his simple life, she would forgive him. He was right. They had no choice. The only other way out of here was death. She would not ask him to give up his life for her. For a cause that was clearly lost.

For now.

She had been wrong about Citric. Blinded by her attraction to him, she had misunderstood and underestimated him. But Citric was about to find out how wrong he had been too. He thought he could take her kingdom and rule it with ease, winning the people over with the simple promise of peace and prosperity. But every ruler worth their crown knows it is not the people who decide who sits on the throne. It's the nobles.

Citric had no understanding of court hierarchy, or how to manage the nobles, or how to play the delicate game of politics. He had no friends at court, no allies. Perhaps she did not need to lead a rebellion against him; he was guaranteed to destroy himself. Or maybe he would anger the nobles enough that they would rebel against him, even without her influence. All she needed to do was sit back and wait.

Martyrdom would not serve her. She couldn't reclaim her kingdom if she was dead. Two nights ago, she had sworn that she would make the necessary sacrifices for her kingdom, no matter the personal cost to herself. Swearing allegiance to that traitor was no different from swearing a marriage vow to a stranger for political gain. She would say the words and she would play the game.

He was in her court now.

Brielle smirked in anticipation, but as her eyes caught on the plate of untouched food in front of the third cell, it slipped from her lips. Nathaniel remained curled in a ball against the wall. He had not said a word or moved an inch since yesterday. Pushing herself to her feet, Brielle walked to the end of her cell and strained her neck to get a better look. She couldn't tell if he was breathing.

"Henri."

Brielle was certain he would ignore her, but there must have been something in her tone that betrayed her concern because he lifted his eyes to her.

"Nathaniel hasn't eaten."

Henri tensed at the sight of the full plate. He got to his feet, his movements noticeably stiff, and walked to the bars connecting their cells.

"Nathaniel."

He didn't move.

"Is he breathing?" Brielle asked.

"Nathaniel." Henri's tone turned urgent. "Guard! We need a healer!"

Brielle watched the guards exchange an anxious look before one of them hurried up the stairway. The remaining one shifted nervously on his feet, clutching the hilt of his sword as if he were expecting an attack.

"For goodness sake, open the door and check on him!" Brielle admonished, but the guard didn't move. "Your new king will be very displeased if you let the Butcher die before he can publicly execute him."

The guard's eyes darted back and forth as he weighed up his options.

"Don't bother."

Brielle exhaled in relief at Nathaniel's voice. Henri swore and ran his hands down his face. He paced away from the bars, only to pivot back to them.

"Why didn't you answer me, damn you?"

Nathaniel didn't reply.

"And why haven't you eaten your food?"

"What's the point?"

Brielle bit her lip. He sounded weak. He was badly wounded, and had obviously lost a lot of blood. If he starved himself, he might not last three days.

"Is that the death you would prefer?" Henri said. "A coward's death?"

"Death is death."

Henri went rigid. Brielle watched him carefully. She could not imagine the emotions he was experiencing, knowing his closest friend was condemned to die. If it was Sienna, she would be prostrating herself on the ground, inconsolable, yet he was as stoic as stone. It was as if he had closed himself off to feeling anything but anger. Perhaps anger was easier to feel than hurt.

She wondered when he had learned that the Butcher was his friend. That his friend had turned into a brutal murderer. Perhaps that was what numbed him, the fact that he didn't recognize his friend at all.

"You have three days to live." Brielle's voice was quiet as she intervened. "How you choose to spend that time is up to you. But if it were me, I would use it to make peace. With yourself. And with those you care about."

Her eyes darted between them hopefully.

"There is no peace for people like me." Nathaniel's words were flat.

"You're right, you don't deserve it." Henri walked away only to turn on his heel again. "You at least owe me some answers. Why didn't you kill me that day?"

"Which day?"

Henri flinched and Brielle's heart quickened at the escalating tension. Clearly, there was history here she did not know about.

Nathaniel heaved a sigh and grunted in pain as he shifted position. "It doesn't matter."

"It matters to me. You had no reservations about killing hundreds of innocent people, but not me? Why should I be any different?"

Silence.

"And don't pretend you had no choice. You had every chance to speak out about your father plotting against the king and you chose not to. You led us both to that battlefield knowing everything that would happen, and you only changed your mind at the last minute because fate drew me out of that tent. If I had stayed, I would have been murdered just like my father."

Brielle's eyes widened in horror. She knew her father had been killed by the enemy's sword, but she'd had no idea that the enemy was within his own army. Nathaniel's father, the commander. They had conspired with King Heroux to assassinate Henri's father. And hers.

"Your father would not have believed me."

"But I would have." Henri pounded a fist into his chest. "I would have believed you. We could have prevented this whole nightmare."

"No, we couldn't have. Anyway, it doesn't matter now."

"Stop saying that it does not matter! You betrayed me!"

"I saved your life," Nathaniel shot back. "Twice."

"Why?!"

Brielle's heart slammed against her rib cage as she watched them; a bear attacking a wounded serpent. She didn't know all the details, but she did know this: Nathaniel had spared Henri's life that day on the battlefield, and yesterday he had surrendered the King's Guard to save him. The emotion in Nathaniel's voice was not feigned. He had no strength left to deceive and no reason to lie. His face was difficult to read, but there was a flicker of something there, hidden behind his eyes, in the words he would not say.

Brielle furrowed her brow. "Citric knew. That Nathaniel spared your life that day on the battlefield. That's why he was so confident Nathaniel would surrender the King's Guard if your life was in danger. He might have even known about the commander's plot against the King."

Henri looked at her as he calculated the implications in his head. "Which means Eve is not his only spy."

She shook her head in wonder and disbelief. How many spies did Citric have? What other secrets did he know?

"You need to swear allegiance to him," Nathaniel said wearily, as if the conversation had exhausted him. "Swear it and walk out of here. Live your life and never think of me again."

Brielle's heart softened a little at his words, but she wasn't sure Henri's heart was even beating.

Citric stood in the cold shadow of the church that loomed in front of him. His eyes assessed the building's façade, from its polished stone steps all the way up to its gable roof. It was an impressive structure. No doubt the life's work of many men, the pride of many masonry artists, and the cost of a small fortune.

Citric ascended the steps one by one, flanked by a dozen of his men, and strolled past the large, open oak doors. Inside, the church was even more remarkable. On either side of the nave was a row of marble columns that delineated the aisles, all the way down the rectangular room. He tilted his head back to see that near the ceiling a band of windows fitted with beautiful stained glass stretched for the entire length of the room. At the far end of the nave, above an intricately carved marble altar, was a semi-circular half-dome roof. It was painted with a breath-taking mural of angels and saints flying amidst the clouds.

"Can I help you?" A bishop approached them, his eyes wary.

The bishop was a short man with a bulging belly and a balding head, but one would think he was a saint himself with how he looked down his nose at them. It was to be expected, Citric supposed. They were pagans after all. They worshiped the natural world instead of some invisible God created in man's image for man's vanity. Citric noted the rings on the bishop's hands: rubies, emeralds, gold. His religious garment, though simple, was made of the finest fabric.

"Yes, Father, I believe you can." His smile was that of a wolf. "The people of the Southern Kingdom are starving and in need of your aid. I'm sure, as a man of God, you would have no hesitation in giving everything in your possession to help them."

At his words, Citric's men began to disperse and the bishop blanched in realization. Citric merely stepped around him, heading for the marble altar.

"No!" The bishop waved his arms frantically. "You are not welcome here. This is a house of God! It is under God's protection."

"I'm sure God would not want his people to starve," Citric tossed over his shoulder.

The protestations of the priests echoed within the walls of the church as Citric's men systematically went from room to room, collecting all the wealth on display, as well as the wealth that was hidden. They would leave no jewel, coin, or tapestry behind. Years of raiding wealthy travelers had taught them to be efficient and effective.

Citric surveyed the marble altar in front of him. A rich red velvet cloth lined the surface, and several gold candlestick holders sat on top, each of them displaying tall wax tapers. He licked his thumb and index finger before pinching the flames out one after the other. The candlesticks would fetch a fair price, as would the cloth.

"This is outrageous! God will smite you and your men!"

Citric slowly turned to see the bishop standing behind him, his cheeks ruddy with fury.

"Do you recall months ago granting sanctuary to two young women?" His tone was casual, but the bishop's eyes narrowed cautiously to slits as he gradually approached him.

"The church offers sanctuary to many people in need."

"You would remember these two women. One of them was the Southern princess."

The bishop's lips twitched in irritation. He did remember them. Sienna had told Citric how she and Brielle had fled the castle in the middle of the night after receiving Henri's message. They had sought sanctuary in this very church.

"I'm sure you offered them your finest hospitality," Citric drawled.

"She was a traitor—!"

Citric's arm shot out to grab the bishop's throat, cutting off his feeble justifications. The bishop's eyes bulged in fear as his fingers clawed at Citric's hand, trying to pry his viselike grip from around his neck. But the bishop's eyes changed from fear to panic as Citric's other hand pried the rings from his fingers one by one.

Pulling him closer, Citric whispered in his ear, "Because they lived, I will spare your life. But if I ever see you near the Southern princess again, not even your invisible God will be able to save you from me."

A second day passed before Citric came to the dungeon. Henri knew he could have called for him, told him his decision and been on his way already. And yet he hadn't. Because if he did, that would be the end. He would never see his friend again, at least not in this life.

Odd how he still thought of Nathaniel as his friend. He was the person who knew him best in this world. His happiest memories, his darkest days, Nathaniel had witnessed them all. He knew the worst thoughts he'd ever had, the endless pit of his inadequacies, his secret desires, and more. Nathaniel had never judged him for any of it. So Henri stayed. Because that was all he could do for his friend; sit in the cell next to him and wait.

They didn't speak again. There was nothing to say. There was everything to say. Brielle had also been mercifully silent. Henri knew she was desperate to talk to him, to sway his decision or come up with a plan, but even she recognized the significance of every hour he chose to spend in this cell. Time is a fickle mistress.

It crawls slowly through pain and whips like the wind through joyous moments. And then life is over.

Henri wondered what joyous moments Nathaniel had had in his life. His happiest memories, his darkest days, Henri did not know them. Nathaniel had never let Henri witness them. He had seen his friend smile only a dozen times in their whole lives, and only ever with him. He couldn't recall if he had ever heard his friend laugh. Probably not. The commander had molded his son into the perfect soldier. Unemotional. Obedient. Loyal. Merciless.

King Heroux had chosen his monster well.

When Citric finally came, Henri was ready, but also not ready. He had made a decision. Yet another choice he would have to live with for the rest of his life. It was too heavy. The weight of his decisions was crushing him, burying him beneath their rubble and devastation.

Citric stood in front of the cell door, absorbing the heavy mood in the room. Finally, he said, "The Butcher will die at sun's rise tomorrow. Will you be joining him?"

Henri pushed himself to his feet and kept his eyes focused ahead, anywhere but on the man slumped against the wall in the cell next to his.

"I will swear allegiance to you."

He could have sworn he heard Nathaniel exhale in relief.

Citric slid his gaze to Brielle. "And you?"

Henri could sense her resistance, even without looking in her direction. It was as if she would rather choke on her own pride than bend the knee to him.

"I will swear it," she bit out.

Citric considered her for a moment and then gestured for the guards to unlock their cells.

"You will both stay at court until you take the oath tomorrow night during the ceremony. After that, you are free to leave if that is your wish."

Free to go live his life while his friend found freedom in death. Henri wondered if Nathaniel would also find peace in death, the peace that had eluded him his entire life. Because, as Henri knew all too well, freedom did not guarantee peace.

The guards opened the cell doors and Henri took a step outside. Despite his conviction not to, he turned his head to his friend and their eyes met. Nathaniel looked pale and weak, but he was alive. At that moment, Henri wondered if he had also chosen to stay. To live one more day in this miserable dungeon because that was all he could do for his friend.

A wave of emotions suddenly pulled at Henri's features. There was so much unspoken between them. Words, it seemed, had always failed them.

"I did it for you." The words tumbled from Nathaniel's mouth in hurried earnestness. "To keep you safe. Everything I ever did was for you."

Henri went rigid as he began to comprehend his meaning. Nathaniel had agreed to be King Heroux's lackey, not for the power and influence it afforded him, but because it put him in the best position to keep Henri safe. He would have been the first person alerted to any sightings of Henri. He would have had a chance to intervene if Henri had been arrested. Nathaniel had turned himself into a monster to protect his friend. They stared at each other, the ugly truth hanging heavy in the air between them.

"I will think of you," Henri promised him, before he turned and ascended the stairs to freedom.

Two guards escorted Brielle to her former bedchamber. As they walked the halls of her home, courtiers abandoned their conversations and stared at her as if she were a rare creature acquired for the royal menagerie. They murmured behind their manicured nails, wild speculations and salacious stories.

Brielle kept her chin high and her spine straight, despite the heat of humiliation in her cheeks. She knew what she must look like. Two days without being able to wash herself, her clothes splattered with dry blood, her hair matted with straw, her skin pale from sitting in a rotting dungeon devoid of natural light. She used to be the sparkling diamond of the Southern court, a princess renowned for her beauty and the decadence of her ladies' court. But that was before she had become a traitor, a rebel, and a prisoner. Now the sparkling diamond had become an ordinary stone, crushed under the soles of men's shoes.

Upon entering her bedchamber, Brielle swept her assessing gaze over the fine furnishings, the large four-poster bed with plush linens, the feathered cushions and chaise longues embroidered with strands of gold. A platter of fruit was laid out on a table in the sitting area and a carafe of fine wine sat next to it. The windows were open slightly to let a cool breeze drift inside, bringing the scent of roses from the garden below. It was strange to see light after three days steeped in darkness. It was intoxicating to breathe fresh air.

"Your Highness." A young servant girl appeared before her, while three others remained standing a few paces away. They all dropped in perfectly coordinated curtsies. "A bath has been prepared for you."

"Thank you."

The servant girl blinked in surprise, and the others exchanged perplexed glances. Of course, months ago Brielle would rarely have extended such curtesy to anyone, let alone a servant. She had forgotten herself. Or rather, she had forgotten who she used to be.

"I-is there anything else you require, Your Highness?" the girl stammered.

Brielle thought for a moment and then began to peel off her dress. The girl immediately moved to assist her, but Brielle held up a hand.

"I can do it." Stripping it from her body, she handed it over to the servant. "Burn this."

"Yes, Your Highness." The girl bobbed another curtsy and fled the room with the garments.

"You may all go. I wish to be alone."

The servants curtsied again and quickly filed out. Brielle wandered over to the copper bathtub and watched the steam rise from the surface of the water in delicate swirls. The sides of the tub were lined with soft linen sheets, and the water was scented with rose oil and fresh petals from the royal garden.

She stepped inside and gradually lowered her body beneath the water. It enveloped her in luxurious warmth, a heavenly aroma filling her senses. Her aching muscles, knotted from lying on a cold stone floor the past few nights, began to unwind. The dried blood caked on her skin melted away.

Normally she would have several servants attending to her, massaging her shoulders, washing her hair, polishing her nails. But things were different now. She was different. Before, every move she made was carefully calculated, every word and deed put on display. She would not have done something if it could not be witnessed, if it did not benefit her in some way. But since then, she had lived a commoner's life, where no one listened to her every word, and her every deed did not matter.

In the beginning it had incensed her, made her feel invisible, *ordinary*. But after a while it had begun to feel strangely freeing. Like breathing for the first time. Yes, she was changed, but she wasn't sure whether she could afford for people at court to see that. Because tomorrow she would have to pull on a silk dress of armor and fix her courtier's mask firmly to her face. She would need to remember how to present herself perfectly. The right words to say, the clever games to play. Because tomorrow she would begin taking back her kingdom.

Eve surveyed the lines of haggard people waiting patiently in front of each station. Children clung to their mothers' skinny legs, their own bodies painfully thin, their skin smeared with dirt. The state of the people was heartbreaking. Fear and despair weathered their faces, while poverty hunched their shoulders and weighed their limbs down like chains as they shuffled their feet forward.

The lines moved slowly, but no one complained. No one tried to push in front or claim more than what was given to them. Citric had charged her with this task the moment the castle was secured: to set up tables in the market square and ration out free basic goods. Food. Clothing. Medicine. The people had come in droves, willing to wait on their feet for hours in order to feed their family a meal or ease the pain of a loved one. Yesterday it had only been the city folk, but word had spread fast and people from neighboring farms and towns now lined the streets.

Eve swayed a little on her feet, exhaustion threatening to take her down again. She had only slept a handful of hours in the past few days. There was so much to do. Thankfully, she was not doing it on her own. The men from the other camps in the Red Wood had witnessed Citric's fiery arrow in the dawning sky several days ago and immediately entered the city, ready to quell any resistance to his reign from the King's Guard. But so far, there had been none. At least nothing overt.

She was sure the guards were grumbling to each other with discontent, now that their rampant crimes had been obstructed and any further offences would be met with swift justice. Men did not like having their behavior questioned, their power diminished. No doubt the day would come when some of them, maybe even all of them, would challenge Citric. But today they stood at their posts and walked their patrols. Citric had strategically dispersed his own men among them. They would hear of any plots to question his authority or seize control.

The women from the other camps in the Red Wood had also come, ready to assist the people of the Southern Kingdom in whatever way they could. They stood at each of the stations handing out goods, while others went to the homes of people unable to walk to the market square. They listened to the harrowing stories of those who had lost loved ones to King Heroux's cruelty. They cried with them and provided solace to those who crumbled in anguish at their feet.

Eve had never witnessed pain and suffering like this before. The conditions under the old Southern king were bad, but King Heroux had swept through the Southern Kingdom like a plague. She had watched helplessly as the people were thrust into abject poverty and oppression, each day worse than the one before. She had dreamed every night of a day when they would finally be able to do something to remedy the injustice.

Part of her couldn't believe it had actually come to pass. That they had succeeded in reclaiming the Southern land. It felt like she was waiting for something bad to happen, for someone or something to rip this progress away from them. No doubt it would come, but they were ready for it.

And then there was the matter of reclaiming the Northern Kingdom. Eve exhaled a breath, feeling the weight of that thought sitting heavily on her shoulders.

A movement in her periphery caught her attention and she instinctively knew who it was. She would know him anywhere, from a long distance or in a dense crowd. His walk. The way his body moved in a fight. His mannerisms. They were as familiar to her as her own. But it was more than familiarity. It was like she could sense whenever he was near. Perhaps because she was always hoping he was near. The past few months had been challenging in many ways, but the silver lining had been him. Knowing that every morning when she woke up and every night before she slept, she would see him.

Citric smiled as he strode toward her, his easy smile that made her heart trip over itself in drunken adoration. He had probably had less sleep than her these past few days. He had been moving quickly from task to task, doing everything he could to secure their hold on the castle and the Southern lands. It had to be exhausting, but he showed no signs of it. He was a walking contradiction. Dressed in leathers and heavily armed as if he expected to go into battle at any moment. Yet he wore a relaxed smile and tossed an apple in the air as if he hadn't a care in the world. When he came to stand at her side, he held the apple out to her.

"Have you eaten?"

Eve gave him a look that told him to stop fussing over her. Even so, she took the apple. She could never refuse him anything.

"How are the people?" His features tightened a little as he surveyed the lines in front of each station.

"Desperate. They just keep coming."

"Have we got enough for them?"

"We have raided the castle, their kitchens and the storage rooms, but we are beginning to run low on some things. Food, mostly."

He nodded thoughtfully and she bit into the apple despite herself.

"I am meeting with the merchants today. I'll secure some favorable trade."

"How deep is the King's treasury?"

"Not as deep as the church's. They were very reluctant to part with it."

Eve smirked at his devilish grin. "Are they men of faith or men of gold? You are simply helping them fulfill their godly duty of charity."

"I told them that. They still did not want to part with it."

With the wealth of the church, combined with the wealth of the Crown, they would certainly be able to secure good trade deals. Which was just as well, because the people would be dependent on them until Citric and the other direct descendants of Sirasinda healed the land and made it fertile again.

"You are tired," he observed with concern. "I'll escort you to your room so you can rest."

Eve opened her mouth to protest, but he was right. Besides, she would never turn down an opportunity to spend time alone with him. She missed it. Craved it. Before he sent her to court to be his spy, they had spent every day for the better part of a year together. Sometimes at Alkhiem among his people, but other times at her country home, just the two of them. And the servants, of course, who were more like family. Not once had they questioned Citric's claim of being a distant relative and heir to the estate after her brother Rowan's death. Nor had they expressed concern about her spending time alone with him or traveling for weeks with him unchaperoned. He was family, after all. They were simply relieved that their mistress was taken care of and they would not lose their positions.

Bonded initially by their grief for Rowan, they had gotten to know each other slowly, and eventually found other common ground. In those early weeks, Citric had asked her so many questions about herself. She had never met a man, besides her father and brother, even remotely interested in hearing her thoughts and opinions. He was just—different. He did not treat her like a child. Or a girl.

He spoke to her of war and violence, death and cruelty. Injustice. Never coddling her ears or sparing the brutal details. After some time, he had goaded her into entering the Red Wood and, despite her abject terror, she had followed him. In truth, she would have followed him anywhere. He had shown her all its natural beauty and taught her how to hunt and live off the land. He had shown her how to make medicines from roots and flowers and tend to people's wounds. It was there he had shared his deepest secrets with her, the history of his people, the cause they were fighting for.

It had felt like a calling. Like a blindfold had been lifted from her eyes and she could finally see the world around her and her purpose in it. Eve had never been suited to dresses and dolls. Her father had reasoned it was because she had no mother to tend to her. She had been raised by a man and an older brother who had indulged her boyish interests. Perhaps that was true, or perhaps she was always meant to live a different life from her gentle mother.

At her request, Citric had taught her how to fight, how to wield any weapon. He had shown her how to observe people and read them as if they were pages in a book. To move without making a sound, to become a human shadow. She had been fourteen at the time; a child, really. But her heart had not been limited by such an arbitrary thing as age. She had fallen irrevocably in love with the wild man who had shown up on her door that day, badly wounded and wearing her brother's silver amulet around his neck.

It was a cruel irony that the worst day of her life was also the best day of her life. Citric had kept his promise to Rowan that he would protect her should her brother die in battle. That promise felt like fate weaving its thread. Weaving Citric's and her threads together.

"You are unusually quiet. Are you troubled by something?"

"No, I'm just thinking," Eve replied as they made their way through the streets to the castle.

"About?"

"The day we met."

Her smile was wistful as she looked up at him, but his face darkened at the memory. She wondered if it was bittersweet for him as well, or just bitter. He had shown up on the doorstep of her estate half dead, having fled the battlefield with three arrows buried in his back. He had deserted the Northern army and tried to bring Rowan's body back to her, but the journey was too long and his wounds were too great. Her brother's body now lay buried in an unmarked grave beneath a blackthorn tree.

Before he buried her brother, he had taken Rowan's silver amulet to give to her. She wore it around her neck every day, until she had to leave to take up her place in Brielle's ladies' court. On that day, she had given it to Citric. She could not wear such a thing at court, but more importantly, she had wanted him to have it. To have something of hers that she loved. To have it resting against his precious heart. He hadn't taken it off since.

"Some days it feels like a lifetime ago," he said quietly.

Only two years had passed, but she knew what he meant. A lot had happened since then. They had come such a long way to restoring his homeland. She had also changed in that time, from a skinny fourteen-year-old girl to a blossoming young woman. Every day her body was filling out with round curves into a womanly figure. She hoped he had noticed.

"And here we are. Victory is ours. I told you I would be your best warrior." Eve nudged his side with her shoulder.

He tossed her a playful smile. "I never doubted you."

Eve beamed under the warmth of his praise, but her joy melted away as they stepped inside the castle. Courtiers bowed their heads or dipped into curtsies as they passed, the ladies dragging their eyes up and down Citric's magnificent form. It made her want to claw their eyes out.

"I hate this place," she cursed.

Citric cast his gaze around at the white-washed stone walls, the high arched ceilings, and the endless corridors. "So do I."

Right. Her hatred had no place beside his. Here stood a grand castle built on the land stolen from his forefathers, their blood and bones crushed into the soil beneath the foundation stones. This castle roiled her stomach for many reasons, but it must be almost unbearable for him to walk its halls.

"Just here," she murmured as she stopped in front of a door and retrieved a small brass key from her pocket.

To her surprise, and nervous delight, Citric followed her inside. His eyes swept over the room as if he were looking for hidden threats. She smiled knowingly and a thrill snaked up her spine at his protectiveness. Eve waited until he was satisfied and his body relaxed a little. She watched as he allowed his eyes to take in the sheer luxury of it all.

"I'm sure this is nothing compared to your rooms. The King's rooms."

"I wouldn't know."

She scoffed before furrowing her brows in question. "Where have you been sleeping?"

"I could ask you the same thing."

Her cheeks flushed, but she followed his eyes as they snagged on a pile of crumpled sheets on the floor beside her bed.

"I can't sleep in the bed," she explained. "It's too soft."

His lips twitched in amusement. "You truly are one of us."

She rolled her eyes at him and took a few aimless steps around the room. She wasn't sure what else to do. Her exhaustion had vanished the moment he stepped inside her bedchamber, replaced by a nervous, fluttering energy. If he wanted to talk to her for hours, she would listen. If he wanted to find out how soft the bed really was, she would not mind.

Not at all.

Her insides warmed at the thought of it and she looked up at him beneath long eyelashes, her heart pounding anew.

"Rest well. Tomorrow will be an important day," Citric said and turned to leave.

Tomorrow. Right. Tomorrow the nobles would swear allegiance to him as their king. Then he would know who was loyal and who was plotting against him. Not by their meaningless words, but by their blood. Only the direct descendants of Sirasinda possessed the ancient sensorium. Even then, the connection was diluted depending on the strength of the bloodline. Citric's bloodline was the strongest among the descendants of his people. Like their ability to connect to the land, to feel it down to the very roots of the trees, to know the movements within the woodland like ripples in a pond, in the same way, when their blood mixed with another's, they could sense them. They could know what was in their heart.

Blood oaths were sacred to the Sirasindans. There were only two occasions in a person's life when they could choose to make a blood oath. When two people chose to spend their life together, they would cut their left palms and take the oath as part of the marriage ritual. When someone chose to follow a leader, they would cut their right palm and swear a blood oath of allegiance. The right hand was for wielding a sword, Citric had explained to her once. The left hand was for caressing a lover.

"Wait," Eve called out to him and he turned back to her. "Tomorrow I want to be the first to swear the oath to you."

She had wanted to swear the oath to him two years ago, but she couldn't afford to have a scar on her palm. She would never have been accepted at court, let alone into Brielle's ladies' court, with such a blatant imperfection. But now, she was free to do as she pleased, and she wanted nothing more than to bind herself to him.

"No. Tomorrow is a public display of power. It's important that Henri and Brielle swear the oath first and the nobles see it."

Eve huffed. He was always calculating, planning things down to the last detail, looking at it from every angle. She could not blame him. He'd had his whole life to think about how he would reclaim this land. Every move he ever made was done with this goal in mind, to save his people and restore their homeland. But she had also been waiting for this her whole life. Waiting for him. And now that they had succeeded in reclaiming the Southern Kingdom, she did not need to be apart from him anymore. They might finally have a chance to change things between them.

Eve reached into her bodice to retrieve one of her hidden blades, the movement confident and, she hoped, a little seductive.

"Then let me do it now."

She approached him slowly and he watched every step she took, heating the molecules in her body like water held over a flame. She stopped a breath away from him and her eyes never left his as she dragged the blade across her right palm. Eve barely felt the sharp, burning sting. It certainly wasn't enough to drag her attention away from his devastatingly handsome face.

He was perfect, even with the violent scar that marred his cheek. It was hard to breathe being this close to him, feeling the warmth radiating from him, inhaling his earthy scent. Meeting her challenge, Citric unsheathed the dagger at his side and sliced open his palm, his eyes never leaving hers. He held his hand up in the narrow space between them, and their palms met as she wrapped her fingers around his. In that moment, she swore she felt something between them ignite.

Eve swallowed hard and steadied herself, ready to say the words she had been longing to say for the past two years. "I swear on the essence of my soul that I will be true and faithful to you as my king. I will serve you with every beat of my heart, with every breath I take, with the strength of my blades and the truth of my words, for all the days of my life. I am yours, body, heart, and soul."

The world seemed to fall silent around them. She was sure that time itself had stopped to bear witness to this sacred moment. Citric's eyes searched hers. She hoped he could see everything in them; every dream and thought and waking moment. It was all for him.

When he spoke, his words were strong and sure. "My blood is now your blood, my life force your life force. You have chosen me, and I have chosen you. Wherever destiny takes us, we will be as one. Let the brother or sister who would break their blood oath be forever cursed."

Eve's mouth parted as if his words had stolen her breath away. She lowered her eyes to his lips, lingering so close to hers. If she inched up on her tiptoes they would meet, soft and gentle. The caress of a feather. The spark of magic.

"Sweet dreams, Evelyn."

Eve blinked and licked her lips as their hands released and he turned away. She watched him walk out of her room, closing the door softly behind him. Her body thrummed at the thought of what had just transpired between them. Her blood was in his veins. She was a part of him now, and he was a part of her. Bound together until death separated them. And even then, her spirit would follow him across the plains of the otherworld for all eternity.

CHAPTER THREE

C itric slapped a hand against his bedchamber wall to steady himself. He felt lightheaded, as if someone had drugged him. Eve's blood had sizzled against his own when it crawled inside his veins. He had never felt anything like it before. Normally when people swore a blood oath to him, he was the one in control. His blood seized theirs and fused a connection, a bond which was usually one sided. He could feel them, but they could not feel him. Unless their bloodline was Sirasindan, in which case the connection went both ways.

But this felt different. Eve's blood raced through his body as if it wanted to take command of his very soul. It clutched at his organs and pumped his heart feverishly until he swore he was going to pass out.

Stumbling over to the bed, he flung his hand out to brace himself on the mattress, but he missed and crashed onto the wooden floorboards. Cursing, he winced against the impact, but made no effort to right himself. The world felt like it had been tilted on its axis. He couldn't stand if he tried. Instead, he stared up at the ceiling and tried to work out what was happening to him.

The moment he exchanged blood with Eve, a wave of emotions had crashed into him. It felt like going from sober to blind drunk in an instant. It was overwhelming. Confusing. Nauseating. He had barely made it out of her room, let alone through the castle and to his own bedchamber. Even now his senses swam in a river of emotions, battling the pull of different sentiments, being dragged under by a riptide of sensations he could not match in strength. All of it dominated by one single emotion: desire.

But it wasn't his.

As much as it slicked his palms with sweat, quickened his heart, and thickened his cock, the desire was not his. Citric closed his eyes against it, trying to take back control of his body by focusing on his breath. Was this Eve's emotions he was feeling? It couldn't be. He had just escorted her to her room to rest. There was no time in the minutes since he had left for her to have found someone to engage in a wildly passionate encounter with. Unless she had a secret lover waiting for her. The thought disturbed him. She was barely old enough for such things. But if she didn't have a secret lover, and he had been the last one to see her ... *oh, fuck.*

Citric groaned aloud as his head pounded with the realization. Desire had consumed him the moment Eve's blood had touched his veins. Eve felt these feelings for *him.* He didn't want to believe it, but there was no other explanation.

If he took a mental step back, he had to accept that Eve was no longer the young girl he had met on the front porch that day. She was sixteen years old. A young woman. It was only natural that she would be curious about—things. Perhaps she had even shared stolen kisses and clumsy fumbles with young noblemen at court.

The thought made him growl out loud but not from jealousy. He would rip apart any young man who took unwanted liberties with her or didn't treat her with the respect she deserved. And he couldn't imagine any young man being worthy enough to deserve her attentions. Perhaps she couldn't either. Maybe that was why she had directed her attention to him. But he would never be able to see her as anything other than Rowan's little sister. He loved her like the sibling he'd never had and would give his life to protect her, but he could not offer her more than that.

Citric stared up at the ceiling as he focused on the rhythm of his breaths and tried to ignore the emotions rioting inside him. How long had she felt this way about him? The intensity of the emotion suffocating his senses told him that it was not a fleeting thought or a slight inclination. If he had to guess, he would say she had harbored these feelings for a long time and he hadn't noticed. Perhaps he hadn't wanted to. She had always been fiercely loyal to him, waiting on his every word, but he had put that down to the unique nature of their relationship. After Rowan died, he had become everything to her. A brother. A guardian. The only family she had left. He thought she viewed him the same way, but clearly she did not.

Now that the blood oath connected them, there was no escaping the uncomfortable truth. He could feel everything she was feeling, whether he wanted to or not. She had known that and still she had sworn herself to him. Perhaps it was her way of telling him how she felt about him without actually having to say the words to his face. Except he had no idea what to do with these feelings. He had never held a sixteen-year-old girl's heart in his hands before. At least not since he was a thoughtless, arrogant sixteen year old himself.

He would need to figure it out, though. The blood oath had opened this floodgate and now he had little choice but to remain silent in the hope it would pass, or break her heart and hope they would both survive the fallout.

Henri could feel the sweat sliding down his back as he shifted anxiously between his feet. His heart galloped hard, as if it were a horse that had bolted from its pasture. It felt like any moment now it would burst right out of his chest.

It was happening again.

There were differences, of course. He was down among the people this time instead of watching from a royal balcony. He was being pushed around by a swelling, feverish crowd, each person vying for the best vantage point, eager to witness the bloody retribution they had been promised. A stage, not a scaffold. Built over the past three days on the green hill just outside the castle walls. Normally executions took place in the town square or in the privacy of the dungeons, but Citric had ordered a stage to be built here on this particular hill. Henri did not know why, but in the end it did not matter. What was clear was that this was more than an execution; it was a performance.

They had built the stage high enough so that even the people at the back of the swarming crowd could see. Two guards held Nathaniel up by his armpits as they brought him forward on unsteady legs. Even from a distance, Henri could see how weak he was. His skin was washed of color, almost gray. Henri swore under his breath. He should be dead already. Most men would have died within hours of that arrow wound, but Nathaniel had fought hard to hold on to life. For what? For this? For his death to be a public spectacle? The sadistic entertainment to a bloodthirsty crowd?

Henri gritted his teeth and tried to hold his ground as the people jostled him about. Even as he did, he pulled his hood closer to his face. He did not want to be recognized. The crowd was out for blood, yelling obscenities and shaking their fists. The promise of violence was thick in the air and the people were breathing it in like poison. If they recognized him, the crowd would surely turn on him as well. The fact that King Heroux was no longer ruling the Southern Kingdom did not absolve him of being a traitor. He had deserted his kingdom and abandoned his people to King Heroux's tyranny. He had betrayed them. No one would be interested in hearing his excuses. Crowds such as these could not be reasoned with.

Years ago, a crowd such as this one had hurled insults at his innocent mother as she was led to the butcher's block. *Whore. Bitch. Cunt.* People that did not know her, as well as people who had been her closest friends. They had so readily believed his father's accusations of adultery. So steeped in their loyalty to their king, they thought it justified their foul debasement of his mother in the last moments of her life. A true queen, she withstood their abuse, head held high, dignity in every step.

She had not faltered when the executioner ordered her to kneel, to lay her head on the bloodstained block of wood. She had not wailed or tried to flee, as some prisoners did. Nor had she made one last plea for the king's, her husband's, mercy. She had protested her innocence every day since he had accused her, to no avail. She knew such a request would go unanswered. Henri wondered now if she had done it all for him, knowing that her young son was watching. She would not have wanted him to see her frightened or suffering or begging for her life. She would not have wanted him to remember her like that. And he didn't. But the memory of the axe coming down on her neck still haunted his dreams.

There was no axe. Henri furrowed his brows at the realization. The guards led Nathaniel to the front of the stage, but there was no block for him to lay his head on. And no executioner. Citric approached from behind as the guards released their grip on Nathaniel and he crumpled to his knees. Henri felt his hands tingle even as his skin turned clammy. He couldn't do this. It was happening again and he couldn't endure it. He couldn't bear to watch someone else he cared about be cut down in front of his eyes. His mother. Fleur. Even his hateful father. The images in his mind never faded. The sounds echoed in his memories. He had been powerless to stop it then, and he was powerless to stop it now.

Always powerless.

A hand suddenly slipped into his, gripping it tight, anchoring him to the moment. Henri looked down at the cloaked figure standing beside him, her gaze fixed firmly on the stage at the top of the green hill. He couldn't see her face but he didn't have to. Brielle didn't say a word and yet he heard everything in the strength of her hand wrapped tightly around his, the determined set of her shoulders, the way her gaze was fixed firmly on the stage. They would endure this together.

Citric walked to the edge of the stage and held his hands up to appease the agitated crowd, who begrudgingly quietened. In the moment of silence, Nathaniel looked out over the crowd. His features held no traces of fear or resentment, but there was an urgency as his eyes searched the faces in front of him. He was looking for someone, Henri realized. He was looking for him. Henri gripped Brielle's hand as he tried to push his way through the throng of people to get to the front.

"People of the Southern Kingdom, you have come here today seeking justice for the crimes committed against you." Citric's voice was stern and commanding as it rang out over the crowd. "This man, the Butcher, is guilty of persecuting you. Enforcing tyranny. And murdering your loved ones. Let his death serve as a warning to anyone who would consider oppressing others for their own gain, who would take that which does not belong to them, who would stand idly by and not fight back against injustice; this is the price you will pay."

It was no use. The people refused to move aside to let him through, lest they lose their precious view. Citric unsheathed his sword and Henri froze. He recognized it instantly. The cruciform hilt was made of heavy iron and the straight double-edged blade was unmistakable: the Sword of Peace. He had admired it once, when it was encased beneath glass and laid into a beautiful oak table. He could never have known the weapon would be the blade to kill his closest friend.

Bile rose in Henri's throat as Citric moved to stand behind Nathaniel, gripping the hilt of the sword in both hands. Brielle squeezed his hand tighter—in comfort or from her own trepidation, he did not know. But then Nathaniel's eyes caught his, as if he had sensed him somehow despite his hooded cloak and the throng of people between them. Henri held his gaze firm and refused to let go, nodding in silent reassurance and understanding as Citric lifted the sword in the air. Nathaniel's blank expression did not change, but Henri swore he saw a softening in his eyes just before the blade was brought down on his neck.

Henri returned to his bedchamber in a daze. His movements were a collection of involuntary reflexes. His mind and his soul were still on that green hill, transfixed by the blood coating the edge of a blade. On the head that had rolled forward into the crowd. He felt like retching his guts up. Scratching his eyes blind until he couldn't even see memories. He felt like punching a wall until there was nothing left but rubble and torn skin and broken bones.

Nathaniel was dead. The people had demanded justice, and Citric had delivered it in a spectacular show. Henri clenched his jaw as he recalled the way the people had cheered as the sword cleaved through his friend's neck. He could not dispute that Nathaniel's death was warranted. He had done unspeakable things in the name of King Heroux. Enforced crippling taxes, set homes on fire, murdered countless innocents.

For him.

To keep him safe.

That thought alone had been enough to keep Henri from sleep last night. He didn't know how to feel about it. Nathaniel had stayed silent about his father's plot to betray the king, and yet he had saved Henri by telling him to run from the battlefield. He knew about the Sodisce. He would have known that Henri would seek refuge there, at least temporarily, but he had not betrayed him to King Heroux. Nor did he meet him there. Instead, he chose to become King Heroux's monster. To commit atrocities against innocent people in order to keep Henri safe. To be in a position to save his life if necessary. And he had. He had surrendered the King's Guard the moment Henri's life was in danger.

It was as if he had been waiting for him that night. Perhaps Nathaniel had seen through the rumors about a sighting of the traitors in Doranth. Maybe he surmised that Henri's spies had planted the rumor to lure half the King's Guard away from the castle. Perchance he had suspected that an attempt would be made to reclaim the Northern castle that night. But not by Henri.

You wouldn't have come on your own. Where is she?

Nathaniel's words had stung at the time but they were true. He knew that Henri would never lead a campaign to reclaim his kingdom. That without Brielle, he would have been content to live a quiet, anonymous life. Maybe if he had, his friend would still be alive.

Henri wiped at his cheeks and was surprised to find them damp. Strolling over to a decanter sitting on top of a small table, he poured a generous amount of the amber liquor into a glass. He gripped the glass tightly in his fist as he remembered those innocent people kneeling in the market square, his friend stalking toward them with a star axe in his hand. The way their bodies fell forward as he plunged that star axe into the back of their necks one by one. Henri pinched his eyes closed against the memory and tossed the liquid down his throat. The liquor burned, but it was not enough to corrode the memories, the emotions, the guilt.

Henri hurled the glass across the room and watched it shatter against the wall. How dare Nathaniel claim that he did those things for him. To protect him. He would rather die a thousand deaths than be responsible for a single moment of an innocent's pain. A tempest of emotions detonated inside him. Henri swept his hands across the table, flinging the glass decanters to smash on the floor, the silver trays clanging against the stone. He picked up the small table and tossed it across the room, watching it break against the wall.

It was all consuming. Fury. Rage. Shame. *Relief.* He stalled in his destruction for a moment, trying to comprehend why he felt so much relief. A whimper escaped his throat as the truth settled over him like a wet blanket being thrown on flames. It was because Nathaniel's words meant that their friendship had not been a lie. Nathaniel had not betrayed him. He had shielded him. He had burned the rest of the world down to do it, but he had protected him in the only way he knew how. He had given him a chance to live the quiet, anonymous life he had always wanted.

After tonight, Henri would be free to do exactly that. All it would cost him was an oath to his friend's murderer. To the man who had seduced Brielle, betrayed her, and stolen her kingdom. All he had to do was not care about any of it.

But he did.

Brielle breathed a sigh of relief as she entered the throne room. She'd had less than a day to orchestrate this evening's celebration, but the servants had scurried at her frenzied commands and the room looked festive enough. It was a wonder the servants had managed to achieve what they had, given that the castle was shockingly low on supplies. Normally, the long tables would be overflowing with food and wine, featuring the best dishes and the most expensive produce. Instead, the tables looked almost bare, presenting the most basic of spreads. Ordinarily, the throne room would be richly decorated, with a dazzling display of candlelight from hundreds of candelabras and elaborate chandeliers suspended from the ceiling. Instead, the chandeliers were noticeably absent and the room was lit by a mere hundred tall tapered candles. To anyone new to court, the room would still look impressive and festive, but to her it looked like they'd been robbed.

Standing in the frame of the great doors, Brielle tensed as the conversations hushed to murmurs and every courtier's gaze turned to her. The princess turned traitor, who fled her own castle in the middle of the night. The princess who had returned to reclaim her kingdom, only to be betrayed by a notorious outlaw vying for her throne. The princess who had not only fallen from her gilded pedestal, but had been quite firmly thrown down. Many in this room would be delighted with her diminished position. They would be thinking there was no possible way she could come back from it.

They didn't know her at all.

As Brielle began meandering through the room, keeping her chin high and her shoulders back, the lords bowed awkwardly to her and the ladies dipped down in the barest of curtsies. It seemed no one was quite sure what her current standing at court was. If she was no longer a princess, they would not have to bow to her. But if she was still a princess, they did not want to offend her by not showing her the proper respect.

Whispers fluttered around the room and those that touched her ears sent shivers down her spine. They were surprised she still had her head. That the new king had not ridden himself of her yet. Brielle forced a tight smile as she walked among them, dipping her chin in polite acknowledgement as she passed by. She had weathered public scrutiny before, been the source of malicious gossip in a crowded room, but this felt different. It felt dangerous. She no longer had her lineage to protect her or her father to defend her. Her place in this court was precarious and she needed to remedy that immediately if she was going to have any chance of challenging Citric's rule.

Brielle surveyed the courtiers, weighing her options. Ladies from her former court stood in small groups, watching her with shrewd eyes and gossiping with sharp tongues. She could not risk approaching them because if they rejected her, it would be over. She knew how this game was played. Everyone was waiting for a sign of whether to accept her or not.

"Your Highness."

Brielle blinked to find a lord bowing low before her.

"Lord Waylan." She tilted her head, smiling prettily.

"Thank God for your safe return to us," he said as he straightened to stand in front of her.

"God himself could not keep me away."

Lord Waylan held his hand out to her. "May I have the honor of this dance?"

Brielle beamed. "Of course."

Placing her hand in his, she let him lead her out onto the dance floor, making sure to make eye contact with as many courtiers as possible. She had not expected it to be this easy, but perhaps she had underestimated her own influence at court. They bowed and curtsied to each other before coming together as the music began. Brielle was out of practice, having spent the past few months living like a renegade in the Red Wood, but Lord Waylan was a confident dance partner. She felt her body responding instinctively to his lead, falling into steps that were as familiar to her as walking.

"My sincerest condolences on the loss of your father, the king. What transpired was nothing short of a tragedy. The whole ordeal must have been terribly traumatic for you."

"It was. I have endured much, but I have risen above it to return to my people."

They parted, each moving away to take steps in a circle before coming back to each other.

"You must be craving stability now."

She was craving vengeance. Blood. Citric's head on a spike.

"Yes, I crave stability for my kingdom. I only want what is best for my people."

He nodded thoughtfully. "I can see the difficult situation you are in. It must be frightening to be so alone. Losing your father and then your kingdom. Having no one to protect you or offer you guidance and comfort."

Brielle's senses pricked and her body stiffened at his words.

"Perhaps I could be of some assistance. You know I am a wealthy man from a good name. I have much to offer a wife."

Her eyes widened in shock and she immediately dropped his hand, stepping back from him. Lord Waylan's eyes darted anxiously around at their watchful audience while the couples surrounding them continued dancing. Brielle quickly regained her composure to resume their dance, but her steps were not as poised as before.

"Lord Waylan, are you suggesting we marry?"

The look he returned her was one of perplexed, wounded pride.

"But I am a princess," Brielle said sharply.

"In name only, I hear." Lord Waylan's grip on her hand and waist tightened. "You have nothing else to claim. You are permitted to live here at court at the new king's mercy, which is sure to run its course very quickly. Then you will have nothing and no one to turn to. You will be thrown out into the streets with the commoners. Not even a lady, let alone a princess. What I offer you is security, comfort, and protection. It is more than you will receive from anyone else in this room."

Brielle scowled and tried to pull herself free, but his hold on her was firm enough to leave bruises.

"I command you to let me go."

"You don't give commands anymore, Your Highness."

His eyes flashed with a predatory anger that sent cold tremors across her skin. The music ended and he released her, bowing low before stalking away. Brielle remained standing there, stunned. She felt the bitter sting of tears in her eyes, but she willed them away and squared her shoulders.

She cast her gaze around to scan the faces of the other lords. She recognized it now, the sinister glint in their eyes. Every one of them had flirted with her in the past, flattered her with pretty compliments, pleaded with her to honor them with a dance. She had enjoyed their attentions regardless of their sincerity because she knew she was safe. They could not touch her. She was a princess and they were beneath her. But now things had changed. They were above her, or so they thought. They believed her to be some wilted flower crushed under Citric's boots. A wounded animal in need of saving. Or caging. They thought her to be desperate enough to consider marrying them. True, she had no wealth to offer them, no land, no kin, but she was the former Princess of the Southern Kingdom. Royal blood was in her veins. That was a prize any noble would covet in a wife.

Everyone's attention suddenly turned to the great doors, where Henri was now standing. Brielle felt her shoulders relax a little as the weight of their scrutiny shifted away from her. Henri looked regal dressed in an embroidered red-and-gold tunic, his hair neatly combed, his jawline cleanly shaven. His gaze drifted around the room as if he were judging it for his approval. He looked disinterested, bored even, as if this whole affair of giving up his throne and swearing allegiance to a new king did not affect him in the least. Which it probably didn't, given his apathy toward his crown, but still, she admired his composure. He looked like he didn't even notice the courtiers' assessing stares and cutting whispers. Perhaps he didn't. He had watched his closest friend be beheaded mere hours ago. Perhaps nothing could really touch him after that.

Brielle's expression fell in sympathy and she lifted her skirts to march across the room to him. She had barely made it to his side before he said, "What is all this?" His tone was reproachful.

"What do you mean?"

"This is supposed to be Citric's allegiance ceremony. I hardly think he would be responsible for this ... display."

Brielle looked around the room innocently. "Citric doesn't understand how things work at court. I am simply helping him."

Henri slid incredulous eyes to her. "Brielle, do not start a game you cannot afford to lose."

"I'm not."

He narrowed his eyes at her. "You forget who you're talking to."

"So do you."

They held each other's stare before he finally looked away, shaking his head and muttering under his breath.

Brielle took a step closer to him as she whispered, "Kings wage war on the battlefield. Queens wage war on the dance floor."

Giving him a pointed look, she walked away to mingle amongst her court.

Henri watched Brielle saunter away from him, looking exquisite in a midnight blue gown with silver trim, her long chestnut hair falling in soft waves over her shoulders. For all her bravado, she remained on the outskirts of conversation, trying to make it appear as though she was above joining their company rather than being excluded from it. But it was clear that she had lost all the power she once had. This was not her court anymore.

Henri knew he should go to her, remain by her side throughout the ceremony so that she at least had one friend. She had been there for him this morning when he needed her most. But for some reason, he could not convince his legs to move. It had taken all the strength he had to simply attend tonight. It was the last place he wanted to be. In the middle of a crowd, surrounded by false allies and blatant enemies. The same people who had cheered as his friend's head was severed from his body.

Months ago, he would have sought oblivion. To drown his thoughts in drink and evaporate his emotions in a cloud of sweet smoke. But he didn't even have the energy to do that. He was tired. So very tired of his life. The choices he had made. The consequences he had to live with. The loss and the grief. In the end, he had nothing to show for it. He had achieved nothing except his own survival. The Northern Kingdom was still under the rule of King Heroux. His people still suffered countless atrocities every day. He couldn't return to the Sodisce because it was in the Northern Kingdom. No doubt the King's Guard was still watching the place, hoping he would return so that they could deliver him to King Heroux. Tonight, after he swore the oath to Citric, he would have his freedom. But now it felt worthless.

"What is all this?"

Henri turned to see Eve standing beside him, her eyes darting around the room in horror. Her expression quickly shifted from shock to anger as her eyes narrowed on someone in the crowd.

"This is all her doing, I presume?"

Henri didn't reply. It was clear that Brielle had used the opportunity of Citric's ceremony to try to re-establish herself at court. To show the nobles that even though they were swearing allegiance to Citric as their new king, Brielle was the one who had organized this celebration to honor him. That nothing happened at this court without her approval.

Eve clenched her jaw in irritation.

"You can't judge Brielle for playing the game when you're an expert player yourself."

He had not forgotten about Eve's betrayal. That she had toyed with him the first night she arrived at Alkhiem, when she hinted that she had been getting well acquainted with Nathaniel. She had known the entire time what his closest friend had become and she did not tell him. She had withheld the truth in order to use it against him at the right moment. Making him a central pawn in their play for the throne.

"I did what was necessary to overthrow an oppressive ruler. Brielle has no goal higher than her own vanity."

"She is fighting for what she believes in, just like you. She believes this kingdom is hers by birthright."

"It's not," Eve shot back.

"A lot of people in this room would disagree with you."

"Then a lot of people in this room will die."

Henri snapped his eyes to her. Her expression was deadly serious. For one so young, she had a fierceness about her that betrayed no mercy. He leaned in closer, his lips pulling back to a snarl.

"If you ever threaten her—"

"You'll what?" Eve countered, lifting her chin and bringing her face closer to his to challenge him directly. "What will you do?"

Powerless.

He would be powerless to stop them if they wanted to harm her. Just like he had been powerless to stop any of his loved ones from dying in front of him. The truth was, he had given up his power long ago when he refused to take an interest in his father's kingdom. When he decided that he would never become king. When he had refused to fight for his people. Power like that, the power of a king, was all-consuming. He had been afraid it would destroy him. Turn him into someone he did not want to be: a monster. Like his father. Like Nathaniel. He had not realized that by giving up his power, he would be helpless to defend the ones he cared about from the monsters who wielded it.

Eve watched Henri's face as his features flickered from barely contained anger to the smoldering embers of despair. *Fool.* It was mystifying why he still defended her. Why he couldn't see Brielle for the spoiled self-centered brat that she was. Despite his stubbornness, and against her better judgement, Eve had actually grown to like Henri. He was no king, but he had proven to have some redeeming qualities. The brief moments they had shared together had resulted in a strange sort of truce between them. Not a friendship but an understanding. Whatever it was, it was gone now. His loyalty was always going to be with Brielle. It was such a waste. She would only ever use him.

"Anyway, it doesn't matter what games she plays. After tonight, you won't be here to witness them. You will be free to start your new life, away from all of this."

Henri shifted on his feet as if the thought made him uneasy.

"Where will you go?"

"What do you care?"

"I don't."

She turned away from him, fuming. He was obviously angry at her for betraying them. So be it. She would do it a thousand times over if she had to. The people of the Southern Kingdom were free, and Citric had reclaimed half of his ancestral lands. They were finally achieving what they had been planning for years. She did not regret any of it. Not one bit. As for his friend the Butcher, he deserved worse than the quick death Citric had given him.

The music ceased abruptly and the courtiers fell to silence as Citric entered the room. No guard followed him, but his hand rested casually on his sword, the Sword of Peace, a reminder to anyone who would challenge him. Instead of the fine court fashion the nobles wore, he was still wearing his leathers. There was no crown on his head. His hair was tied back into a rough ponytail at the nape of his neck, with errant strands breaking free at the sides. Eve's heart kicked in her chest at the sight of him strolling through the crowd toward the throne.

His throne.

As a direct descendant of Sirasinda he was the rightful custodian of the land, but he would never be one of them—a polished peacock of a king. He would always be a warrior with a rebel heart and a wild soul. A king for the people. Her king.

Citric stalled in front of the throne as if he couldn't bear to sit on the gilded seat that had overthrown his ancestors. Instead, he remained standing and turned to address the crowd.

"How did you know?" Henri's whispered words were urgent in her ear.

Eve shot him an irritated look. She had been waiting for this moment for years and he was ruining it.

"Know what?" she hissed.

"That Nathaniel would surrender the King's Guard if my life was in danger?"

Eve released a long-suffering breath. "Are you still so blind? He was in love with you."

She watched as the color drained from his face and his lips parted, speechless. He was so ignorant it beggared belief. When they first arrived at the Southern court, Nathaniel had been difficult to get a read on. He had seemed completely void of emotion and lacking in the normal weaknesses that most men had in abundance. Trying to uncover information about him was frustrating to say the least. But then she had realized something. The absence of information and weakness and emotion told her everything she needed to know. Because Henri was the one thing his world revolved around. And although such a thing could be dismissed as mere duty, Eve had suspected there was more to it.

She had observed him carefully that week and her suspicions were proven right. Because she knew what it looked like to be in love with someone who was oblivious to her affections. To want someone to notice her so badly, but at the same time be terrified at the thought of them knowing the true depth of her feelings. To hide it all beneath a cool, ambivalent mask, to explain her actions away under the guise of duty and loyalty. The signs were veiled and fleeting, but they were there. In the careful distance Nathaniel maintained between them. In the way he averted his eyes whenever Henri flirted with a lady. She recognized his pain and his longing.

Henri's breath was warm against her cheek as he snarled, "If you are so good at seeing the truth, then you would know that Brielle and Citric slept together."

The words stopped Eve's heart in her chest. Her stomach plummeted to the floor. She blinked up at Henri, stunned.

"I thought not," he spat.

"Lords and ladies of the former Southern Kingdom," Citric began as his eyes roamed the uneasy crowd before him, "I am Citric, the new king of this land. A land that was once known as Sirasinda. The land of my people. Generations ago, my people lived in peace and prosperity on this land for many years, until one day a great army came against us. They did not approve of our way of life, our connection with the land, our beliefs. But most of all, they coveted what was ours. They slaughtered my people and destroyed our homes, our sacred sites. Then the two men who led the army divided the lands into North and South and pronounced themselves kings. The Old Treaty was written to ensure that they never came against one another, that one side could never claim the entire breadth of our lands. Our history, our very existence, was lost. Rewritten. But we have never forgotten. We are the rightful custodians of this land and we reclaim it as ours. Tonight, those who recognize my claim will swear an oath of allegiance to me. They will be welcome to remain on our land, provided they abide by our laws and customs. Those who do not recognize my claim and swear an oath of allegiance to me are not welcome and must leave our lands immediately. Those that refuse to leave will face my justice."

Unsettled murmurs bubbled up among the crowd, but Eve hardly noticed them. It wasn't true. It couldn't be true. Brielle represented everything Citric hated. He would never be attracted to a girl like her.

"Those who wish to swear the oath to me should come forward now."

His gaze cut through the crowd to fix on Henri, a silent command in his eyes. Henri stepped forward, his movements slow and deliberate, allowing the eyes of the crowd to follow him as he made his way toward the throne. He stopped to stand in front of Citric and they regarded each other for a tense moment before Henri kneeled before him. The crowd inhaled a sharp breath of disbelief.

"I hereby rescind my claim to the throne of the Northern Kingdom. I swear on my faith and my honor and before the witnesses here tonight that I will be true and faithful to you as my king, pledging to you my undying loyalty, the strength of my sword, and the truth of my words, all the days of my life."

Henri stood and Citric reached for the dagger at his belt. The crowd stiffened but Henri didn't so much as flinch. He simply took the blade from Citric and cut a line across his right palm. The people stirred, clearly affronted by the sight of such a pagan ritual. Citric, in turn, drew the blade across his own palm and then clasped hands with Henri in strength.

"My blood is now your blood, my life force your life force. You have chosen me, and I have chosen you as a blood brother. Wherever destiny takes us, we will be as one. Let the man who would break his blood oath to his brother be forever cursed."

Henri turned back to the crowd and surveyed them for a moment, as if making sure the message was received loud and clear. As he strode forward, they parted in front of him, watching in bewilderment as he left the throne room. At his swift departure, they turned to each other, exchanging anxious glances and fevered whispers.

"Who among you will be next?" Citric challenged.

The crowd shifted fearfully as silence fell over them like a death shroud.

"I will."

Eve's head snapped with the rest of the crowd's in the direction of Brielle. She stepped forward, her gait regal, her eyes never leaving Citric. Eve's whole body itched to rush out and stop her, but she knew better than to make a scene. She glanced at Citric, hoping he would reject her offer and humiliate her. He didn't need her oath. She could never be a threat to him. But he didn't say a word as she approached to stand before him. Their eyes lingered on each other and Eve's stomach turned to acid. Brielle slowly lowered herself on both knees before him. The sight looked sensual somehow. Even Citric appeared to be spellbound by the sight of her kneeling at his feet.

"I hereby withdraw my claim to the throne of the Southern Kingdom. I swear on my faith and my honor and before the witnesses here tonight that I will be true and faithful to you as my king, pledging to you my undying loyalty and the truth of my words, all the days of my life."

She rose elegantly and clasped her hands demurely in front of her. Citric's expression was imperceptible as he reached for his blade.

"There is no need to bind my oath in blood, my king. I would seal it with something far stronger."

Brielle stepped forward to press a whisper of a kiss against his cheek. Eve's mouth fell open as the crowd gasped in shock. Brielle pulled away slowly, spearing Citric with a charged look before she turned to face the crowd, her smile coy and triumphant.

CHAPTER FOUR

C itric watched her walk away from him, back into the crowd of stunned courtiers. His body had gone rigid as she pressed her lips lightly against his stubbled cheek, but at least one part of his body had twitched. Even now he could feel it swelling beneath his breeches, intoxicated by her perfume which still lingered in the air around him. The image of her kneeling before him replayed in his mind, arousing him further. He had hardly heard a word she said during the oath taking, too distracted by the view of her perfect breasts peeking out from beneath her laced bodice, her soft lips hovering tantalizingly close to his cock. They had not pleasured each other in that way the night before taking the castle and now he regretted it. Sorely. The thoughts came to his mind fast and hot and relentless. Her lips kissing the tip of him, her lips parting to take him into her mouth, the wetness of her tongue coating his column.

A nauseating wave of jealousy and outrage struck him.

Fuck.

The murderous expression on Eve's face shocked him to his wits. So he had been right, then. The emotions he felt the other night were Eve's. He recognized the texture of them, the intensity. Her outrage was warranted. He had lost himself for a moment there. But the jealousy—

Regaining his composure, Citric speared the crowd with a taunting look. "Who will be next?"

The lords reluctantly stumbled forward one by one to swear the oath. They repeated the words as one would repeat a nursery rhyme. Which made sense, as they probably would have learned it from their tutors as children in order to be able to swear an oath to their king when they came of age. But this oath was different. The lords cringed when they drew their own blood to the surface and recoiled in disgust as they clasped hands with him, mixing their blood with his. Citric felt each of them seep inside his veins, fusing with the sensorium. He began to catalogue each of them, the way the tongue catalogues flavors. It would take time to recognize each tether, but after years of practice, he was a fast learner.

The lords retreated quickly when their oath giving was done, disappearing back into the safety of the crowd and allowing another lord to step forward. Citric knew he should be paying closer attention to them, to what the sensorium could reveal about each of them, but his mind kept straying back to Brielle. To that featherlight kiss that had seared his skin.

He should have expected Brielle would take his oath ceremony and turn it into a grand spectacle. It was an attempt to undermine him and reinstate her position at court, to reclaim some shred of dignity and power. But he could have never predicted the kiss. Clearly her attempts at regaining her pride and social influence had failed, so she had done something unexpected. It was a masterful move. The court had already deemed her ruined the moment she lost her kingdom. As a woman without wealth or title, she was no longer worthy of their time or company. So she had taken control of her own demise by ruining herself publicly, thereby putting herself back in a position of power.

Citric had to give her credit. The move was bold, but it was also desperate. No nobleman would have her now. By taking such familiar liberties with him, she had insinuated that they meant something to each other. Not enemies or former allies gone sour, but lovers. No nobleman would marry a woman who had already given herself to another man. They would consider her spoiled goods. His blood heated violently at the thought. It made him want to break bones. Citric knew Brielle considered every lord here to be beneath her and he would never argue with her on that point. But by declaring herself his lover, she had thrown her fate in with his. No nobleman would marry her, but no courtier would dare touch her either, for fear of reprisal from their new king. No one would dare touch a king's possessions.

The truth hit him like a blow from his blind spot; she had done it to protect herself.

His fierce gaze locked onto her as she stood at the back of the throne room with a wineglass perched in her hand. She stood alone. The courtiers were keeping their distance from her, not willing to talk to her, but also not willing to throw her out.

The moment the last lord swore the oath to him, Citric stormed down from the dais and stalked across the room toward her. Her only response to his thundering approach was to leisurely sip from her glass of wine. The sight of her wet lips sent an erotic charge to his manhood.

"Who was it?" he demanded, his voice fatally calm.

"Who was what?"

"Who threatened you?"

Her perfectly poised features faltered slightly as she cast her eyes around the room, clearly concerned that they were being overheard. He watched her gaze carefully as it scanned the faces of the lords in attendance, but she gave nothing away. Ever the practiced courtier.

She lowered her voice. "I don't know what you're talking about. The only person who has threatened me recently is you."

He pressed his lips into an aggravated line. "Now that you have sworn the oath to me, you have my protection. You didn't need to ruin yourself for it."

Her head whipped up to him, her eyes flaring like embers. "I didn't ruin myself. You ruined me."

"I seem to remember you begging me to."

A fetching shade of rose-petal pink adorned her cheeks. "I meant when you stole my kingdom from me."

"I don't think that's what you meant at all."

Citric lifted his hands to trail his knuckles down her arms, slowly caressing her soft, exposed skin. He heard her breath catch in her throat as her brown eyes bored into his. He wondered what other parts of her body had also responded to his touch. If the walls of her sex were slick with wanting. If the sudden silence and stillness in the room was any indication, she wasn't the only one mesmerized by him. Conscious of eyes upon them, he leaned in closer to whisper into her ear. He couldn't help but inhale the perfumed scent of her neck, and his cock grew broad in response. "If anyone threatens you, you will tell me."

Her voice was satisfyingly uneven as she replied, "Is that a command from my king?"

"From your lover." His carnal words melted into her ear.

Citric could have sworn she shivered, but she recovered quickly to step back and pierce him with a lethal look. "I can protect myself. The question is, who will protect you from me?"

She tilted her head to reinforce her point before sauntering away from him. He watched her perfect figure sashay from the room, along with every other courtier, and in that moment he understood the power she used to hold over this court.

Her words did not surprise him. Citric did not need the blood oath to know that Brielle was scheming to reclaim her crown. He had never been under any illusion that she would accept defeat graciously. He just didn't know how being the king's lover helped her cause.

Brielle hesitated in front of the door and cast her gaze down the length of the empty hallway at the other doors on either side. She was standing in the guest wing of the castle, which hosted a number of bedchambers usually reserved for visiting royals and dignitaries. It was her best guess for where Henri had been staying, but she had no idea which room he was in or if he was even here at all. She drew in an anxious breath and forced her knuckles to rap on the door.

Silence.

It was late. After swearing the oath to Citric and watching the lords reluctantly swear theirs, she hadn't stayed much longer at the allegiance ceremony. There was no need, she had made her point. She left as soon as was socially acceptable and rushed here, to a hallway of doors, in the hopes of finding him. Henri hadn't even looked her way before departing the throne room after swearing his allegiance to Citric. She thought he would have at least sought her out to say goodbye now that he had obtained his freedom. He was grieving the loss of his friend, she understood that, but surely that made saying goodbye to her even more important.

Brielle knocked on the door again, this time a little firmer. "Henri."

Silence.

Unless he was still mad at her. Brielle moved down the hallway to the next door and rapped on it resolutely. She knew he hadn't been impressed by her scheming tonight, not that he had stayed for the full performance, but he should know her better than to expect her to accept defeat. She would never accept it. She would do everything in her power, diminished as it was, to rectify the wrong done to her. Henri wanted her to be safe, to embrace a simple life, but to her, that would be worse than death.

"Henri," she called out as she knocked on the door again.

Silence.

Brielle moved to the next one, her delicate knuckles now clenched into a formidable fist to pound on the door. The thumping sound echoed down the hallway. She didn't even know what Henri planned to do with his freedom, where he planned to go. She had been so caught up in her own schemes she hadn't thought to ask him. He wouldn't dare travel to the Northern Kingdom. Which meant his only option was to sail across the sea to another country. Perhaps he would start another business. Except he had no coin. She would have to give him some. Her room had largely been stripped of wealth and she no longer possessed her jewels, but she would find something to give him.

"Henri!" she cried, desperation seeping into her voice.

He wouldn't have left without saying goodbye.

He wouldn't have.

Silence.

Brielle's eyes stung with tears, and this time she let them fall onto her cheeks. Because she was alone. In an empty hallway. In what used to be her home, her castle, her kingdom. Lord Waylan was right. She had nothing and no one. Not anymore.

Henri sat on the ground with his back against the door, listening to Brielle call out his name. She sounded frantic and loud enough to wake the entire guest wing of the castle. He knew he should open the door. She clearly needed him. But he didn't move. Not even when her fist pounded on his door, sending violent vibrations against his spine. He didn't have the energy to deal with whatever schemes she wanted him to join her in and he was afraid that if he opened the door, he would lash out at her. His eyes traveled over the shattered glass still splayed across the floor of his bedchamber. A sheen of sticky residue now glazed the wooden floorboards and the smell of stale alcohol coated the air. It was safer for Brielle if he did not open the door. Besides, he did not want her to witness him like this.

After a few minutes, the hallway outside went quiet and his muscles relaxed a little. Void of distraction, his mind stumbled back to Eve's haunting words.

He was in love with you.

Upon hearing them, he could have sworn that time itself stalled. He didn't believe it. He had opened his mouth to admonish her for fabricating such hurtful accusations, thinking she had said it to wound him, but the look on her face told him she believed it. More than believed it, she *knew* it.

Nathaniel. His friend since childhood. In love with him.

In all their years of friendship, Henri had never once seen Nathaniel pursue someone romantically. Even when Henri came into manhood and was relishing his first sexual experiences, his friend did not join in his boastful retellings. Nathaniel had never commented on the beauty of the ladies at court. He had never sought out any company but Henri's. At times, Henri had wondered if his friend ever experienced sexual urges at all. But of course, he assumed that his friend was just extremely discreet. He had good reason for discretion, given who his father was. Now Henri suspected the truth was far simpler. More painful. Nathaniel had not pursued anyone because he could not have the one person he desired.

Part of him still couldn't believe it, didn't want to believe it. Not because he found the thought repulsive, but because he couldn't bear the implications of it. It meant that his friend had been in love with him, perhaps for years, and he never knew it. He could not imagine what that had been like for Nathaniel. The agony he would have felt. He could not reconcile all the things that his friend's desires would have cost him.

A chance at happiness.

His life.

It was why he was willing to burn the rest of the world down in order to keep Henri safe. Because he loved him. Henri had never felt that way about anyone. Perhaps he had come close, once. For Brielle, he had been willing to do almost anything. Except reclaim his kingdom. That decision had cost them both. If he had aligned with her when she first came to the Sodisce then perhaps none of this would have happened. They would have found a way to take back their kingdoms and Nathaniel wouldn't have had to become a monster to protect him. Henri would have given up his chance to live a normal life, but his friend would still be alive. His people would be safe. Brielle would have her kingdom and he would have the power to protect her against her enemies.

His choices had condemned them all. He had made them based on fear and his own selfish desires, and the price paid was severe. For everyone. Henri clenched his hands into fists as he stared at the shards of glass on the ground. He could not fix what he had broken, but that did not mean the pieces couldn't be reforged. Tonight, he would make another choice. One that he would not regret. Because he refused to be powerless any longer. And because it was not too late to reclaim his kingdom.

Eve kicked off her blanket in frustration. She had been tossing and turning in bed for hours, her mind battered by relentless thoughts, each a more punishing blow than the one before. Citric's eyes on Brielle as she lowered herself demurely before him. Brielle pressing her perfectly painted lips to his stubbled cheek. Citric taking Brielle to his bed.

Eve grabbed a pillow and pinned it to her face before releasing a feral scream. Her lungs expunged, she tossed the pillow violently across the room and lay there panting. Eve didn't want to believe it was true, but Citric had been the one to teach her how to read people. How to notice every detail in a facial expression. The slightest change in body language. Her eyes did not lie. Something had happened between them. Perhaps it had only been a fleeting moment of passion. A simple kiss. A mistake. Eve pinched her eyes closed.

"Please don't be in love with her. Please don't be in love with her," she prayed to any god who would listen.

Opening her eyes, she didn't feel any better for her prayers. She did not want to believe that Citric could be foolish enough to fall prey to Brielle's pretty face and charming manipulations. Despite taking the oath, Eve had no doubt that Brielle had not given up on her quest to reclaim her kingdom. She never would. With her power at court extinguished, she did not present a threat to Citric in that way, but what if she captured his heart? What if he fell in love with her?

"No!" Eve screamed as she clenched the sheets in her fists.

Citric could lose everything. She wouldn't let that happen. Eve slid off the bed and marched outside her bedchamber into the hallway. She didn't care that she was only wearing her white linen nightgown and that her hair was a wild, tangled mess from her fitful attempt at sleeping. She needed to speak to Citric. Now.

Eve stormed through the rabbit warren of hallways until she came to the king's rooms. There were no guards posted out front, but that did not surprise her. Citric had no need of guards to protect him, nor would he probably want them hovering. She yanked open the heavy doors and marched inside. It was dark. No candles were lit, but there was a sliver of moonbeam peeking through the curtains on the far side of the room.

"Citric," she called out as she strolled over to yank the curtains back, flooding the room with moonlight.

A hand seized her mouth as another yanked her body back against a solid male form. Her eyes widened in horror as three men appeared out of the shadows in front of her, swords and daggers in hand, black masks covering their faces. To anyone else, that might have been enough to disguise them, but Eve had made sure to carefully study every man in the King's Guard, especially ones that were formerly King Heroux's men. These men definitely belonged to him.

"Where is the outlaw king?" one of them demanded.

Eve struggled against his hold, but he was at least three times her size and she was stupidly unarmed. She mentally kicked herself. She knew better than to go anywhere unarmed. Especially in the castle.

"I'll only ask you nicely one more time, girl." The man's breath was hot and foul against her cheek.

"We know you're his little spy." One of the other men sneered as he stepped closer to her. "Tell us or we will make you tell us." He lifted his knife to her face so that it gleamed in the moonlight. Pointing the tip of the blade to her collarbone, he drew a line slowly down the front of her chest between her breasts. "And we will enjoy it."

The men snickered.

"What do you say boys, a round each?"

Eve jerked her head back into the man's face before she bit down on his hand.

"You bitch!"

He released her, but before she could move, she felt an explosion of pain against her cheek as she was knocked clear across the floor.

"You'll pay for that."

Eve tried to ignore the black spots in her vision as she scrambled to her feet, but the men were already on her, dragging her backward by a fistful of hair, and clawing at her nightgown. She couldn't even think to scream as she kicked out against them, her hands flying, trying to grasp something, anything she could use as a weapon.

The tearing sound of steel filled her ears as a sword punctured through the chest of one of the men. Eve gasped in surprise but she didn't hesitate. She grabbed the blade as it fell from the man's limp hand and swung it round to hack into the legs of the second man towering over her. He roared in pain as he stumbled backward, giving her enough time to get to her feet and plunge the sword into his heart. As he went down, she whirled around to see the third man lying lifeless at Henri's feet.

Henri rushed to her, a bloody sword clutched in his hand. "Are you all right?"

Eve lifted her chin defiantly, though her lips trembled with fear and adrenaline. "I'm fine."

His eyes searched her body for injury and his mouth pressed into a tight line at the sight of the savage rips in her nightgown.

"They were looking for Citric," she explained, her voice shaky.

"Where is he?"

"I don't know."

In her haste to confront him, she had forgotten that Citric was not sleeping in the king's rooms. She had no idea where he was sleeping.

"Why are you here?" Eve furrowed her brows warily, sword ready in her hand.

"I came to talk to Citric."

His tone was even, but there was something lacing it.

"In the middle of the night?" she pressed.

"Same as you, I suppose. Couldn't sleep?"

She clenched her jaw. "No."

Eve thought she saw a flash of sympathy cross his features, but it disappeared in an instant. He still hadn't forgiven her, then.

Henri kneeled beside one of the men and yanked the mask down from his face. "Who are they?"

"From the King's Guard. Formerly King Heroux's men."

"So this was an assassination attempt."

The door crashed open and Henri moved to shield Eve with his body, but he relaxed at the sight of Citric. Citric's eyes were wild as they scanned the scene before locking onto Eve.

"Are you hurt?" he demanded as he rushed to her side.

"No." She averted her eyes away from him.

The situation couldn't get any more embarrassing. She had been caught trespassing in his bedchamber in the middle of the night and had been ambushed whilst unarmed. Citric had taught her better than that.

"How did you know that Eve was in danger?" Henri asked as his brows slammed together.

Citric's gaze flicked to his and then he looked away, as if he was reluctant to answer the question. "I felt it."

"What do you mean you felt it?"

Citric looked back to Eve, but she was still refusing to meet his eye.

"The direct descendants of Sirasinda possess an ancient sensorium. An additional sense that is activated by blood. When our blood mixes with another's, we are forever bound to that person through a blood bond. We can sense them. To some extent, we can experience what they experience, feel what they feel. It's not exact. How we perceive or interpret an experience can be wrong, just like any other sense. Like when you think you hear or see something, only to find out it was not what you thought. I sensed both of you were in danger. That knowing led me here."

Henri stared at him, wide-eyed, his expression a mixture of awe and dread. "Blood magic. So the stories are true."

"Yes."

"That's why you wanted the nobles to swear a blood oath to you, so you would know who poses a threat to you." At Citric's curt nod Henri's face turned dark. "Don't you think they have a right to know about this invasion of privacy before they swear allegiance to you?"

"If they are loyal to me, they have nothing to hide."

"It's a violation," Henri insisted.

"It's necessary," Citric returned.

Henri shook his head and rubbed his chin in irritation. Eve observed him carefully as his mind appeared to grapple with the implications. After a moment he gestured to the dead bodies at his feet and said, "You didn't feel them coming?"

"King Heroux's men from the King's Guard," Eve explained to Citric.

"The King's Guard have yet to swear oaths to me. Something I will remedy immediately."

Eve could feel Citric's eyes on her, willing her to look at him, but she couldn't. She was too embarrassed. She tried to lift a torn scrap of linen back across her shoulder, but it fell limp, exposing the top of her breast. Henri retrieved a blanket from the end of the bed and wrapped it gently around her shoulders. She peeked her eyes up at him in silent thanks.

"I'm sorry." Citric's voice was strained with guilt. "I should have been here."

"Where were you?" she replied.

She was not angry that he was not in his room, that they had found her instead of him. She did not blame him for what happened. But she was hurting, and that was entirely his fault.

"In the Red Wood."

Right. She should have known he would be sleeping in the Red Wood to maintain his connection with the sensorium. And to avoid having to sleep here, in this castle he hated so much.

"You've been sleeping in the Red Wood?" Henri challenged. "If you don't want to leave the Red Wood, then why lay claim to the Southern Kingdom?"

"I have already explained why," Citric shot back angrily. "Generations ago, this entire country was like the Red Wood. My people cared for the land and it provided for us. After the slaughter, our numbers were few. We barely survived. We hid in what was left of our land, what little they had not burned or claimed for themselves. They called it the Red Wood for the river of blood that soaked the woodland floor. After that day few people dared to enter it, fearing the wrath of vengeful spirits. We have been waiting lifetimes to reclaim what was stolen from us."

"Citric shares a blood bond with his land," Eve clarified. "For centuries his people have shed their blood and buried their bones in the soil of the Red Wood. He is bound to it. He can feel it and everything that happens in it, as if it were a part of him. His people stay connected to the land by caring for it, passing down their history through stories, rituals, and traditions. The stronger the connection, the more fertile the land becomes, the stronger his people are."

Eve watched as Henri digested her words. It was a lot to take in, she knew.

"Is that why the land in the Northern and Southern Kingdoms has become less productive over generations?" Henri asked.

"The land knows it was stolen," Citric replied. "It became a prisoner of war to its foreign rulers and has slowly wasted away over the years. But now that we have reclaimed it, as my people return to their land, the direct descendants of Sirasinda can start the healing process."

"You can heal the land?" Henri narrowed his eyes skeptically. "Make it fertile again?"

Citric tilted his head in affirmation. "It will take time, but it can be done."

Henri paused for thought. "Except you have only reclaimed half of your land."

"King Heroux is living on borrowed time." Eve's voice turned lethal. "The Northern Kingdom will be ours. Not that any of this concerns you. You're leaving, remember?"

Henri cast her a veiled look before turning back to Citric. "That's what I came to talk to you about."

Brielle strolled down the castle corridors, ignoring the nobles who bowed and curtsied to her face but then murmured insults behind her back. After her performance at last night's allegiance ceremony, her position at court had been firmly reinstated.

For now.

It was clear to everyone that she meant something to their new king. He had spared her life, allowed her to retain her title as princess, and permitted her to live at court. And then there was the kiss. So delicate a gesture and yet so grand in its meaning. Nobody would ever dare to be so presumptuous with a king, unless ... she would let their minds run wild with speculation. It may have destroyed what little reputation she had left, but it also bought her time and a measure of safety. No lord would threaten her or seek to marry her if they thought she was favored by the king. Even so, she knew her reprieve was temporary. With Henri gone, she only had herself to rely on. It was time to make her next move.

Brielle swept into the council chamber to find the room filled with councilmen, their disgruntled chatter coming to an abrupt halt at her unexpected presence. Her eyes moved involuntarily around the room and she stumbled a step as the memory of what happened in this room played out before her eyes. Meaty hands wrapping tightly around her throat as she gasped for air. Blood splattering across her face as she plunged a dagger into a man's neck. A pool of blood at her feet, seeping closer and closer to her shoes.

"Can we help you, Princess?"

Brielle cleared her throat and tried to compose herself. "Not at all, Lord Bailey. I'm here for the council meeting."

She pretended not to notice as the lords exchanged glances with each other. Instead, she walked down the length of the oak table to take the seat at the very end. The men bristled, affronted at the bold act. Citric, being king, would take the seat at the opposite end of the table. She couldn't wait to see his face when he saw her sitting across from him.

"Your Highness, you are not part of this council," Lord Bailey said as the councilmen crowded around her.

They looked as if they wanted to remove her with their bare hands, but she knew none of them would dare.

"I sat on this council for months while my father, the king, went to war against King Heroux."

"Yes, your father appointed you regent in his absence. Your father is now dead. We have a new king," Lord Bailey explained as if he were talking to a small child.

"Indeed, we do. I can assure you, the new king values my opinion very much."

An uneasy quiet filtered among them. Brielle unfurled her lips into a satisfied smile.

"Then perhaps you can speak to the king about returning the church's wealth."

Brielle's smile faltered at the sight of the bishop who stepped out from among the crowd of lords. The last time she had seen this insufferable man, he had led Sienna and her to a crypt beneath the church instead of offering them rooms for sanctuary. Sienna had given him her rings in exchange for food, water, and information.

Schooling her features to hide her contempt, Brielle replied, "Citric does not recognize the authority of the church, bishop. Or respect our God."

She basked in the pleasure of the shocked murmurs as the lords cursed amongst each other.

"As you witnessed from the blood ritual that took place last night, he is a pagan," she continued. "And let us not forget that he was an infamous outlaw for many years. His lust for riches is well known. In fact, he has managed to strip a lot of the castle's wealth in a matter of days."

"I heard he has pilfered our storage rooms and handed our supplies out to the commoners," Lord Walter said, outraged.

"If that is true and King Heroux lays siege to the castle, we will all die," Lord Rylan exclaimed.

Brielle sighed dramatically. "Unfortunately, it is true, and I doubt he will return any of it. But he is the new king, as you say, Lord Bailey. We must respect his reign."

Lord Bailey worked his jaw as he pondered the matter. "He hasn't been crowned yet."

The men nodded and murmured in agreement.

"Only the church can coronate a new king, and we refuse to do so until he returns our wealth," the bishop declared, slamming his hand on the table for emphasis.

"Which he will never do," Brielle added sweetly.

The lords considered each other carefully.

"Then perhaps we should appoint a new king," Lord Bailey suggested cautiously. "Now that there is no line of succession, we could form a witan to elect and approve the appointment of a new king."

Brielle's features tightened. "There is a line of succession."

"How would we nominate candidates, Lord Bailey?" Lord Walter asked.

"It should include only those with the strongest claims to the throne," Lord Bailey replied.

"My house owns the majority of land in the Southern Kingdom," Lord Ambrose boasted. "That gives my house the strongest claim."

"You may have the majority of land, Lord Ambrose, but in terms of wealth, my claim would be stronger than yours," Lord Walter insisted.

The council chamber erupted into argument, voices climbing over each other for attention and validation. Brielle pinched her lips into a thin line. Was she invisible? Did they not see the obvious answer right in front of them?

"My lords," she called out, drawing their attention back to her. "The strongest claim to the throne is, and always will be, through royal blood. I am my father's daughter."

Lord Bailey barely contained the scorn from his face. "You are a woman, Your Highness. A woman cannot rule a kingdom."

"Then I will marry," Brielle seethed through her teeth. "I will secure a strong alliance with another kingdom."

Lord Bailey scoffed in disdain. "I hardly think you will be able to secure a marriage proposal given … recent events. Let alone from a king."

Brielle's cheeks flamed.

"In any case, we don't have time to secure a marriage alliance," Lord Walter insisted. "King Heroux will be at our gate any day now to reclaim the Southern Kingdom. We need to have a strong ruler, one who is ready to lead us into battle to defend our kingdom."

"I will go to war." Brielle pushed herself to her feet and spread her fingers across the table in determination. "I will fight for this kingdom until my last breath."

The lords stared at her with a mixture of contempt, pained endurance, and disgust.

"You have courage, Your Highness," Lord Rylan attempted to placate her. "But we need a man's courage."

Brielle looked around at the faces in the room. Even compared to a pagan outlaw for a king, even confronted by the promise of a devastating war, they did not consider her fit to rule.

They would never consider her fit to rule.

Brielle pushed her chair back, the legs scraping against the floorboards, before she marched for the door.

"Where is this outlaw king?" Lord Bailey exclaimed, annoyed. "Does he not possess even the most basic manners to arrive on time?"

Brielle turned on her heel. "Oh, don't you know, Lord Bailey? Citric does not recognize the authority of the nobles either."

With that, she swept out of the room.

CHAPTER FIVE

B rielle stalked the halls aimlessly for a few minutes, trying to expel the fury from her body. Despite her indignation, she knew she should not be surprised. On her father's death, she had learned how little the lords respected her position at court. They would have handed her over to King Heroux in a heartbeat, or murdered her themselves if it meant one of them could ascend the throne.

She had naively hoped that saving them from the rule of King Heroux and reclaiming her kingdom would prove to them that she was fit to be queen. When that had failed, she had hoped that when faced with the prospect of a pagan outlaw for a king, they would finally realize she was their only hope and support her claim. But no. They couldn't see past their own small-mindedness and personal ambition. They couldn't see past her sex. Well, she'd be damned if she let any of them rule her kingdom.

Brielle advanced on a pair of King's Guard posted on the corner. "Where is the king?"

It was only then that she noticed something was not right. The guards looked rattled, their skin pale, their words nervous.

"He's out in the bailey, Your Highness."

Brielle frowned curiously and made her way out of the castle. Descending the stone stairs, she spotted Citric standing across the way in front of the stables, talking with a few of his men from Alkhiem. As she strode toward them, one of the men inclined his head in her direction and Citric turned. His expression hardened, as if the conversation he was having with his men was serious and now the sight of her only added to his problems.

At her approach, the men silently dispersed. Brielle let out a frustrated breath. She was sick and tired of being excluded from everything.

"What is going on?" Brielle demanded.

"Nothing." Citric's reply was curt as he took up a casual stance.

She glared at him. "Everyone seems to be on edge, especially the King's Guard. Are we expecting an attack?"

"We should always be expecting an attack," he returned coolly. At her deadpan look, he explained, "This morning every man in the King's Guard swore a blood oath to me. At least, most of them did. Those that refused or gave false oaths were taken to the dungeon."

So that's what had rattled the guards. They had been forced to partake in a pagan ritual, swearing a blood oath to their new king, and then watched as their brothers-in-arms were imprisoned when their new king did not believe their professions of loyalty.

"I suppose they will face your particular brand of justice on the green hill?"

"They will. As will all traitors."

Brielle narrowed her eyes at him. If that was meant to be a warning, she did not take kindly to it.

"Careful that you don't forget to make friends, as well as execute traitors."

"I have no need of friends," he said dismissively, and began to walk away.

Fuming, she hurried to follow after him. "Yes, you do. You need the nobles on your side if you are going to keep your crown."

"You do not care if I keep my crown."

"That is not true. I swore my allegiance to you, didn't I?"

Something flickered across his face, and Brielle instinctively knew he was thinking of the kiss. It had clearly had an effect on him. That knowledge ignited butterflies in her stomach, butterflies that she swiftly stomped on.

"You missed the council meeting this morning," she accused as she continued to follow him.

"I didn't call a council meeting."

"At the beginning of every week, there is a council meeting. You need to attend. The nobles are turning against you."

"So that's what that was," he muttered. "And I suppose you had nothing to do with that?"

"I don't need to stoke this fire. It's raging pretty well on its own thanks to you, and it's about to get out of control. They fear your pagan ways and think you don't respect them."

"I don't!" He rounded on her, furious. "They cannot call themselves men. Not one of them stepped forward to defend the people against King Heroux's tyranny. Not one of them stepped forward to defend you when your father was murdered."

Brielle blinked, taken aback by his rage in defense of her.

"I-I know that," she stammered, "but they are necessary to win over."

Citric hissed and stalked away, but she kept pace with him. "They possess the land, the wealth, the influence. You cannot hold the Crown without their support. And why are you still wearing those clothes? You look like an outlaw, which is not helping your cause. You need to look the part of a king and wear fine clothes. And you need to be crowned, immediately. Which, by the way, the bishop is refusing to do until you return the church's wealth. You need to stop robbing everyone blind!"

Citric stopped so abruptly she almost ran into him. His expression was wry with amusement, which only served to irritate her further.

"What?" she spat.

He cocked his head, his gaze assessing her. "Are you my royal adviser now?"

She bristled at the thought, but the alternative was unacceptable. She would not allow any of those misogynistic malcontents to rule her kingdom.

"You clearly need it."

A smirk danced on his lips. "Come with me."

He started walking in the direction of the gatehouse, but Brielle hesitated. "Where?" she asked warily.

He didn't respond.

Huffing out a breath, she reluctantly caught up with him and they walked in silence as they passed beneath the gate.

Stepping out into the city, away from the protection of the walls and the King's Guard, Brielle began to feel nervous. This was not right. A king casually strolling out of his castle into the city streets without cause or ceremony, without even a host of guards at his back. It was unheard of. Reckless. Stupid. Anything could happen. Riots, robbery, abuse of every kind. Citric was the best warrior she had ever seen, but he was still only a man. Against a city of commoners and vagrants, they would both die very quickly.

As they walked through the dusty, noisy streets, the people watched them curiously, but they didn't gawk at them or pause in their tasks. It was as if they were used to the sight of him, their new king, walking the streets as if he were one of them. In fact, they smiled at him, called out greetings and blessings on him. They even called out greetings to her, which made her uncomfortable. Citric, on the other hand, nodded back at every single one of them and placed a hand over his heart in acceptance of their good wishes.

Feeling slightly dazed, she asked again, "Where are we going?"

"Just here."

They came to a stop at the entrance to the market square. Brielle could see a number of tables set up where traders and farmers would normally be selling their wares. Instead, people stood patiently in long lines behind each table, being served by women who handed out what looked to be basic goods. Other people formed lines in front of several large cauldrons where women were cooking what smelled like soups and broth.

Brielle didn't recognize any of the women, but she knew they were not from the Southern Kingdom. They dressed like the women of Alkhiem, and the smell of the food was intimately familiar. If she needed any further confirmation of her suspicions, she found it when she noticed Eve standing behind the women, as if she were supervising the operation. But instead of watching the women, Eve's gaze was firmly fixed on Brielle and her expression was murderous.

Trying to ignore the daggers being thrown her way, Brielle turned her attention back to Citric. "What is this?"

"Your people have been neglected for too long. The poor, the elderly, the children. They have all been suffering, dying of disease and poverty. My people are doing what we can to help them."

Her lips parted in astonishment and she surveyed the scene again. "I don't recognize these women. Where did they come from?"

"Alkhiem isn't the only camp in the Red Wood. There are many."

Brielle arched her eyebrows, surprised.

"But we are running low on supplies," Citric went on. "It's going to take time to restore the land, for farmers to return to their fields and yield decent crops. I am gathering all the wealth I can and using it to make profitable trade deals. We will need to house and feed the people until the land is ready to provide for them. Just outside the city, beyond the western tower, we have started to erect tents. Anyone who wants to seek refuge is welcome."

Brielle stood dumbfounded at his words, combined with the sight in front of her. She had never witnessed anything like it. The people looked wretched, as if they were hanging onto life by a string. The whole scene looked like the aftermath of war, where people became displaced and desolate.

In truth, the war was yet to happen.

"This is very kind of you, but what will happen when King Heroux retaliates against us? We no longer have enough provisions for the castle to withstand a siege. We have no room for all these people to seek refuge inside our walls."

"I will make sure King Heroux does not cross the border. Now that we have the Southern army, we can face him on a battlefield of our choosing and reclaim the Northern Kingdom."

"War costs money. Men, armor, horses, provisions."

"It's fortunate I'm a notorious outlaw who has built up his wealth over many years."

Brielle glanced at him sidelong to see a smirk tug on the corner of his lips. "This was your plan the whole time. To accumulate enough wealth from robbing nobles to wage war?"

His eyes danced mischievously and she couldn't resist the small smile that bloomed on her lips. He stared at her thoughtfully for a moment before clasping his hands behind his back.

"I'm discussing such plans with my council tonight. People I've chosen personally, whose opinions I trust and respect. I want you to be one of them."

Brielle looked up at him wide-eyed but his expression was completely serious. She turned away slowly, her thoughts and emotions suddenly a churning sea inside her. Was she really going to give up the fight for her kingdom so easily? Become one of Citric's trusted inner circle and help him secure his throne?

Her throne.

"If King Heroux had not invaded, you would have eventually waged war on us," she said tentatively, her words hanging heavy in the air between them. "Would you have killed my father?"

She couldn't bring herself to look at him because she knew what his answer would be.

"If he refused to give up his claim to the land and swear the blood oath to me, yes."

Brielle sucked in a thin breath. "And me? Would you have killed me?"

"No." His answer was swift, certain.

"You said only days ago if I did not swear my allegiance to you, you would kill me."

Citric's fingers suddenly gripped her chin, gentle but firm, and guided her face back to him until their eyes met. "But we both know I never would have done it."

Her heart thundered at his words, his touch. Did she know that? He had fooled her once before. Lied to her. Betrayed her. Done things she never would have thought him capable of.

Doubt must have shown on her face because he released her chin and his features hardened. "If you were successful in overthrowing me, like I know you have been trying to do, would you have killed me?"

Brielle hesitated, the words stuck in her throat. His betrayal had enraged and wounded her like nothing else before in her life. The only thought that had brought her comfort was revenge. In those heated moments, she would have gladly ordered his execution. But would she have been able to go through with it? If the council had supported her claim today, and if she managed to take back her throne, would she be able to harden her heart enough to rid herself of the threat he posed to her? And if she did, would she regret it?

"You have certainly changed from the princess I met in the woods that day."

She couldn't tell if that was a compliment or not. It didn't sound like it.

"I have learned much about the world since then, and much about myself."

She had led a campaign to reclaim her kingdom. Fought for her life and killed her enemies. Been betrayed and imprisoned by people she trusted. Been excluded and rejected by her own court. And abandoned by one of her closest friends.

Brielle inhaled a deep breath to steady herself. "The night before we infiltrated the castle, I made a vow that I would make whatever sacrifices were necessary, no matter the cost to myself, to ensure the safety of my kingdom. You betrayed me, and I will never forgive you for that."

Citric's expression remained imperceptible, but something flickered behind his eyes.

"I do not know the truth of your claim on my kingdom, but it is not the most pressing issue right now. The Southern Kingdom is facing many threats; least of which is a war with King Heroux and a potential uprising from our own nobles. You and I want the same thing: peace and stability for the people. That is all that matters." Brielle turned to walk away before tossing over her shoulder, "For now."

Her heart pounded as she walked away from him. She could feel his stare boring into her back, causing her fingers to fidget nervously, but she hoped he didn't see that. She hoped she looked as confident as she sounded. In truth, she was closer to tears than treachery. Ever since she learned of Citric's betrayal, she had been consumed by anger. She regarded his actions to be a betrayal of her as a sovereign ruler, not her as a woman. She had not allowed herself to be just a girl, deceived by ... well, she wasn't sure what he was to her. They had spent one night together, with absolutely no promises for the future. Really, it was silly that she had any feelings for him at all.

Brielle walked past the lines of people in the market square to approach Eve, who shot her a look that was less than welcoming. Brielle ignored it and tried to insert some civility into her voice.

"How can I help?"

It was the first time Brielle had spoken to Eve since the day she had betrayed her. There had never been any hope of friendship between them, but now it seemed like Eve hated her even more than before. Brielle hadn't thought that was possible, but if she had to guess why, she would bet the kiss had something to do with it. It was clear to anyone with a set of eyes that Eve desired Citric.

Brielle's little performance at the allegiance ceremony would have gotten under her skin.

Eve's face twisted in mock confusion. "The Southern Princess wants to help her people all of a sudden? Why is that, I wonder? Is it to gain their love for the coup she is preparing? Or is it to impress the new king?"

Brielle released a long-suffering sigh. "Neither. Now, how can I help?"

Her voice turned ice cold. "We don't need your help."

"I can do whatever task needs doing. I am willing to learn."

"You had your chance to care for these people and you didn't. So go back to your castle and plot your schemes, but know this: you will never win. Not this kingdom and certainly not him. Not while I am by his side."

Put firmly in place by the heat of her words and the venom in her voice, they regarded each other before Brielle lifted her chin and walked away.

Eve stoked a log on the fire, not because the flames were dying, but because she was still restless with irritation. She could hardly believe her eyes when she saw them together in the marketplace that morning. Citric standing beside Brielle as if they were not enemies, showing her the efforts of his people to help her people. A people she had ignored and neglected for years. They had stood so close to each other, too close for her liking, and at one point they had even smiled at each other. But then the conversation between them must have soured because their body language changed. She'd felt relieved to know that they were arguing and incensed that Brielle was causing trouble again. Why was Citric even giving her his time? There was so much to do and so little time to achieve everything and he was spending precious moments with *her*. Eve tossed another branch into the flames, sending sparks flying.

Henri shot her a curious glance from where he sat on the opposite side of the fire. She narrowed her eyes at him, daring him to ask her. He didn't, and she was glad. At least one of them had the common sense not to aggravate her.

"He's here," Leif announced and stopped his nervous pacing at the entrance of the cave.

When no one appeared, Henri tossed Eve a questioning look.

"Leif can sense Citric through the blood bond they share. He's a direct descendant of Sirasinda, so the connection goes both ways."

Moments later, Citric appeared out of the shadows of the woodland and swung down from the saddle of his dun mare. He tied the reins to the branches of a nearby tree where the other horses were grazing. Approaching the cave, Citric nodded curtly to Henri and clasped Leif's arm in greeting. When his attention turned to her, Eve tried to keep the scowl from her face. If he thought she was upset, he would want to know why and she couldn't tell him. Not without sounding ridiculous. Worse than that, he might think she was upset because of the attack. But she had already forgotten all about that. At least, she was trying to. Unable to force a smile, she turned her head away in indifference.

"Henri, do you remember Leif?" Citric clapped a hand on his friend's shoulder.

Henri returned a brittle smile. "I never forget a man who threatened me."

At the sound of another horse's approach, Eve's head whipped up and she shot to her feet. A white mare came into view and Eve squinted in the dark, trying to make out the figure. Her eyes widened in recognition before they snapped to Citric.

"What is she doing here?"

"I invited her."

Brielle dismounted from her horse, tied the reins next to the others, and surveyed the mouth of the cave with trepidation. As she approached, a gentle wind sent fallen leaves spiraling around her skirts.

"Why?" Eve hissed, clenching her hands into fists at her sides.

"Because we need more allies, not more enemies."

Brielle suddenly froze. "Henri?"

She rushed toward Henri and he stood to catch her in a tight embrace, his expression somewhat perplexed. Eve's gaze flicked to Citric, curious to see what his reaction would be to this display of affection. He watched them embrace, but his features betrayed nothing.

"I thought you had left," Brielle breathed into Henri's shoulder. She pulled away from him but held his hands in hers as if she didn't want to let go of him just yet.

Eve's eyes darted between them and Citric, taking note of every micro reaction.

"I couldn't leave while King Heroux still rules the Northern Kingdom. I will fight for my people's freedom and then I will be free to live my life as I choose."

Brielle gave him a small, grateful smile and squeezed his fingers.

"Citric." Eve's voice was cutting as she called his attention back to her. "She is not our ally. She should not be here."

"I don't like you either," Brielle retorted. "You betrayed me, and you used Henri. Don't think I will ever forget or forgive that. But this isn't about us, and this campaign does not require us to like each other."

"I don't trust you!" Eve bit the words out one by one.

"Enough." Citric's tone conveyed that he was bored with the argument.

Eve pressed her lips into an indignant line. How could he do this? It was impossible not to see how stupid this was. Brielle was doing her best to undermine and discredit Citric, manipulating the nobles to turn against him and back her claim for the throne. And now she was here. Citric trusted her enough to let her know their plans. It was unfathomable. No doubt she would take every word and twist it to her own advantage, dismantling them from within. How had she even convinced him she was an ally? Eve wouldn't have thought he would be so easily deceived by some sweet words whispered into his ear or some temptress moves in the bedroom. The very thought of Brielle doing such things made her feel equal parts sick and murderous.

Citric indicated for everyone to sit down around the fire. "Brielle, this is Leif."

Brielle nodded to him in greeting. "Why are we meeting here?" She glanced around the small cave as she took a seat next to Henri.

"You have to ask that?" Eve sneered.

"We can't risk being overheard in the castle," Citric replied. "I think it was you who once said that even the walls have ears."

"And you would sense anyone unfamiliar entering the woods trying to spy on us," Henri added, to which Citric gave a confirming nod.

Brielle frowned. "What do you mean?"

"I'll explain another time," Citric said.

"Sure. Let's just tell her all our secrets," Eve fumed.

"They are my secrets to tell." Citric's voice betrayed his waning patience.

Eve clenched her jaw. It was bad enough that Brielle would learn their plans to reclaim the Northern Kingdom, but now he was going to tell her about the blood magic and his connection to the Red Wood. He might as well give the kingdom back to her right now! The Sirasindans had kept the ancient sensorium a secret for centuries. Until last night, Citric had only ever told one person outside of Alkhiem: her. She still remembered the moment he laid his deepest secrets at her feet. She had felt overwhelmed and honored by it. Like he had chosen her. Like she was special.

"Now that we have secured the Southern Kingdom," Citric began, "we must look to taking the North. We cannot allow King Heroux to cross the border into the Southern lands. We must choose a battleground and lure him out of his stronghold with the promise of war."

"Where did you have in mind?" Henri asked.

"Just beyond the border, near Nistan." Leif unfurled a map across the ground, placing small stones on the four corners. Pointing to an area on the map, he explained, "It gives us the advantage of the high ground and allows easy movement of soldiers to the front."

Henri leaned forward, resting his elbows on his knees as he surveyed the map. "I know the place. It's a good choice."

"Then it's decided. I will send a raven to King Heroux tomorrow stating our terms. The army will need to be ready to march by the end of the week," Citric said.

"Are we sure King Heroux will agree to our terms?" Brielle queried. "The last time we tried to engage him in battle, he used a secret alliance instead of an army to defeat us."

"Things are different now," Citric replied. "King Heroux suffered heavy losses from his campaign against Airedeen, so it made sense to find an alternative way to conquer the kingdoms. Since then, he has replaced his losses with the Northern army. A seasoned war lord is always eager to see battle."

Brielle frowned, unconvinced, and turned to Henri. "What have your spies gathered about his numbers and his plans to retake the South?"

"I haven't heard from them. They've gone quiet." His tone suggested that the silence worried him.

"Your spies knew nothing about the commander's plot with King Heroux," Brielle mused out loud, as if thinking something through.

She did not appear to notice Henri's features tightening in response to the criticism.

"What are you saying?" Eve demanded.

"I don't think King Heroux will meet our terms for war. He did not accumulate all his land and wealth by simply winning battles. He is cunning. A good strategist will always choose the path with the greatest chance of success and the smallest chance of losses."

"What other option does he have except to meet us on the battlefield?" Leif asked.

"I don't know." Brielle bit her lip pensively, and Eve rolled her eyes. "But what if we presented him with one? An opportunity for a new secret alliance?"

Brielle looked across at Henri and hesitated. Eve narrowed her eyes curiously as she watched them both. It was like Brielle didn't want to suggest her plan out loud.

"Send Henri as your emissary." The words tumbled from Brielle's mouth as if she had forced herself to spit them out.

Eve's eyes widened in horror. "What?"

"King Heroux will kill him," Citric countered.

"Not if Henri presents himself as a potential ally. If Henri can convince King Heroux that he is willing to betray you in exchange for becoming his new right hand, then we will have a spy in the very center of his court. We will know his every move."

Henri stared back at Brielle, his expression grave, and Brielle seemed to wither beneath it.

"King Heroux will never believe that," Eve scoffed. "He murdered Henri's father and stole his kingdom."

"But I betrayed him in his attempt to reclaim it and then I killed his closest friend," Citric interjected, before fixing his gaze on Henri. "You swore allegiance to me and volunteered to be my emissary so that I would trust you, but really you want vengeance against me."

Henri's eyes hardened on Citric as a muscle ticked in his jaw. "Well, when you put it like that."

Eve's wide eyes darted between them in chilling disbelief. Surely Citric could see that this plan had no merit. He would be sending Henri to his death. King Heroux would kill him on sight. And even if he didn't and Henri somehow managed to convince King Heroux he was switching sides, what was to stop him from actually switching sides? If King Heroux promised him the return of the Northern Kingdom in exchange for betraying the Southern Kingdom, would Henri really turn him down?

Henri had always claimed he did not want to be king, but perhaps he had changed his mind. In fact, she was certain something about him had changed. Only last night he had sworn an oath of allegiance to Citric in exchange for his freedom, a freedom he had coveted his entire life, and yet he had not left. He had stayed. Moreover, he had sought Citric out to pledge his sword to his cause, a cause he had never cared about before. Not really. He had never fought for anyone, except Brielle, and he had no hope where she was concerned if she and Citric—

Her stomach lurched and Eve tossed another branch into the flames to distract herself from the images that flashed in her mind. Then again, perhaps Henri and Brielle were in on this together. Maybe this was their scheme for revenge. To establish Henri as a spy in King Heroux's court, while Brielle remained a spy in Citric's court. Both working together to undermine from within. Eve's eyes darted between them warily. Both of them looked ruined by the proposed plan, their expressions grim, but they could be playacting.

Henri exhaled a heavy breath. "If I can't convince King Heroux, he will kill me."

Eve observed Brielle's features crumple in anxiety.

"If you can convince him," Citric countered, "it might win us the war and save countless lives. The choice is yours."

Henri placed a folded blanket on his mare's back, making sure it covered the withers. Reaching for the stirrup, he placed it over the horn and put the girth over the seat of the saddle before hoisting it onto the horse's back. His mare waited patiently as he positioned it evenly across the blanket.

The journey to the Northern castle would be a long one. He would need to travel through the Red Wood for as long as possible to avoid detection, but eventually he would leave its sanctuary and head out onto the open road. From there, it would only be a matter of time before the King's Guard intercepted him. They would take him to King Heroux to be executed and to claim their reward. That would be his one chance to convince the king that he was more useful to him alive than dead. It was ironic that he had spent months evading capture by the King's Guard and now he was planning to hand himself over to them.

Henri released the stirrup from the saddle horn before pulling the girth down off the seat. He slung the girth underneath his mare's belly and fed the cinch strap through the ring.

"Your Highness."

Henri turned at the voice to find three lords standing just outside the stall. Ominous. Whatever this was, it couldn't be good.

"It's just Henri now," he replied.

"A shameful injustice." One of the men shook his head as he lowered his voice to a conspirator's whisper. "To force a true heir of the Northern Kingdom to renounce his claim to the throne."

Henri tensed. "And you are?"

"Lord Willoughby. This is Lord River and Lord Condor."

The lords inclined their heads to him in a subtle show of respect. Henri cast his eyes around the bailey, noting the people that may be watching and listening to this treasonous interaction.

"What can I do for you, my lords?"

"We want you to know that not everyone in the castle supports the outlaw king," Lord Willoughby said in a hushed tone.

"Many of us do not want a pagan for a king. We respect the old ways. A king should have a royal lineage, royal blood flowing in his veins," Lord River explained.

"We are prepared to do what is necessary to ensure that you reclaim your rightful place," Lord Condor added. "Both the Northern and Southern Kingdoms could be yours."

Henri stood there for a moment, stunned. A faction of the nobles wanted to rise up against Citric and make Henri king. He glanced around the bailey again, but Citric and his men were nowhere in sight. Surely Citric could sense these traitors in his court. They would have sworn a blood oath to him.

"How many of you are there?" Henri asked carefully.

"Enough," Lord Willoughby replied confidently.

Henri considered them for a moment. "I am grateful for your loyalty, my lords. I will have need of it when the time comes. I am leaving to gather more support for my cause, but I will return. In the meantime, do not do anything without my approval. The outlaw king should have no doubts about your loyalty to him."

"Of course, Your Highness."

They inclined their heads again and exchanged satisfied looks with each other before walking away. Henri watched them go, still slightly bewildered by what had transpired, but he quickly sobered at the sight of Brielle strolling toward him. He turned back to his mare and began tightening the saddle straps.

"You're still mad at me, then?"

Henri softened a little at the hurt in her voice. "I'm not mad at you. You devised an impressive plan."

"That puts your life in danger."

"Always." He tossed her a rogue grin, but they both knew it was forced.

She had a point. Every plan she had ever formulated to reclaim her kingdom had put his life in danger. He had lost the Sodisce because of her brazenness. He had been imprisoned and faced a traitor's death because of her stubbornness. Now he was being sent into the serpent's lair as a spy because of her cunning.

"I'm sorry—"

He held up a hand. "Please, don't."

She bit back the words even as her eyes pleaded with him to understand. He did. He really did. Henri turned and glanced down at her hands, which were clasped in front of her. Her fingers were picking at her nails anxiously. She never used to do that. Back when he first met her, when she ruled her infamous ladies court, she had never let any weakness show. Now she looked torn and vulnerable. She was afraid for him. He wanted to take her hands in his, like she had last night. He could still feel the warmth of her body pressed against his when she embraced him, so relieved to find that he had not left her. Now he really was leaving her and he might never return.

"Queens must make difficult choices sometimes. Sending soldiers into battle, risking the lives of the people they care about the most."

"I am not a queen." Her voice broke and she averted her gaze to the ground.

Henri cupped a hand to either side of her cheeks and raised her tearful eyes to meet his. "Don't you dare let anyone tell you you are not a queen. You are the most powerful queen I know."

His lips seized hers. She released a small sound of surprise, but then her mouth opened to him and her body melted against his. Emboldened, Henri explored her mouth with his tongue, tasting the essence of her. Her lips were soft and sweet, just as he dreamed they would be. Her skin felt like silk beneath his fingertips. Their mouths moved together as one, hot and insistent. Henri felt his manhood swell and his balls tighten as his arousal peaked. He wanted to forget that there was anything else in the world except them. He wanted to explore every inch of her skin with his mouth, to adore her body for hours, but he restrained himself with all the willpower he possessed because he knew that this fleeting moment was all he could have right now. This divine kiss which would live on his lips until his dying breath.

Their lips parted an inch, both of them breathless, but neither one of them pulled away. Henri smiled a little when he saw that Brielle's eyes were still closed, as if she did not want the moment to end.

"I will come back to you," he promised, pressing his forehead against hers.

Brielle's eyes opened slowly and she searched his face, finding the conviction of his words in his determined expression. Henri waited for her to say something back. To promise him that she would wait for him, that she would think of him, dream of him. That she would hold this kiss in her heart until he returned.

But she didn't say a word.

Henri pulled away and turned back to his mare, trying to distract himself from the absence of her words and what that meant.

"Did you swear the blood oath to Citric?" he asked.

"No," she replied, clearly surprised by the change in direction of the conversation. "Why?"

"Good. Never swear it. There is something you need to know."

CHAPTER SIX

B rielle felt a little lightheaded as she walked the corridors of the castle. A servant had relayed a message that Citric wanted to meet her in the council chamber, so she was walking in that direction, but her mind was elsewhere. Her thoughts ricocheted between Citric possessing blood magic which connected him to an ancient sensorium that the Red Wood also possessed, and the fact that she had just kissed Henri.

Or rather Henri had kissed her.

But she had definitely kissed him back.

She couldn't stop thinking about it. His lips pressed against hers. The way he had held her so carefully in his arms, as if she were a precious vase. Henri. She had kissed Henri.

Brielle stepped mindlessly into the council chamber. It took a moment for her to register the sight in front of her; the entire council was seated at the long oak table, with Citric at the head of it, all of them staring at her.

Waiting for her, she realized.

Citric unfurled a slow, dangerous smile. "Lady Brielle."

It immediately set her nerves on edge.

He gestured to the vacant seat at the far end of the table. "Please join us."

The councilmen shifted in their seats and muttered to each other in disapproval. Brielle ignored them as she forced her feet to move toward the seat. It wasn't the nobles' overt displeasure that constricted the air in her lungs, but rather Citric's casual demeanor. Sitting down, Brielle folded her hands in her lap and tried to remember to breathe.

"My lords, Lady Brielle has told me of your discontent at my lack of attendance at these council meetings." He waved a hand in a half shrug. "I did not know about them. I did not call them. But Lady Brielle has since explained to me their importance. That every man here is a man of wealth and influence, and that these council meetings are held to discuss important matters of the Crown."

His gaze shot down the length of the table to fix on her with lethal precision. Worry flooded her chest and her palms began to sweat. She knew that look.

"Except men like you have not earned such a privilege," he continued. "You failed to lift your banners to defend your kingdom when your king was betrayed and murdered. You neglected to protect your princess and future queen. You did nothing to stop the enemy from entering your city walls and subjugating your people."

Brielle's heart hammered against her chest as she gripped the armrests of the chair with her fingernails.

"I have no need of men like you. This council is hereby disbanded."

Her stomach plummeted as the councilmen shot to their feet in outrage, calling out insults and cursing his name.

Brielle scrambled to her feet. "My king."

Her words were drowned out beneath a torrent of abuse, but her eyes pleaded with Citric to take back his words immediately. He simply held her stare with a knowing smile.

"You cannot rule this kingdom alone!" Lord Bailey shouted.

"I am not alone. I will form my own council with people I trust. People who have earned the right to be there. Not because of their family name or their wealth or their lineage, but because their loyalty is without question, their bravery in the face of tyranny unmatched. I only see one person in this room who has earned the right to be on my council," he said, his eyes spearing her from across the room.

Flattered, nervous butterflies stirred in Brielle's stomach.

"You cannot do this!" Lord Walter insisted.

"We will not allow it!" Lord Ambrose echoed.

"The church will not support this!" the bishop added.

At the sight of the bishop, Citric narrowed his eyes to lethal slits. "Didn't I warn you what would happen if I saw you near her again?"

The bishop paled. Citric rose suddenly, his hand on the hilt of his sword, and the bishop quickly stepped behind the nearest noble. It was a brave gesture on Citric's part, considering he was grossly outnumbered. Others would call it foolish. Brielle would call it typical.

"You have all sworn oaths to me. I warned you. If you wish to remain on our land, you will abide by the laws and customs of my people. Our customs do not recognize the hierarchy of men based on wealth and status. This council is disbanded. If you do not respect my decision, you should leave. Now. Before your blood is spilled."

Brielle swallowed hard as the tension in the room tightened like a noose around her neck. She hardly dared to glance around at the faces of the lords. The most powerful men in the Southern Kingdom had just been degraded and dismissed.

By an outlaw.

By a man of common birth.

The lords began to file out of the room one by one, their faces contorted with anger and the promise of revenge. She tried to weather their silent threats as they left, but she knew her features betrayed her horror at what had just occurred.

The moment they were alone, Brielle opened her mouth to speak, but there were too many words she wanted to say, most of them not fit for a lady to utter. Citric watched her, amusement dancing across his features. She snapped her lips together, furious.

"Do you realize what you've done? This is not how things work!"

"It is now."

"Oh no," she laughed manically as she marched around the table to confront him. "No, no, no! They will kill you! They will revolt against you! You can't hold this kingdom without them!"

"I can and I will."

"You have plunged us into civil war!" she yelled within an inch of his smug face.

His voice was deadly calm as he replied, "If that's what it takes, then so be it."

Brielle recoiled in disbelief.

"Why are you protecting them?" Citric's expression darkened within a split second. "They would have given you over to King Heroux. They never would have supported your claim to be queen. Men like that, and systems like this, infect society until everything is rotten from the inside out."

Society tries to tell us who is worthy and who is not. All to control us, to ensure we live our lives by their rules. To retain their power, they force women to take up the smallest space in the room, if they are permitted to be in the room at all.

Father Bastien's words surfaced in her mind. He was right. She was living proof of it. But she also recalled his warning.

Some women accept this and bend accordingly, but others do not. Either way, there is a cost.

Of course, there was a part of her that was richly satisfied that the councilmen had been so thoroughly humiliated. She loathed every single one of them. But there was another part of her, a wiser part, that knew the cost of such action.

"Your society is no better," she accused. "What do the women of Alkhiem do? Prepare food, wash clothes, mind the children."

His tone was a low warning. "You know nothing of my people."

"And you know nothing of my people."

Their stares held each other, neither one of them willing to back down.

"You are tearing this kingdom apart," she breathed, desperate for him to understand.

He leaned in closer, fixing his steely eyes on hers. "I am rebuilding this kingdom. In order to do that, I must first tear it down. Wall by wall. Stone by stone. I will reduce this kingdom to rubble if I have to."

Citric stormed outside to the castle yard, adrenaline still coursing through his veins. He needed to train, to expel his anger before he changed his mind and annihilated every member of the council, starting with that bishop. *Fucking cowards.* They had been lucky to leave with their lives. When they dissented openly in front of him, it was all he could do to hold back his wrath.

And Brielle, she had defended them. Despite everything they had done to her and all the ways they had failed her, she had pled their case. Fear was the only explanation he could find for her actions. He understood that breaking traditions founded on ignorant beliefs and bigoted social systems was unnerving, but these traditions did not serve her. Nor had they served her people. Change was necessary and he had no time for playing politics. He would not rule a kingdom filled with spineless traitors who hid behind their wealth and breeding. Nor would he subject his people to their self-serving doctrine.

Leif spotted him across the yard and the look they exchanged confirmed that he felt everything through the blood bond. Leif hastened toward him, checking that his weapons were secure in anticipation of what Citric might need from him.

"I want the lords watched," Citric commanded when Leif arrived at his side. "They are against us, but I'm not sure how or when they will strike. Send two men to watch Brielle day and night."

"Do you suspect she will join the lords and betray you?" Leif's brows knitted together.

"No. I suspect they will target her because of me."

He had never meant to put her in danger, but when she all but declared herself to be his lover, she had unwittingly put a target on her back. The lords were pitiful excuses for men, but they weren't fools. They would never challenge him directly. That much was evident from their reaction in the council chamber. There had been a dozen of them and one of him, but they did not band together to try to take him down. Instead, they had slithered away to converse amongst each other and devise a more sinister plan. No doubt they would go after the weakest chinks in his armor: the people he cared about the most. Fortunately, most of the people he cared about could defend themselves, but Brielle would not stand a chance against them.

Citric suddenly winced against the onslaught of emotion that assailed him. He searched the castle yard until he saw Eve marching toward him, fury in her eyes.

"We need to talk," she said.

"If it's about the council I just disbanded, it needed to be done."

"Good riddance. No, it's about this idiotic plan to send Henri north."

"What about it?" Citric tried to focus on calming down. He was already enraged and now that he was absorbing Eve's emotions, he was on the brink of going over the edge.

Eve threw her hands up in indignation. "Can't you see that this plan is utter madness? Either King Heroux will kill Henri or Henri will betray you by switching sides."

"Henri is loyal to us. When he said he wanted to help liberate his people, he was telling the truth. If his loyalty changes, I will feel it."

"What if you don't? Or what if Henri stays loyal, but he is simply a puppet in all of this, oblivious to the plans of the princess who is pulling his strings?"

"What do you mean?" Leif asked, a note of concern in his voice.

Eve huffed as if she resented having to explain herself. "Brielle was the one who came up with this ridiculous plan. She is also the only one who hasn't sworn a blood oath to Citric. We don't know whose side she is truly on or what she is planning. Sending Henri to spy in the Northern court could be a part of her grand scheme to reclaim the Southern Kingdom."

"She doesn't know about the blood magic," Leif countered. "At least she didn't seem to last night."

"She is devious." Eve shook her head as her lips twisted into a bitter smile. "If she didn't know already, Henri would have told her by now. Don't you see? They are in on this together! You're a fool if you think she'd just let this go."

"I know her well enough not to think that," Citric returned. Eve recoiled as if she'd been slapped and her heart clenched in pain. It hurt him to feel it, deeper than any flesh wound. "But I also don't think she'd put her own ambitions ahead of her people's safety, not anymore. She wouldn't do anything to put her kingdom at risk."

"You mean your kingdom." Eve's eyes narrowed shrewdly, as if she were suddenly questioning his loyalty.

"This argument is pointless," Citric returned, annoyed. "Henri has left already."

"What?" Eve spluttered.

"I ordered him to leave at first light. If Henri's loyalty changes, I will feel it. In the meantime, I am having Brielle watched day and night. Does that satisfy you?"

"Let me watch her. I know her the best out of anyone here. I know how she thinks, what her next move might be."

"No." Citric didn't need the blood bond to know how much Eve loathed Brielle. Her emotions would get in the way of her being an objective spy. More concerningly, if it became necessary for her to defend Brielle against an attack, he was not sure she would. "I have another task for you."

Brielle paced in front of the windows of her bedchamber like a caged lion. She didn't know if she wanted to cry or scream or break something. Probably all three. Henri had left on a mission that would most likely see him killed and Citric was systematically, unapologetically, destroying her kingdom. She had tried to advise him on how to keep the peace, to keep his crown, but he clearly did not want to listen to her. The arrogance of him! To think he knew this kingdom, her people, better than her. She wanted to smack that smug look right off his face. He would probably let her try and that enraged her even more.

Perching her hands on her hips, she forced herself to look out the window into the gardens below. From here, the world looked calm and peaceful. The flowers were in bloom, the lawns were meticulously manicured. It was not too long ago that she had hosted elaborate garden tea parties by the lake and her worries had centered around finding a suitable king consort and making sure her ladies did not outshine her. Now all of that felt like a distant memory. Another life entirely.

If she was being honest, though, her unraveling was fueled by more than just her concern for Henri, the threat of war, and a potential coup from the nobles. Citric possessed blood magic that connected him to the land.

His land.

The land of his people.

It was unbelievable, and yet she knew it was true. She had seen it without understanding it. When they traveled through the Red Wood, she had marveled at his knowledge of the wood. He knew every inch of dirt, every river, every tree. He knew where the men would find game to hunt and where edible vegetation grew. He knew where every danger lurked, both seen and unseen. She needed no further proof to know that his claims were not false. Which meant—she was not the true heir to the Southern Kingdom.

She did not have royal blood.

She was not a princess.

She was simply the descendant of a man who had taken something that wasn't rightfully his. All she was, and everything she had ever believed herself to be, was a lie.

Brielle braced herself against the window seat as the truth knocked the air from her lungs. All her life she had feared being plain. Weak. Ordinary. And now she was. With Citric as king and without a legitimate claim to the throne, she no longer had a purpose. Or a place at this court. For the first time since her kingdom had been taken from her, she had no cause to reclaim it.

Her hand flew to her mouth and a devastated sob broke through the wall of her fingers. It seemed to open the floodgates of tears that followed and soon she was gasping for air as her heart shattered into a million pieces. This life, this purpose, was all she had ever known. She had been born to a great destiny; to rule the Southern Kingdom. What was her destiny now?

She didn't know how long she cried for, but eventually her tears dried up, leaving her raw and hollow. The world around her became a solemn, silent witness to her pain. Her soul felt vacant as she leaned against the glass pane of her window and looked down below. All of it—the gardens, the castle, the land, the people—was no longer hers.

Brielle was at a loss for what to do with herself. It would take weeks for Henri to arrive at the Northern court. Longer before they would hear any word from him. If he was able to send word at all. She would not be able to endure it, sitting here in this room, waiting to hear whether he had lived or died. She needed to *do* something. She needed a purpose. Citric had no use for her, he did not want her counsel. Eve did not welcome her help with the camp. She had nothing left.

Her features set in sudden determination as she pushed off the windowpane. She may not be a princess or have a claim to these lands, but she was born in the Southern Kingdom and that made it her home. These were her people and war was coming. She would not abandon them. She would fight, even if she did not lead the battle charge, even if her name would be lost to history. Because history may be written by the victors, but war was won by the nameless.

Weeks Later

Henri stumbled forward as the rope around his neck was firmly yanked. The guard leading him seemed to derive sadistic pleasure from pulling on it every couple of meters, despite the fact that there was no need. He had been a model prisoner since the day they arrested him, the very picture of compliance. Besides, it wasn't like he would stand a chance against them if he tried to run. He had a dozen guards on either side, escorting him through the corridors of the heavily fortified Northern castle. His hands were bound tight enough to rub his skin raw and his body ached everywhere from the nightly beatings he had been receiving.

After weeks of riding through the Red Wood, he had begun traveling north on the King's Road. It had taken less than an hour for the King's Guard to find him after that. On sighting the guards hurtling toward him with their swords raised, Henri had simply dismounted from his horse, removed his weapons, laid them down on the ground at his feet, and raised his hands in polite surrender. Even so, it did nothing to prevent their assaults against him. The guards knew they needed to deliver him to King Heroux alive, but beyond that, they could do whatever they liked. This was their chance to get revenge on a prince and they had relished in it.

Henri almost preferred the nightly beatings to the reality of returning to what had once been his home. His chest had clenched violently at the sight of the Northern castle in the distance. Unlike the Southern castle, which sat on an open plain surrounded by soft hills, the Northern castle was perched on the edge of a rocky cliff overlooking the sea. Henri had hoped never to return to it. To never again see this cold, towering fortress that reminded him so much of his father.

As the guards escorted him to the throne room, his heart slammed against his bruised ribs. Many times he had walked this route, summoned by his father to answer for his latest public transgression, or to attend political affairs where his presence was required and his silence was mandatory. But he had never been escorted to the throne room by a dozen King's Guards before. Or led by a leash around his neck as if he were a village dog. If only his father could see him now. The bastard would turn in his grave.

Henri tensed as they marched through the open doors into the throne room. Old habits, it seemed, did not die as easily as kings. The room was large but it wasn't welcoming. Unlike the Southern court, it did not boast elaborate furnishings and colorful tapestries fit for royalty. It was cold and practical, void of a woman's touch, he supposed. The only color was the gray stone of the floor and walls. It captured his father's essence perfectly; the seat of power for a cold, pragmatic ruler.

Except now someone else sat in that seat of power. Henri's eyes immediately locked on to the man sitting on his father's throne. He was leaning forward slightly, with both hands resting on the hilt of his sword which was standing upright before him. Despite the crown upon his head, his blond hair fell unkempt around his face. His beard was long and thick, but his mustache was meticu-lously groomed into two plaits the length of his beard.

Of course, Henri should have expected it. Before he became a famous warlord, conquering kingdoms to add to his ever-growing empire, King Heroux was a Merovian king, otherwise known as the long-haired kings. For them, their long beards and mustaches symbolized their status as kings. Their subjects were not allowed to grow facial hair unless they were nobility, and even then, there were rules as to how long they could grow it. It was rumored that if one cut the long-bearded hair of a king, they would remove his claim to kingship itself.

As the guards led Henri to the throne, King Heroux watched him through narrow eyes that seemed to be permanently in a state of suspicion. The King's Guard bowed collectively and Henri tried not to wince in pain as he bent forward to join them.

"The former prince of the North." King Heroux's voice was rough like gravel. "You are a hard man to kill."

It was true enough. Henri had escaped him on the battlefield where he was supposed to be slaughtered alongside his father. He had escaped him again when the King's Guard had raided the Sodisce.

Henri grimaced as he straightened. "Then it's lucky for you I surrendered."

"Is that so?" King Heroux directed the question to the guard still holding Henri's leash.

"We found him traveling north on the King's Road, Your Highness."

King Heroux flicked his gaze back to Henri in a silent demand to explain.

"I come as an emissary for King Citric. He wants to set terms for war."

"An emissary." King Heroux rolled his tongue around the word as if he did not like the taste of it. "He could have sent a raven. Or a low-ranking soldier for me to kill. Why send me your head?"

Henri shifted his weight casually to evidence that he was unaffected by the implied threat. "I volunteered."

"Did you now?" King Heroux cocked his head as he stroked the length of his beard.

A shadow seemed to fall across the room as the king considered the situation before him. Henri knew the next words out of the king's mouth would either command his immediate death or a temporary reprieve. It took a lifetime of courtly skill to maintain his confident, impassive façade while he waited for his fate to be decided.

Finally, King Heroux flicked his hand. "Everybody out. Leave the prince with me."

Henri released a silent breath of relief. The guards hesitated, eager to collect the reward for their efforts, but none were foolish enough to challenge a king. Henri's leash was abandoned on the ground as the guards filed out of the room. The echo of the great doors closing behind him set his teeth on edge, but Henri was careful not to show it as he focused on the king in front of him, who was watching him closely beneath hooded eyes.

"So, the outlaw king wishes to play a new game with me."

"He wishes to kill you. And reclaim these lands, which he believes were taken from his people generations ago."

King Heroux's expression remained stagnant, which meant Citric's claim had already reached his ears. Interesting.

"And what do you want, prince?"

Henri recalled the image of Nathaniel's face seconds before Citric's sword took his head. "Revenge."

King Heroux nodded reflectively. "I killed hundreds of soldiers from the great Northern army and took your kingdom for myself.

I had your father slaughtered in his own war tent by the man he trusted the most. I turned your closest friend into your enemy. And I smoked you out of your whore's house like a common sewer rat."

Henri felt his stomach turn to acid at every word. Keeping his expression neutral, he replied, "You did, but it's not you I want revenge against. I never wanted to be king of the North, you are welcome to it. The loss of a few soldiers is of little concern to me. I hated my father so you did me a favor there. As for the Sodisce, I was getting bored of it anyway. But Citric betrayed me, and that I cannot forgive."

"He betrayed you when you tried to reclaim your kingdom," King Heroux pointed out. "Revenge is not the only thing you want, prince."

Henri tilted his head in acknowledgement. "You are right. Though I meant what I said, I don't want to be king. But I have come to realize the cost of being a man without power. I refuse to live my life like that, at the mercy of others. My terms are simple: make me your right hand in the Southern Kingdom, and I will win you this war."

King Heroux stroked the length of his beard in contemplation. "An interesting offer. But I can win this war without you, so you have no value to me."

Henri shifted his weight again and glanced around the room as if he were bored. "You may be able to win this war, but you won't be able to keep the Southern Kingdom without someone to hold it for you. Your Butcher is dead. I'm willing to become the devil himself if it gets me what I want."

King Heroux's gaze lingered on him as if he was searching for a spot in his armor through which to strike. "I have many loyal, capable men under my command. Why should I give the task to you?"

"Because I will earn it. You may have the numbers to win the war, but why lose men when you don't have to? I know Citric. I know how he thinks. I know his weaknesses. If we play him right, we could retake the Southern Kingdom without losing a single soldier."

King Heroux suddenly pushed himself to his feet and stalked down from the dais, gripping the sword in his hand. He halted abruptly at Henri's side as if he had meant to walk past him and leaned in closer until Henri could feel his stale breath on his skin.

"We will see how useful you are, prince. If you have overstated your worth or if you are stupid enough to try to betray me, I'll carve out your heart."

Eve wandered through the tents that had sprung up just beyond the western tower like green grass after heavy rain. Over the past few weeks, hundreds of people had migrated here seeking shelter, food, and protection from King Heroux's rule. Every day, more people arrived; entire families, entire communities. Citric had managed to secure some profitable trade deals, so they were able to offer the people basic rations and supplies, but Eve wondered how long it would be before the supplies ran out.

Unfortunately, finite supplies were not her only problem. The more people that arrived, the more complicated the situation became in the camp. Entire families were living in tents barely big enough to sleep in. Along the western plain, the tents were lined up in rows, one after the other, allowing little privacy between families and groups. People were beginning to bicker. They lacked purpose. While some were willing to use their skills to help contribute to the camp, others simply sat in despair or stewed in anger at their situation. Buckling under the stress of displacement and an uncertain future, tempers were running short. Not only within the camp, but between the refugees and the city's residents. Citric's men had had to intervene in several fights in the past week alone. Now the King's Guard were permanently stationed around camp, as well as within the city and around the castle. They would actively roam through the camp and the city at all hours of the day and night to ensure the peace.

It was relentless work. Everyone was feeling the pressure of various demands and the drain of not having enough to meet those demands. Enough resources. Enough space. Enough hope. But what choice did they have? They could not turn people away.

And then there was the Southern court. Ever since Citric had disbanded the council, the court had become the most dangerous place to be. Fortunately, she was able to avoid it most of the time, dedicating every waking moment to the western camp and the flood of refugees crossing their border. But when she dragged her tired limbs to her bedchamber at night, she could feel the tension suspended between the walls. It was in the silence of the hallways. The passing of looks behind her back from courtiers and servants alike. The castle used to be filled with petty court politics and salacious gossip, but now it was filled with fear and the spark of righteous anger.

The lords were definitely up to something, she was sure of it. In the days after the council was disbanded, they had all gone to ground, keeping a low profile. Some barely even attended court at all, and when they did, they tried to avoid the king's notice. But in the past few days, they had all returned and were walking the corridors of the castle like they owned it. They were meeting together openly, defiantly. Whatever the reason was, it could not be good.

Eve felt a tingling awareness tugging at her consciousness before she spotted Citric in the distance, talking to his guards. Her steps faltered. It was too late, though. She had caught his eye and so couldn't pretend she hadn't seen him. She scowled, muttering a very unladylike curse under her breath as she stood there awkwardly, unsure what to do with herself. Since their argument a few weeks ago, things had been strained between them. He did not appreciate his decisions being openly questioned and she could not fathom why he was being so stupid. It was killing her to feel estranged from him like this, but she refused to hold her tongue. He would always hear the truth from her, whether he liked it or not.

Evidently, he did not.

Her only comfort was that things between him and Brielle were worse. In fact, they appeared to have been completely broken beyond repair. Eve had barely seen Brielle in weeks. She hadn't left the country, unfortunately. Eve wasn't that lucky. Brielle returned to her rooms every night, but what she did with her days, Eve did not know. If it were up to her, she would follow Brielle's every footstep and listen in to her every conversation, but Citric had tasked her with overseeing the camp. She didn't have a spare minute to dedicate to watching Brielle.

"Did you want to speak to me?"

Eve startled at Citric's sudden appearance in front of her.

"No," she replied tersely and sidestepped him.

He let her walk past him before he called out to her. "Evelyn."

She faltered. Her name. On his lips. It melted her heart every time. Somehow it sounded different when he said it. Like walking in a dream, like the promise of hope.

"Do you need me?"

Yes. She needed him more than she would ever admit out loud. She needed him to be the leader that the people deserved, to listen to her when she pointed out the disastrous decisions he was making. She needed him to *see* her. Now that things were broken between him and Brielle, she wanted more than anything for him to see her as a woman. As the woman who had been standing by his side for years. Who had given him everything and always would.

Why couldn't he see her?

Eve had hoped the blood bond would tell him what words could not convey, but nothing had changed between them since the blood oath. He had not treated her any differently. He still looked at her the same as he always had. Maybe it made her a coward, but she couldn't bring herself to purge her feelings to his face. The very thought terrified her because then she would know for certain how he really felt about her. There was no going back after that, and she would rather have the agony of not knowing than the devastation of knowing he did not feel the same.

Turning to face him, her expression tightened. She would never get used to his hair being pulled tight into a braid against his skull. She missed his wild tangle of auburn hair flowing past his shoulders. She missed when it had been just him and her.

"We need more supplies," she said tartly.

"They should arrive here in the next few days."

She nodded. "Any word from Henri? He should have arrived at the Northern court by now."

"No. It will be difficult for him to get word to us. King Heroux will be watching him closely until he gains his trust."

"And Brielle?" She was loath to ask, but couldn't help herself.

Citric cast his gaze out across the western plain into the Red Wood. "She is occupying herself."

"I bet," Eve muttered under her breath. "Are your men still watching her?"

A slight shift of his features told her they weren't. He had likely diverted them to patrol the camp and keep the peace. Leif and the other direct descendants of Sirasinda had been sent to the surrounding farmlands to begin healing the land, which meant they were short on men.

In answer to her sour expression he said, "I am watching her."

Eve bristled. Somehow the words did not sound like he was watching her to determine her treachery.

"She is not our only concern. The lords are up to something. Can you feel it?" Eve asked.

"I feel their resentment and hatred toward me, but it's difficult to interpret when and how they will act on it."

Eve frowned, concern suddenly etching her face as she looked at him a little closer. She didn't know why, there were no obvious outward signs, but in that moment she knew something was wrong. Citric was exhausted. And not just the exhaustion that came from establishing a new kingdom, building a refugee camp, dealing with disgruntled nobles, and planning a war. It was the blood oaths, she realized. In the past few weeks, he had exchanged blood oaths with dozens of lords and an entire garrison of King's Guard. It had taken a toll on him, overloaded his senses.

Eve didn't know what it felt like to use blood magic, but she imagined it would be similar to using a muscle. The more pressure the muscle was under, the more strained it became. It would likely take time for Citric to adjust to the barrage of new stimuli assaulting him. To be able to discern between the people he was sensing in order to accurately interpret what he was feeling and from who.

"So arrest them now, like you did with the King's Guard you knew to be traitors," Eve suggested.

"No. I could justify doing that as it followed a direct attempt on my life. I can't arrest and execute nobles without cause."

"You are king. You can do whatever you want. You know they are traitors. Don't give them the chance to betray you."

Citric returned a knowing smile. "I'll be fine."

She gritted her teeth. Why was he being cautious about this? The Citric she knew would have taken their lives without a second thought. He did not believe in justifying his actions to anyone and if anyone had an issue with a decision he made, the matter would be resolved on the training ground. With blood.

It was all Brielle's fault. Even with things broken between them, her claws were still firmly inserted under Citric's skin. She was messing with his head, making him question himself and his decisions. She was changing him. Eve scowled and her fingers flexed as if in preparation to draw her blade. If anything happened to Citric because of Brielle's meddling manipulations there certainly would be blood to pay. And Eve would be the reaper.

CHAPTER SEVEN

B rielle fitted the arrow into the deck of the crossbow and lifted the weapon to her eye-level. She took a steadying breath, settled her aim, and let the bolt fly. It split the ribbon nailed to the tree fifty yards away. Brielle smiled, triumphant.

Her skills had significantly improved over the past few weeks, to the point where she rarely missed a target. She was getting quicker at reloading as well. She practiced doing it over and over again to make sure she would be able to perform under pressure. Because unless Henri could convince King Heroux to trust him, it was only a matter of time before war would be upon them.

Since Henri left and Citric disbanded the council, Brielle had returned to the Red Wood to practice with the crossbow every day. She'd even started throwing her short daggers at targets, though her aim was far better with a crossbow. Either way, she would be ready when war came. She pictured each target as a different enemy she wanted to slay. King Heroux. The councilmen. Everyone who had ever tried to diminish her power. It felt good to release her anger with every bolt that left the bow. Coming to the Red Wood to train was more than just an emotional outlet, though. It was a daily ritual, her own personal communion. As a result, her body was getting stronger, her arms more muscular, her aim more precise. At the very least, it distracted her from thinking about Henri.

Retrieving her waterskin from the ground, Brielle took a long drink. She could divert her mind easily enough during the day, but when the sun faded, night ominously crept up on her, stoking her worst fears. Henri being assaulted. Tortured. Beheaded in the town square for all to see. His broken body displayed on the ramparts for the birds to feast on. Brielle choked on the water. He could be dead right now and she wouldn't know it. Every breath she took could be his last.

She pinched her eyes closed, willing the thoughts to scatter from her head. Every day, she fought the urge to find Citric and ask if he had heard anything. Mainly because she was fairly sure he hadn't, but also because she did not want to speak to him. By disbanding the council, he had drawn clear battlelines and her silence and avoidance of him was all she could do to protest. It was meaningless, she knew, but it was the only power she had. He probably hadn't even noticed or cared. He hadn't sought her out. In fact, she hadn't even seen him since the day he disbanded the council.

He was likely too busy trying to manage a volatile kingdom. It had changed dramatically in the past few weeks. Tensions were high with so many unfamiliar faces roaming the streets, combined with the shortage of resources and the fear of retaliation from King Heroux. She felt it every time she rode out through the city gates toward the Red Wood. The castle was worse. The nobles used to hide their contempt behind good graces and a well-practiced courtly mask, but now they openly sneered at her and uttered insults just loud enough for her to hear as she walked past. *Whore* seemed to be the favorite. It was so unimaginative she almost pitied their lack of intelligence. One thing was clear, though: it was not safe to leave her rooms unarmed.

Brielle whirled around at the sound of a horse galloping hard across the western plain toward the Red Wood. It only took a moment for her to recognize the rider as he slowed his dun mare to navigate through the tree line.

She glowered in annoyance as he stopped to dismount. "Are you having me followed now?"

"No." Citric casually sauntered over to her, his eyes noting the crossbow in her hands. "Do I need to have you followed?"

"How did you know I was here?" Before he could answer, it dawned on her. "You sensed me because I'm in the Red Wood."

He cocked his head. "Henri told you."

"Of course he did. We have no secrets from each other."

"Secrets are useful sometimes." He cast his gaze out into the distance at the ribbon speared to a tree with a bolt. His brows twitched, seemingly impressed.

"I suppose you know everyone's secrets through the blood bond. Except mine." She gave a saccharine smile.

It was divine providence or dumb luck that she had refused to slice her palm that day and swear the blood oath to him. She'd had no knowledge of the implications at the time, she just didn't want to mark herself. That decision had proven to be invaluable.

"Are you afraid of what the blood bond might reveal to me?" Citric's voice was sultry as he took a predatory step toward her.

Her heart catapulted at his sudden invasion. His eyes raked over her, stripping her bare unashamedly. She didn't move. Couldn't. Didn't want to. It was like she was suspended in time, being held captive by the magnetic force of him.

"For me to know how your body reacts when I'm near you?"

She wanted to deny that he had any power over her at all, but her treacherous body had already betrayed her and surrendered itself wholeheartedly.

"What thoughts go through your head," he purred as he leaned in close to whisper in her ear. "What you dream about at night."

His hand pressed lightly against her waist and she shivered as it moved slowly up her corset, his fingertips brushing over the swell of her breasts.

"The memory of how I touched you. How I made you come again and again."

A molten warmth pooled in her core as her sex began to throb in delicious anticipation. Because she did remember. She had tried not to think about it, but there had been moments of weakness. At night, beneath the sheets, when her hand would wander. It had provided her with release, but it was nothing compared to what his hands could do. What his lips could do. What his manhood could do. The pleasure only he could give her.

Brielle instinctively licked her lips and his hand gripped her chin, tipping her face up slightly, as if he wanted to watch the movement up close. His finger traced back along her jawline, his eyes never leaving the sheen on her lips, which were inches away from his. She could feel the heat of his skin in all the places that their bodies almost touched. It was a vicious torture. She desperately wanted him to touch her. To take her.

"There's so much more I want to do to you."

Yes, she almost breathed out loud, as her eyes closed in ecstasy. She wanted him to do everything to her. To feel him inside her, hard and hot and deep. She wanted to yield herself to him completely.

Betrayed.

He had betrayed her.

The thought slammed into her mind and her eyes shot open. He had taken what he wanted from her once before and then betrayed her without a second thought. He had lied to her and imprisoned her and threatened her. Granted, his claim to the Southern lands was legitimate, but it did not change the fact that he had deceived her.

"You've done enough to me." Her voice was sharp as she ripped herself out from underneath his spell. "Fool me once. I will not be fooled again."

She stepped away from him and tried to cool the lust from her senses. The evidence of his arousal was clearly visible through his pants, though she tried her best not to look. Tried and failed. The sight made her core throb anew.

Citric's brows knitted in confusion before his features darkened. "I am not trying to fool you, Brielle. I have no secrets left from you."

"That doesn't mean I can trust you. I told you I would never forgive you for betraying me and I meant it."

"I am sorry for how things happened between us," he tempered, clearly trying to control his impatience. "It was never my intention to hurt you. I asked you if you were sure. I warned you that in the morning, everything would change. We agreed we owed each other nothing."

"You owed me your loyalty! You lied to me!"

"I never lied to you. I told you I would help you reclaim these lands, restore the peace, and protect the people. I have kept my word. I told you I did not desire to be king. That is still true. I didn't do this for my own ambition. I did it to take back what was stolen from my people."

Brielle scowled and crossed her arms over her chest. He was twisting things to suit himself.

"Don't stand there and pretend like you are so different from me. We are the same. Name one thing you would not do to ensure the survival of your people."

He had a point, she accepted reluctantly, if only to herself. She was yet to find the line she wouldn't cross to protect her people.

"What do you want? If you came here hoping for a rendezvous with your lover, you have wasted your time."

He studied the wrath on her face, as if debating whether he should press his suit or not. "I have some news I thought you would like to know."

"Henri," she breathed, every other thought forgotten. "Is he all right?"

"I have no news from him. But I haven't lost my connection to him, so he is still alive at least."

Brielle's shoulders sagged a little in relief. "You can feel him through the blood bond? Feel what he feels?"

"I have a connection with him, yes."

"Is he scared? Hurt?"

"Do you really want to know?"

"Yes," Brielle said firmly.

"The answers may cause you unnecessary pain."

"Since when do you care about causing me pain? Answer me!"

Something flashed across Citric's features, as if her words had stung. "He was in pain for several nights. Then I felt fear. I believe he is at the Northern court and since he is not dead, I'm assuming he has found a way to convince King Heroux not to kill him."

Brielle's face paled in horror. Henri was hurt and scared and completely alone. *Alive.* He was alive, she reminded herself. But it didn't lessen the knowledge that he was suffering. She forced herself to nod in acceptance even as her stomach churned like curdled milk.

"What is your news?" she asked quietly.

Citric suddenly went deathly still. His eyes darted back and forth as if he were concentrating on something in his head. A thought. A sound. A feeling. Then his eyes switched to look out across the western plain.

"What's wrong?" Her gaze followed his to see at least a dozen men on horses spearing across the plain toward them, with swords raised.

Brielle didn't have time to draw breath before Citric pulled an arrow from his quiver, shifted into a side stance, and let it fly.

"Run!" he ordered. "Get to your horse!"

The arrow hit one of the men with force. Citric was already releasing a second arrow as the man fell to the ground to be trampled beneath hooves. Brielle's eyes widened in terror. She fumbled loading a bolt to her crossbow as she hurried to take a stand beside Citric to form a line of defense. She lifted her crossbow to eye-level and tried to remember to breathe as she aimed and released the bolt. To her astonishment, it hit its mark and the man slumped forward in the saddle, clutching his chest. By that time Citric had already released several more arrows, but the remaining men were closing the distance fast and would be upon them in a matter of seconds.

Brielle reloaded a bolt and fired, hitting another target before the assailants burst through the tree line into the Red Wood. There were too many of them. Far too many.

"Get to your horse now!" Citric bellowed as he released another arrow and then tossed his bow aside to draw his sword.

Brielle swung her crossbow on her back and ran for her white mare, which was tied to a nearby tree. The clashing of swords rang out behind her. She didn't know how many men Citric was battling, but she did know he was grossly outnumbered. She would need to ride fast to get help. Brielle's fingers scrabbled to untie the reins before she hoisted herself up into the saddle. She quickly yanked the reins to turn the horse around, but then she felt hands grabbing at her dress, trying to pull her down. Brielle shrieked and kicked out at the men surrounding her. Her thoughts were panicked, but her eyes didn't lie. She recognized their faces; the councilmen.

"Don't you fucking touch her!" Citric roared.

But they did. Their hands grabbed at her skirts and legs and arms before they managed to pull her down from the saddle, kicking and screaming. She hit the ground hard, but barely registered the pain as she tried to twist her body out from beneath their grasp. It was no use, they were too strong. She couldn't land a blow or get to her hidden daggers because they had her arms pinned.

Brielle could still hear the collision of metal, but she knew Citric would not be able to hold out against them much longer. It was a miracle he wasn't dead already. Lord Ambrose hurled her to her feet, twisting her arms painfully behind her back, and pointed a long dagger to her abdomen. Lord Bailey stood beside him, a smug, satisfied smile spread across his hateful face.

"Citric!" Lord Bailey shouted.

Lord Ambrose roughly spun her around to face Citric, who was battling three men. The sickening sound of cracked bone reverberated through the wood as he head-butted one before swinging his sword to cut down another in a furious frenzy of blood. He kicked the third in the gut, sending him flying backwards into the dirt.

"We have your whore!" Lord Bailey called out, sneering at her in disgust.

Citric froze as his eyes cut to her direction. The men surrounding him halted, panting, clearly relieved by the moment's reprieve.

"Let her go." Citric's tone was dangerously low, his words promising certain death.

Lord Ambrose pressed the dagger harder in answer, and Brielle couldn't help the whimper that escaped her lips.

"I will gut her right here in front of you," Lord Ambrose warned. "Throw your weapon down."

"You fucking coward!" Citric raged. "Hiding behind someone weaker than yourself. You want revenge? Take it! Fight me like a man!"

"I don't need to fight you to win, you stupid pagan. This kingdom is ours. There is no place here for your kind. Now, I won't ask you again."

Lord Ambrose pressed the tip of the blade harder and Brielle squirmed to avoid it piercing her skin. Citric unleashed a roar, the sound echoing throughout the wood like a furious, wild beast. Then Brielle heard a thud and Lord Ambrose fell to the ground behind her, a knife lodged in the side of his skull. She lifted her eyes to find Eve hurtling toward them on her horse, her knives flying. Citric had already resumed battle, so Brielle plucked the dagger from her belt and plunged it into the man closest to her. She didn't look to see who they were; they were the enemy and they would kill her if she didn't kill them first.

Eve didn't slow her horse as she slid from the saddle to the ground in one swift motion and began slashing through the men with precision. Brielle retrieved another dagger from her bodice, only to find Lord Bailey glaring at her, his expression murderous. Her heart fell out of her chest.

"You bitch! Did you really think we would let you rule?"

He stalked toward her, clearly enjoying the sight of her terror. There was no way she could overpower him and yet she had to try. In seconds he would be on her. She clutched the dagger in her hand and stood her ground as adrenaline flooded her veins.

"That little knife of yours is not going to save you," he taunted.

The look she returned was deadly serious. She had killed men before, she reminded herself. She would survive this one.

"What did you call her?"

Lord Bailey's steps faltered when he saw Citric prowling toward him, the promise of death in every powerful movement. He was a terrifying sight covered in blood, his muscles rippling. Behind him the councilmen lay slain on the woodland floor and Eve stood in the middle of them, her sword dripping. Brielle's attention snapped back to Citric just as he disarmed Lord Bailey in one brutal move by striking him in the throat. Lord Bailey staggered backwards as he choked and spluttered, clutching his throat with desperate fingers.

"Say it again, coward."

Citric's fist landed a punishing blow to his face and she heard something crack as Lord Bailey fell to the ground. Citric did not relent, he unleashed himself, his fists raining down on him as if he couldn't hold himself back. Brielle was sure he was going to kill him, but then suddenly Citric stopped. He stood over Lord Bailey's body, his knuckles split and his chest heaving from exertion as his eyes took in the carnage he had inflicted with primal satisfaction. Lord Bailey lay slumped against the ground as if his body was no longer made of bones. But he was still breathing. Citric slowly kneeled down beside him.

"I told you not to fucking touch her."

Lord Bailey didn't have time to reply before Citric started breaking his fingers one by one. Brielle lifted her hands to her mouth in horror as Lord Bailey released a torrent of blood-curdling screams. She averted her eyes to Eve, who returned her a hard, unsympathetic look.

It was true Lord Bailey had tried to kill her. He had mocked and dismissed her claim to the Southern Kingdom. To save his own skin, he would have given her over to King Heroux in a heartbeat. He had called her a bitch and a whore. Now that she thought about it, those words stirred a memory of another man who had uttered such insults. A King's Guard who had driven a knife across the throat of a woman at the Sodisce. A woman who had protected Henri with her life, protected them all, and paid the ultimate price. That guard had called her a whore. Nothing but a whore. But she had proven to have more courage and bravery than that guard would ever know. *Whore. Bitch. Cunt.* These were the words men used to demean women, to try to strip them of their power.

The screaming stopped. Brielle couldn't bring herself to look at what was left of Lord Bailey's fingers.

"Brielle." Citric's words were as cold and dangerous as thin ice. "This man's life is yours to take."

"W-what?"

"In our customs, when a person wrongs another, they are entitled to take their revenge. He threatened your life. His life is yours to claim."

Brielle flicked her gaze to Eve, who dipped her chin in agreement, her expression as sharp and unforgiving as her blades. When Brielle turned back to look down at Lord Bailey, she could still feel Eve watching her, no doubt curious to see what she would do. Lord Bailey deserved to die, she knew that. For his treason. For every wrong he had ever committed against her and her people. Yet carrying out an execution with her bare hands, not in the frenzy of battle or self-defense, but in a calm moment of justice, felt beyond her.

Brielle steeled herself. This was the duty of queens, to pass judgment and be willing to carry out the sentence with their own hands if necessary. She may not be a queen in title anymore, but that didn't change the fact that she had been raised to be a queen. Any trepidation she felt was quickly reforged into action.

She approached Lord Bailey, her short dagger in hand. "Looks like no one is going to save you from my little knife."

To her surprise, Eve came to stand beside her in solidarity. A look passed between them before they both stared down at the pitiful man crumpled at their feet.

Eve's finger traced the edge of her dagger from the hilt to the very tip as she mused, "I should cut out your tongue before you die."

Lord Bailey released a strangled sob and tried to plead for mercy, though the words were muffled through blood and broken teeth.

Brielle encased her heart in iron as she kneeled down in the cold earth and yanked his head back by his hair.

"Say it again," Brielle demanded, her voice sounding like nothing she had ever heard before. Ruthless. Powerful. The voice of a queen.

He blubbered, shaking his head profusely, begging for his life.

"Say it!"

The word formed on his shaking lips, but before he could utter it, she plunged the dagger into his throat.

"Or you could just do that." Eve raised her brows, surprised but satisfied.

Brielle turned away from the sight of blood spurting forth from Lord Bailey's punctured throat and let his lifeless body fall to the ground. Standing up, she found the scene around her was not much better to look at. The slain bodies of the councilmen littered the ground.

A disbanded council was bad.

A dead council was worse.

"I think the only lord not among them is the bishop," Brielle pointed out.

"I'm sure he gave the mission God's blessing." Eve rolled her eyes before turning back to Citric. "Didn't you feel them coming?"

His features darkened like a storm. "Not until it was too late."

"You're hurt."

Brielle's gaze followed Eve's to see a nasty gash along Citric's ribs. His blood was soaking through his leathers and black cotton shirt.

"It's nothing. How did you know we were under attack?"

Eve hesitated. "I sensed it."

Citric's expression matched Brielle's own confusion.

In answer to their questioning looks, Eve explained, "I sensed you were in danger. The feeling led me here."

Brielle's gaze lowered to Eve's hands. Sure enough, there it was: the slice across her right palm. It looked freshly healed, as if it had only been done weeks ago. Brielle had never noticed it before, and she would have on one of her ladies.

"The blood bond," Brielle murmured, turning to Citric. "Eve sensed you were in danger."

"That's not possible." A haunted look fell across his features. "Your bloodline is not from Sirasinda."

"Stand there," Eve instructed him, indicating to a spot in front of the hearth.

Citric obliged as she quickly moved around his bedchamber, collecting a bowl of fresh water and a clean looking linen shirt. Setting the bowl on a nearby table, she took a dagger to the shirt, ripping it into a collection of short and long strips. She was vaguely aware that Brielle was hovering somewhere nearby. She had no idea why Brielle was still here, but she didn't have the time or energy to challenge her presence and send her away. Citric's wound needed to be inspected and cleaned, then she would collect the herbs she needed to make a poultice. Eve scrunched a short scrap of linen and plunged it into the bowl.

"Shirt," Eve commanded as she turned to face him.

Citric gave her a look that told her she was being bossy, but she simply lifted her brows, daring him to say it to her face. The corner of his mouth tugged into a wry smile before he undid his leather straps one by one and lifted his shirt over his head. Eve tried to keep a straight face, just as she tried to ignore the fireflies that took flight in her stomach. Her hands trembled a little as she wavered between the awkwardness of touching his bare skin and her desperation to touch him. She pressed her lips into a firm line. She could do this.

"You need to see the court physician," Brielle insisted.

"Eve's knowledge of healing surpasses most physicians," Citric replied.

Eve flashed him a proud smile as she approached to inspect the gash across his ribs. It was vicious, but it wasn't deep. He wouldn't need stitches. She placed a hand against his muscled abdomen, somewhat unnecessarily, as she began to clean the wound.

After a moment, Citric asked, "What did it feel like?"

She knew what he was talking about. "Like ... a tugging in my mind. Like a truth demanding to be known. It was ... instinctive and insistent. I knew exactly where you were and I knew you were fighting for your life."

"You must have someone in your family lineage who is from Sirasinda," Brielle said simply.

"Even if she did, it doesn't explain why her connection is so strong," Citric countered. "Any connection to the sensorium should have diluted with every generation born outside of Sirasin-da."

"Maybe I've strengthened it somehow," Eve suggested. "You brought me to the Red Wood two years ago. It has always felt like home to me. I have learned your ways, listened to the stories hand-ed down by the old ones, adopted the rituals and traditions as if I were born into them. I am more Sirasindan than I am Southern."

Citric's brow creased in consideration, but she could tell he remained unconvinced.

"You buried Rowan's body beneath a black thorn tree in the Red Wood," Eve said quietly before giving a little shrug. "Perhaps burying his bones in the earth strengthened my connection to it."

"No." There was a distance in his eyes as he tried to puzzle it out. "There is only one way your bloodline could retain such a strong connection to the sensorium over time. Your ancestor must have been a hunna."

Eve stilled, shocked by the thought.

"What's a hunna?" Brielle asked.

"A wise woman, a gifted healer, and mother to our people."

"Mother to the people," Brielle repeated the words slowly. "You mean a queen."

"Sirasinda never had kings or queens. Hunnas led our people because their connection to the land and the sensorium were the strongest of all of us. But my people haven't had a hunna in gen-erations."

Eve turned away, as if in a daze. Her hands mechanically plunged the bloody cloth into the water before wringing it out again, but her thoughts were spinning. Despite her shock and disbelief, it made complete sense. She had never been suited to a lady's life of silk dresses, simpering manners, and graceful dances. She loved the woodland and all its wildness. She had dedicated herself to learning the art of healing. The people of Alkhiem were her people. The cause of reclaiming the land for Sirasinda was her cause.

"The blood oath must have activated your connection to the sensorium," Citric concluded.

Eve returned to cleaning his wound. "I took the blood oath weeks ago and I didn't feel anything until today. I can't feel anything right now. I feel normal."

"It will take time for you to connect to the entirety of the land. To recognize the sensations and interpret them correctly. You likely connected to me so easily because of the blood oath we share and our close proximity to each other."

Very close. Her hands were currently on his naked body and she could smell the sweet scent of his sweat beneath the copper tang of his blood. His body radiated warmth and brute strength and raw sexual power. It was making it hard to concentrate around him. Her movements were becoming flustered. She almost startled as Brielle came up behind her to get a closer look at the wound.

"Are you sure you don't want to see the physician? That looks serious."

Eve shot her a murderous look.

"At least you won't have to ask me where I got this scar from," Citric smirked, his voice sultry.

Eve's eyes snapped up at him and then glanced back to Brielle, whose cheeks were most definitely blushing. Their gazes held each other captive, as if locked in a memory.

Desire.

She felt an ignition of desire. Not hers ... oh God. She was feeling Citric's desire. His desire for ... *oh God.* Eve pressed hard against the wound and Citric hissed as he jolted.

"Sorry," Eve said flatly before turning to Brielle. "You don't need to be here, you know."

"Citric!"

Eve and Brielle both spun around at the familiar voice that echoed down the hallway promising certain retribution. Sienna marched through the doorway of Citric's bedchamber, breathless and furious, her belly twice the size of when they last saw her. Jameson followed a few paces behind his wife, his face drawn and haunted.

"Sienna!" Brielle rushed to her friend and they engulfed each other in an awkward hug, given the size of her belly.

"This is the news I wanted to tell you," Citric muttered.

He must have felt them traveling through the Red Wood and wanted to tell Brielle they were close to arriving. Eve hadn't felt them, though. If she was connected to the sensorium, shouldn't she have felt them?

"Are you all right?" Sienna asked as they pulled away from each other.

"I'm fine. Better now that you are here."

"Jameson said you were locked in the dungeon." Sienna speared Citric with her steely gaze as her voice turned brittle. "That you had betrayed her and threatened to execute her."

Citric's features remained unapologetic. "I did what was necessary to reclaim our land."

"You are a traitor! A liar and a betrayer! Both of you."

Eve blinked as Sienna turned her wrathful words on her. It surprised her to find that they stung. Sienna was the only lady of Brielle's court she had truly connected with. Unlike the other ladies, Sienna was genuine and kind. She had welcomed her to court and looked out for her, almost like an older sister would.

"I'm glad you are well, Sienna. I see my people took good care of you." Citric cast a pointed look in Jameson's direction. "You are welcome to stay here at court, but you will find the kingdom has changed."

"Yes, I saw as much when we rode through the city."

"Where is Henri?" Jameson interrupted.

"He's ... alive," Brielle replied uncertainly. At Jameson's worried expression, she added, "I'll explain later."

"What happened to you?" Sienna asked, as if she had only just noticed Citric's bloody wound.

"There was an assassination attempt," Eve said. "Another one."

"What do you mean another one?" Brielle's eyes widened in fear.

"It doesn't matter," Citric replied firmly.

"King Heroux's men tried to kill Citric a few weeks ago in his bedchamber. Instead, they found me," Eve said smoothly.

Brielle's lips parted in surprise. Whether it was due to the knowledge that there had been another assassination attempt or the fact that Eve was in Citric's bedchamber, she didn't know. She hoped the latter. She hoped Brielle's mind wandered with the possibilities of why she had been there.

Sienna turned to Brielle, her expression begging an explanation.

"Citric disbanded the council. Which resulted in them revolting against him and ambushing us in the Red Wood in the hopes of taking the Crown for themselves."

"What?!" Sienna gasped, and Jameson swore.

"The castle's wealth and supplies have been depleted," Brielle continued.

"What kind of reign is this?" Sienna cried.

"Sienna," James reproached, his tone gentle, but the look Sienna turned on him was withering.

"Citric hasn't even been crowned yet," Brielle went on. "The bishops refuse to crown him because he robbed the church of their wealth."

Sienna opened her mouth to protest, but hesitated. "Well, I can't say I disagree with that one."

"Citric has used the wealth to feed the starving, home the displaced, care for the sick and protect the innocent. His reign is one of peace and equality," Eve shot back.

Sienna leveled her with a hard look. "A good ruler knows that the ends do not always justify the means. This is not the Red Wood. This is the Southern Kingdom." She grabbed Brielle's hand and directed the next words at Jameson. "I will be staying in Brielle's bedchamber tonight. We have much to talk about."

She began leading her friend out of the room before she tossed over her shoulder, "We brought your priest."

It was only then that Eve noticed Father Bastien was standing behind Jameson. He lifted his hand in awkward greeting. As his wife charged past him, Jameson simply lowered his head in anguish.

CHAPTER EIGHT

C itric absorbed Jameson's suffering like he was inhaling bitter smoke. He could almost taste the elements of guilt, hurt,
fear, and longing. Something had obviously changed between him
and Sienna, and Jameson was desperate to fix it, but by the looks
of it, Sienna was unforgiving. Citric switched his gaze to Father
Bastien in silent question and the priest returned a resigned, for-
lorn look. Whatever the problem was, it had been going on for
quite some time.

Eve resumed cleaning his wound in silence.

"Leif is coming," Citric announced to nobody in particular.

He had felt Leif's fear and panic when he was fighting in the Red
Wood. His friend would have sensed that he was in danger, but had
been powerless to do anything about it. Citric had sent Leif and
the other direct descendants of Sirasinda to the surrounding farms
to begin healing the land. They had been too far away to come to
his aid, but Citric had felt Leif racing back as fast as he could.

As if Citric's words had summoned him, Leif burst into the
room, his face ashen with worry. His eyes immediately landed on
Citric and narrowed in on the sight of his wound. "What happened?"

"The councilmen tried to take their revenge."

"And failed," Eve added. "They're dead now."

Leif's features cinched in confusion. "You didn't sense them coming?"

Citric speared him with a severe warning look before turning his attention to Jameson. "Jameson, show Father Bastien to a room where he can rest."

Catching on, Father Bastien added somewhat eagerly, "Yes, I would very much like to rest."

The last thing Citric wanted to deal with right now was having to explain the blood magic to Jameson. Or the fact that he was tethered to Citric for the rest of his life. The ruse was barely necessary, though, as Jameson didn't appear to notice Leif's slip of the tongue or Father Bastien's awkwardness. Clearly other concerns occupied his mind.

Citric waited until Jameson and Father Bastien had left and were out of earshot before he turned back to Leif. "I felt the threat, but not until it was too late."

"Why? What's wrong?" Leif pressed.

"Nothing's wrong," Citric growled.

Eve arched an eyebrow before she pointedly dropped the cloth into the bowl of bloody water. "The blood oaths with the lords and the King's Guard have taken a toll on you and put a strain on your connection to the sensorium."

His features twitched in confusion before he remembered that she could feel him too. Their connection went both ways.

"Can't you sense that about him?" Eve turned the question on Leif like an accusation.

"No," Leif replied, somewhat perplexed. "I can feel his emotions, but an individual's connection to the sensorium is private, personal. No one else can feel it."

"Except a hunna," Citric replied. "Their connection to the sensorium is the strongest of all of us."

It was why, historically, the people of Sirasinda swore blood oaths to their hunna. The hunna's connection to the sensorium was strong enough to bear the weight of many tethers. His was not, apparently. In Alkhiem, his men had sworn blood oaths to him as their leader and he had always been able to handle them. But the numbers of his men were nothing compared to the numbers of the lords and the King's Guard combined.

Eve's expression was curious as she considered his words. "I felt it this morning. Outwardly you looked fine, but somehow I knew that your senses were overloaded. You're still adjusting to all the new connections and sensations, trying to decipher between disgruntled feelings and credible threats."

"How could you know that?" Leif frowned, curious.

"Eve sensed I was in danger and came to our aid," Citric explained. "She is a hunna."

Leif's mouth fell open. Eve shifted on her feet uncomfortably.

It took a moment for Leif to regain the ability to speak. "How is that possible?"

"There is no other explanation for how she is able to form a connection with me, given the fact that generations of her family have lived outside of Sirasinda."

Leif and Eve exchanged heavy looks.

"This changes everything," Leif breathed.

His meaning was not lost on Citric. It did change everything.

Eve's eyes suddenly widened in fear, as if a thought had only just dawned on her. "Since your connection to the sensorium is compromised, you can't be sure that you will feel it if Henri switches sides."

They both looked to him for an answer, for reassurance. He could not give it to them. They wouldn't believe him anyway. He could no longer pretend that he was in complete control when the truth was he had not felt this vulnerable in a long time. He should have sensed the councilmen's threat before they ever had a chance to put their plan into action. He should have killed them all weeks ago and been done with it. Mercy cost lives. He knew that better than most. It had almost cost Brielle's life. The thought ripped his beating heart out by the arteries. If anything had happened to her, he would never be able to forgive himself. It tortured him to know that those fucking cowards had laid their hands on her.

"What can we do?" Leif asked him.

Citric's features tightened. "Nothing."

Hope that Henri did not betray them.

"Spend tonight in the Red Wood," Eve suggested. "Connect with the land and the spirits. They always help you. When was the last time you did that?"

Weeks. It had been weeks since he spent any real time in the Red Wood. His days were filled with managing a kingdom on the precipice of self-destruction, and his nights were spent guarding the door of Brielle's bedchamber because he didn't have any men to spare for the task. He had barely slept in weeks.

"Go. I'll guard her tonight," Leif said, sensing every word he would not say.

Eve shot Leif a sharp look before she attempted to school her features into cool disinterest, but even without the blood bond connecting them, Citric could see her emotions were simmering just beneath the surface. *Jealousy. Rage. Hurt.* He needed to talk to her about it, but he didn't want to wound her. And he didn't want to lose her. Eve had been a significant part of his life for the past few years. His promise to Rowan would only be fulfilled when he breathed his last breath in this world. Until then, he would always take care of Eve as if she were his own flesh and blood. But he could not offer her more than that, and a part of him feared what she would do when she realized it.

Brielle watched her friend curiously as they strolled the halls to her bedchamber. Sienna was clearly exhausted. She had been traveling for weeks on horseback through the Red Wood while pregnant, but there was something else not right about her demeanor. There was an edge to her that Brielle had never witnessed before.

"You still occupy the queen's rooms," Sienna remarked as they walked inside.

"Citric never asked me to move, so I didn't."

Brielle helped her friend lower herself down onto a daybed lined with cushions. Sienna let out a small, undignified groan as she laid back against them. Fetching a pitcher of water, Brielle poured a glass and held it out to her.

"Thank you." Sienna took the cup from her hands and drank deeply.

Casting her eyes around the room, Brielle spotted a plate of biscuits that the servants had left for her. She retrieved them and passed the plate to Sienna. While Sienna eagerly nibbled on a biscuit, Brielle took the opportunity to admire her growing belly.

"She is getting bigger," Brielle observed.

"She's very active for a girl. She moves around a lot."

"That seems like a good sign. It must mean that she's healthy."

Sienna's lips formed a proud smile as she ran a hand over her belly affectionately.

"I'm so glad you are here," Brielle sighed. "These past few weeks have been ..."

There was no word to describe it. Difficult, yes. Challenging, very. Heartbreaking, certainly.

"Tell me everything," Sienna encouraged gently.

It was almost impossible to put into words everything that Brielle had been through since that morning they had infiltrated the castle. From being betrayed and imprisoned to discovering the Butcher's identity and watching his bloody execution on a green hill. From being ostracized at court and rejected by the council to formulating a plan to send Henri to the Northern court as a spy. Not to mention discovering Citric's connection to the Red Wood via blood magic and an ancient sensorium, before becoming the target of an assassination attempt by a coup of nobility. Then came the latest revelation of Eve being a hunna, the first in generations for Citric's people. What that meant, she wasn't entirely sure. By the time Brielle had finished, the biscuits were gone and Sienna looked a little pale.

"Jameson told me he swore a blood oath to Citric. Does that mean Citric shares a connection with him? That he can feel what Jameson feels?"

Brielle gave an imperceptible nod. "Though it doesn't take blood magic to see that something is wrong between you and your husband. What happened?"

"What do you mean what happened? He left you in a dungeon to be executed! I charged him with your safety as his queen and he abandoned you!"

Brielle recoiled, surprised at her friend's fury. She had never seen her angry before. The closest Sienna ever came to anger was to give a look of disappointment or disapproval. Perhaps a stern but sensitive reprimand. This reaction was completely out of character for her.

"You can't hold that against him. He was desperately worried about you. You're his wife and you were with the enemy. Of course he would put your safety above all else."

"If anything had happened to you ..." Sienna shook her head as her voice wavered and tears filled her eyes.

Brielle reached for her hands and held them tightly in hers.

"I don't know whether I would have been able to forgive him." The words tumbled out of Sienna's mouth like a confession and she began to sob.

Brielle's face crumpled in sympathy. "Of course you would have. If something had happened to me, it wouldn't have been his fault. He served me as best he could. We were betrayed. Besides, it doesn't matter anymore. I am very much alive."

Sienna squeezed her hands and forced a brave smile through her tears. "Good. Now, what is your plan to reclaim your kingdom?"

The words caught in Brielle's throat. "I don't have one."

Sienna's expression mirrored her own disbelief as she heard her own words echo back to her. It didn't sound like something she would ever say. Yet it was true.

"The land belongs to Citric's people."

"You have accepted that?" Sienna asked carefully.

Brielle nodded. "It doesn't change the fact that they are my people and I will fight for them. Just not as their queen."

Sienna stared at her, pride gleaming in her tear-stained eyes. But then her gaze fell as if she wanted to say something but wasn't sure whether she should.

"What is it?" Brielle prompted.

"Jameson mentioned something else. About you and Citric." The tea.

"Oh." Now it was Brielle's turn to avert her gaze. "It was one night. The night before we infiltrated the castle. I just—I wanted to make a choice for myself for once, before I gave myself in service to my kingdom for the rest of my life. It was a mistake."

"It happens." A shy smile of understanding graced her lips. "Was it at least a good mistake?"

Brielle's insides kindled as she recalled the hunger of Citric's mouth against hers, his skillful hands roaming her body, his manhood plunging into her as he rode her to ecstasy.

"A very good mistake, then."

"I kissed Henri," Brielle blurted out before bringing a cushion up to hide her face.

"Wait, what?" Sienna's eyes widened in shock. She pulled at the pillow to bring it back down.

"Or rather, Henri kissed me, but I definitely kissed him back."

Sienna gaped in confusion. "Brie, do you have feelings for Henri?"

"Of course I have feelings for Henri. I care about him a great deal."

"But do you feel for him in *that* way?" Sienna pressed.

Brielle's thoughts stuttered. She couldn't deny that she was attracted to Henri. From the first day they met, something had sparked between them. But it had also changed over time. They wanted different things from life, had forged different paths, and that always seemed to put them at odds with one another. But he had fought for her. Many times. He was fighting for her now. She wasn't so naive as to think that he had agreed to become a spy solely to free his people from the tyrannical rule of King Heroux. He had also done it for her. Because she had asked him to. Because it meant that she would be safe.

Yes, she had feelings for Henri. But it confused her to think of how different they were to the feelings she experienced when she was with Citric. Despite everything he had done to her, she still wasn't immune to him. She wished she was, but there was just something about him that kept drawing her back under his power. He had lied to her. Betrayed her. Threatened her. But he had also defended her. Trusted her. Challenged her. Championed her. He had made her body feel things she hadn't known even existed. Awakened desires deep inside her that had haunted her sleep ever since. Just breathing the same air as him was electrifying.

Sienna arched a curious eyebrow, as if she could read her thoughts. "I see. Well, I think it's safe to say your suitors have never included a fallen prince or an outlaw king before."

Henri tried to calm his nerves as he was escorted from the dungeon by a dozen King's Guards. Where exactly they were escorting him, he did not know, but he assumed King Heroux had summoned him. So far, he had been treated well. Kept as a prisoner, but with his own private cell, regular edible meals, and a noticeable lack of torture. That could all change in an instant, though. Henri knew he needed to secure King Heroux's trust today. It was imperative for him to advance from prisoner to trusted ally so that he could roam the castle freely and gather the information he needed.

Obtaining King Heroux's trust would not be easy. Henri knew he needed to give him something that no one else could. To prove his worth above all other men already loyal to him. It was a deadly game he was playing and now was not the time to play it safe. He needed to show his hand, every card, everything he was willing to sacrifice, in the hopes it would be enough to get what he needed.

The King's Guard marched him around a corner and instinctively he knew where they were heading: the war room. It was the room where his father and the commander would plot strategy against the never-ending enemies of the North, both real and imagined. His father had seen betrayal around every corner, in every face and word and deed. The cost of being king, Henri supposed. But then again, Brielle's father had not been paranoid. He had formed a council of trusted advisers that he would consult with and listen to. The North had no such council. The commander was the only man his father had ever trusted. It was an irony of epic proportions that the one man his father trusted had been the one man to betray him.

Henri fortified himself as they entered the war room. His hands were no longer bound, his neck mercifully free of rope, but the King's Guard were still cautious of him, as evidenced by the number of men currently surrounding him. King Heroux was leaning over a table lined with maps and carved wooden figurines designed to represent soldiers and resources. He waved the guards away, but two remained, one on either side of the door.

Definitely still cautious, then.

"It's time to prove your worth, prince." King Heroux's tone was laced with impatience. "You told me you could win me this war without losing a single soldier. Now you are going to tell me how."

Henri approached the table, his stride casual and confident. "By destroying the thing Citric loves the most: Alkhiem."

The king observed him carefully as Henri walked around the table, dragging two fingers along the outline of the Red Wood on the map. "His people live in small camps spread out across the Red Wood, but Alkhiem is their main city. It's not much to look at; it's a city of tents. But there is a ruin there, an ancient temple that is significant to them. I don't know why and I don't care. The point is, destroy Alkhiem and you will deal Citric a fatal blow."

King Heroux tilted his head in consideration as he threaded his fingers through his long beard. His mustache remained bound in two long plaits, but today the ends of the plaits were decorated with silver beads. "What are their defenses?"

"It's a city of tents, it has no defenses. No fortification of any kind. A few hundred men at most. They are skilled fighters, but they are not soldiers. They would be no match for your army."

"And you know where this Alkhiem is?"

Henri nodded seductively. "I propose you accept Citric's terms for battle to meet just beyond the border near Nistan, but instead of meeting him, send your army to the Red Wood. Citric is cunning and obviously has the patience and foresight to play the long game. But slaughtering his people and burning the Red Wood to the ground, effectively repeating history, will tear him apart. I have seen the man become the beast. Do this and he won't think, he'll just react, blinded by the need for revenge. Which means he'll be vulnerable and easy for you to kill."

King Heroux grabbed a wooden figurine representative of an enemy army and indicated to the Red Wood, which spanned the entire length of the map. "Show me where Alkhiem is."

"If I did that, you would have no need of me," Henri countered with a sly smile.

King Heroux's features twitched with irritation as he toyed with the figurine in his hand. "Very well."

He walked over to a stone window where a small cage sat on a wooden bench beneath it. A black raven was perched inside, its beady eyes watching them curiously.

"Send a message to the outlaw king telling him I accept his terms for war."

Henri hesitated a moment before moving to the bench to find paper and ink waiting for him. He didn't know why, but he felt anxiety crawl up his spine. He'd expected to fight harder to convince King Heroux that the plan had merit. But perhaps the Northern army was not as strong as he assumed it to be and King Heroux was keen to find a way to preserve his numbers. Henri's hand was steady, despite the king watching over his shoulder, as he wrote out the short message and signed it. He dried the ink with sand, rolled up the paper, and attached it to the raven's leg before releasing the bird into the sky.

"You have proven yourself useful to me, prince." King Heroux's voice held a note of pleasant surprise.

"Good. Then I hope that we can come to a better arrangement. As much as I have enjoyed the hospitality of your dungeon, I would prefer more comfortable accommodations befitting an ally to the king. And I have no need of minders." Henri cast a look back at the King's Guard stationed at the door. "I'm not likely to get lost in this castle."

"Trust must be earned, prince."

Henri turned back to him, a cold sensation prickling his skin. "I believe I have just done that."

"You have proven your worth, not your loyalty," King Heroux countered before beckoning the guards with a crook of his fingers.

Henri watched them disappear through the door, only to reappear moments later escorting three people inside: a man, a woman, and a young girl barely ten years old. In chains. Dread flooded Henri's veins.

"You told me you were willing to become the devil himself. The man I choose to hold the Southern Kingdom for me must be willing to do whatever it takes to quell those who would rise up against me. The Butcher was my loyal dog. He killed his own father at my command."

King Heroux unsheathed his sword and held the pommel out to Henri. His stomach hollowed out as Henri eyed the blade with trepidation.

"Your trial is simple; kill these people, who mean nothing to you, and I will trust you."

Henri stood there, unmoving. He knew his confident courtly mask had slipped, that traces of shock and revulsion were clear in his eyes. It was a test and he was failing. He knew he should do something, say something to try to recover, but he didn't know what to do. The people stood before him in tattered clothes, their heads bowed in resignation, the woman cradling the child close to her body in a feeble attempt to protect her or calm her. The child did not cry, though. She had probably been crying for hours. Days. Weeks. He didn't know. But he could see that there was no fight left in these people.

His mouth was suddenly dry and he forced himself to swallow as he tried to find some words to say. "What crime did they commit?"

"Does it matter? Your king has given you an order."

"A man who passes the sentence should know the crimes committed."

He was stalling. They both knew it.

"They failed to pay their taxes."

The exorbitant taxes that most people could not afford to pay. The taxes that paid for King Heroux's endless war campaigns, that would pay for this war campaign. The weight of Henri's decisions fell on him. He had allowed this man to take his kingdom. Hell, if he was being honest, a part of him had been relieved that the kingdom had been taken from him. He had failed to fight for it, to protect his people, and this was the consequence. The death of hundreds of innocent people. Men. Women. Children. He hadn't witnessed the atrocities with his own eyes, hidden away in the escapism of the Sodisce. He hadn't suffered through the pain alongside his people. But now the harsh truth was standing right in front of him and he couldn't escape it.

He had no choice. If he killed them, he would gain King Her-oux's trust. If he didn't kill them, King Heroux would kill them anyway. He knew that as sure as he knew his own name. Then King Heroux would kill him. He would have failed his people, again, and left them at the mercy of a tyrant. Brielle would be in danger. He couldn't protect her if he was dead. Henri reached for the sword, all too aware that his palms were slick with sweat. King Heroux watched his every move.

His mind flashed back to when he had watched the Butcher slaughter innocents the night before they infiltrated the castle. Henri hadn't had a choice then either. If he had intervened, he would have been caught, killed, and the entire campaign would have been put at risk. He had convinced himself that day that the campaign was more important than a handful of lives, no matter how innocent. That truth had not changed. Yet those deaths, and his failure to act, still haunted his dreams.

He recalled challenging Nathaniel about his choice to become the Butcher. Nathaniel had claimed that he'd had no choice. That the only choice was to die or become a monster, so he had become a monster. He had done it to protect him, the man he loved. If Henri killed these innocents, he would be no better than Nathaniel. He already had the blood of hundreds of people on his hands, *his* people. In one way, the choice did not matter. But in another way, it was the only thing that did matter. These people would die today, he knew that. But not by his hand.

Henri swung the sword in a swift, graceful arc that nicked at the throat of King Heroux even as he threw himself backward to avoid the blow. The King's Guard immediately drew their swords, but King Heroux commanded them to stay back as he grinned at Henri. "He is mine."

The King retrieved a hidden sword beneath his long coat and took up a defensive stance. Of course he hadn't really given Henri his only weapon. He wasn't a fool and Henri could never be that fortunate.

"I see that the devil is really an avenging angel."

"No, I am just a man. But I am not a murderer."

Henri swung his sword overhead and King Heroux deflected the blow. Steel met steel as they clashed and broke apart, circling each other. The king charged at him, pushing his weight forward, and Henri lost his footing to fall on the ground. He recovered by rolling into a somersault that landed him back on his feet, his sword at the ready. Henri advanced and the cry of ringing metal filled the room. He attacked and parried, finding a momentum he had never felt before, a strength and grit fueled by injustice. As King Heroux deflected another blow, Henri brought his fist up to smash into his face. The king stumbled backward, surprised, blood now gushing from his nose to stain his braided mustache.

Rage glowered on the king's face. "Kill them!"

"No!"

Henri tried to get to them, but King Heroux was already striking out at him in a fever of blood lust. Henri heard the swift sounds of steel slicing through skin and bone behind him even as he defended himself from the king's wrath. It was never going to be enough. No matter what he did. It was always going to end like this, at the bloody edge of a sword. But at least he had chosen to fight and die protecting his people. It was an honorable death for a fallen prince.

Citric kneeled in the damp earth of the Red Wood and laid his palms flat against the ground. It had been too long since he had felt this land's heartbeat beneath his skin. As a soldier in the Northern army, he had spent long periods separated from the woodland, his connection fading every day until it was nothing more than a phantom limb. Whenever he could, he had returned to the woodland and the connection replenished like green grass after the season's rain. But this felt different.

He had known for weeks now that something wasn't right. He was off-center, unbalanced. It had been easy to dismiss it as the product of trying to rule a kingdom on the brink of war, manage a court of nobles he would rather slaughter, and deal with a princess he would rather fuck than fight. Which made everything else that much harder to do. Citric had tried to sustain his connection to the sensorium by collecting moments whenever he could. He had slept in the Red Wood rather than the king's rooms and that had sustained him for a while, but that had been weeks ago. Ever since the night of the attack on Eve, Citric had ensured that anyone who wanted to try to kill him could easily find him.

He had thought he could manage his connection to the sensorium like he had before when he was in the Northern army, but he had underestimated the toll the blood oaths would have on him. He had never managed this many before. The tethers leeched onto him, sucking at his senses, splitting his awareness in every direction. He could feel the tethers fraying at the edges, his perceptions blurring. He hadn't wanted to acknowledge it because it was unacceptable. He was responsible for ensuring the safety and survival of his people. And not only his people, but the people of the Southern Kingdom as well. So many depended on him. His strength. His decisions. All of which hinged on his blood magic and connection to the sensorium. He could not afford weakness. He could not afford to lose control.

Burying his hands deep beneath the soil, Citric grasped at the earth as if the sensorium was something tangible he could latch onto. It wasn't. Like the land it came from, the blood magic could never be contained or controlled or possessed. Only embraced. His people did not own this land. They had never claimed to. No, his people did not lay claim to the land, they laid claim to the responsibility of caring for the land. Protecting it. Nurturing it. Worshiping it as the source of all beginnings and ends. As the source of life. The sensorium was nature's gift to them.

Citric closed his eyes and opened his soul to everything that surrounded him. From the myriad of insects that crawled along the ground, to the seeds that would soon birth new life, to the withering bark on the trees and the wind that filled his lungs with notes of peppery leaves as he drew each breath. *Home.* This land was his home. The womb of his people. The lifeblood of everything. Citric felt the land stir beneath his palms, awakening to his touch. He felt its pulse tremble in his veins as it sought him out, causing his blood to surge. He felt the spirits of his ancestors caress his soul as they filled him with peace beyond this mortal world, the wisdom of the sky, and the strength of the past and future combined. His thoughts began to empty out of his mind as his essence left his body—but then it all rushed back in at once.

He opened his eyes violently to the knowledge that she had entered the Red Wood. Citric felt the imprint of her feet on the ground with every step she took. He was aware of her reaching out to him through the blood bond, following their connection like a string that would lead her straight to him. And it did. It took mere minutes for Eve to find him, despite the heavy darkness of the night. The moon was barely a slit in the ebony sky above them and the stars were masked by cloud cover.

When Eve saw him, she hesitated. He remained on his knees in the dirt, silent and still, as if he were one of the trees that had stood there for hundreds of years. Though it was too dark to see her face, Citric could feel her conflicting emotions. She did not want to disturb him, but her curiosity had gotten the better of her. Citric returned a smile that she couldn't see, but he knew she could feel it through the blood bond. It told her he was waiting for her. Eve approached tentatively before kneeling on the ground in front of him and sitting back on the heels of her boots.

Citric knew why she had come. While he was trying to gain control over all the new connections and sensations he was experiencing, Eve was barely feeling anything at all. She had told him that, despite her connection to him, she didn't feel any different. She couldn't feel the Red Wood like he could. The blood oath should have awakened her connection to the sensorium weeks ago, but it was only when he was in danger that the connection had screamed to the surface of her awareness.

"What can you feel?" he asked quietly.

Citric watched the whites of her eyes as she glanced around, as if searching for a feeling to latch onto.

"Nothing."

"But you can feel me."

Her attention returned to him and she nodded self-consciously. "What can you feel?"

Citric inhaled a deep breath, breathing in the woodland like secondhand smoke. "Everything. I can hear the trees talking to each other above and below ground. I can feel the animals and the vegetation, the cycle of life and death. I can sense when the woodland feels threatened and when it feels at peace."

It was the reason why he had spared Brielle and others that first night they had camped in the woodland. He had been alerted to their intrusion and potential threat, but by the time he arrived with his blood brothers to deal with them, the wood was calm. At peace. So he had let them live. It hadn't escaped his attention that since that night the woodland would sometimes react to Brielle's presence. It was always subtle, like a shifting of the breeze or a playful wind, but he had noticed it. The wood saw her as a friend.

"That sounds ... overwhelming."

Citric tilted his head to the side in acknowledgement. "At first. It can feel uncomfortable or confusing. Like a vision of bright colors that do not make sense or like walking from darkness out into daylight. But you learn to adapt to it and then you don't even notice it. It becomes like every other sense. It just is."

Eve's throat bobbed as she swallowed deeply. He could feel the nervous tremors of her anxiety. She wanted to learn about her connection to the sensorium, but it was more than just personal interest. She felt the weight of everyone's expectations on her, along with the fear of not being able to meet them.

Citric inclined his head to his hands, which were still splayed in the dirt. Eve leaned forward and buried her fingers in the soil between his fingers, their hands almost touching but not quite. He felt her heartbeat quicken at their close proximity to each other.

"Concentrate," he urged her, his tone firm but gentle.

She closed her eyes and her features tightened in determination. Citric could feel her searching for it, stumbling around in her awareness, keen to latch onto any sensation in the hope that it would be what she was looking for.

"The sensorium is in your blood. It is a part of you, just like it is a part of this land. Do not look for it, recognize it. You have recognized it before. You said the Red Wood always felt like home. That my people have always felt like your people; our cause, your cause. Because you are Sirasindan. You felt the truth before you knew it."

Her eyes crinkled and shifted beneath her eyelids as if something had caught her attention.

"You know who you are now. A part of you has always known. You are a hunna, the first in generations, mother to our people."

She did know, he could feel it. All of a sudden it was the only thing she knew. He watched as her fingers buried deeper into the soil as if she might disappear beneath it. It was like an anchor sinking into water, an arrow being released from a bow; nothing could stop her now from going deeper and further. The world around her changed in an instant as a million sensations burst through her at once. Citric felt it all as she did, every microsecond, every new consciousness. She could feel every drop of water in the smooth stream that flowed for miles to the east. She could hear the scratching of the animals underground, making homes for themselves. She could sense the rays of sunlight that had been trapped by the leaves of the trees during the day, feeding the insatiable hunger of the woodland. She was aware of the exchange of nutrients from root systems that spanned unimaginable distances. The sensations were infinite. The knowledge visceral.

"It's incredible," she breathed, her eyes still closed.

He smiled. "It is."

"There's something else." Her brows furrowed as she tried to interpret what she was experiencing.

"The spirits of our ancestors."

He felt their presence gather, stronger than ever, because he was feeling what she was feeling. He wondered if they had always known about Eve's lineage or if they were just as surprised as he was to learn about it. Whatever the answer, they rushed inside her now like a force. Citric had always experienced the spirits as a calming presence, providing clarity and a quiet strength when he needed it the most. But this just felt like raw power. The fate of worlds.

The weight of history. Citric felt Eve buckle beneath the pressure of it, and his fingers grasped hold of hers to ground her firmly to the earth.

He wasn't sure how much time passed before the spirits released her. It felt like only minutes but it could have been hours. When Eve opened her eyes, she looked different. Like her soul had aged a lifetime. Citric wasn't sure what to say to her, what she needed from him, but he was aware that their fingers were still intertwined. She didn't seem to notice, though.

"Eve."

Her eyes blinked back at him but they still seemed far away. "Can I stay here with you tonight?"

He gave a vague, concerned nod. "I promise you, you will never be alone in this. I will be here, always."

Eve offered a small, grateful smile, but it looked detached somehow. He was about to say more when he felt the echo of a sudden, blinding pain.

Not his.

The connection snapped into bleak focus as the truth laid out Henri's bones before him, like a carcass to dissect.

CHAPTER NINE

E ve glanced around the cave in the Red Wood. It was noticeably cramped thanks to Citric's ever growing council. Sienna
sat uncomfortably on a log with Father Bastien at her side and
Jameson stood behind her. Brielle paced anxiously near the rear of
the cave while Citric and Leif stood at either side of the entrance,
as if they were wary of another ambush. The recent assassination
attempt had proven that threats still lingered everywhere and vig-
ilance was necessary.

"We're safe," Eve confirmed, and Citric and Leif turned in her
direction. She sat on a log opposite Sienna with an arm draped
casually over a drawn-up knee. "I'll feel it if anyone enters the Red
Wood."

She felt everything now. She had hardly been able to sleep last
night because she was experiencing so much. Too much. The
woodland did not sleep. The trees, the animals, the earth continued to shift and talk and breathe beneath her. She had tried to
drown it all out by focusing on one thing: the man sleeping beside
her. But then she couldn't sleep for a whole new reason.

It had felt like old times, when it had just been the two of
them, living in the Red Wood. They used to spend every moment

together. Every day he would show her a new part of his world, teach her a new skill, share his deepest secrets with her. Just like he had last night. She hadn't wanted to go to sleep for fear of missing a single minute of being beside him. She had dreaded the dawn.

Citric retrieved a note from inside his tunic and held it aloft. "I received word from Henri last night."

Brielle immediately stopped pacing at the back of the cave. "Is he all right?"

"King Heroux has agreed to our terms for war."

Eve raised her brows in surprise. "Which means he convinced King Heroux to attack Alkhiem." She begrudgingly gave Brielle a sidelong look. "Turns out the master of spies is a pretty good spy himself. Your plan worked."

It was the closest thing to a compliment she would ever give her. Brielle's body relaxed a little and Sienna threw her an encouraging smile.

Eve turned back to Citric. "When do we march out?"

"Tomorrow. The Southern army is ready, they only await orders. Alkhiem is preparing for war, making sure defenses are in place."

Eve nodded as restless energy coursed through her limbs, both hers and the woodlands. This was what they had been working toward for years. One final battle and the whole country would be theirs. Sirasinda would finally be restored to her people.

Citric turned to address Jameson. "You will stay here to ensure that order is maintained and the people are well cared for. The numbers crossing the border to seek refuge with us have not slowed. They need strong leadership."

Jameson's expression was neutral as he nodded his acceptance, but Eve could see the flicker of gratitude in his eyes. He would have been a good warrior to have fighting beside them, but Citric was gifting him a small mercy. Jameson would not want to leave his pregnant wife again.

"Father Bastien, you will stay here and help him. The people are in need of your compassion and spiritual guidance."

Father Bastien tilted his head in understanding and exchanged a hopeful smile with Jameson.

"You will need to be crowned king before the army marches out tomorrow," Brielle insisted. "Most of your army are from the South, not the Red Wood. They need a king to follow if they are going to march into battle. Especially if they are going to enter the Red Wood. They are probably more terrified of that than going to war."

"But you said the bishops are refusing to crown him." Sienna frowned.

"We have our own priest," Eve pointed out and turned her attention to Father Bastien.

Father Bastien lifted his shoulders in a shrug. "I am ordained by God. I suppose I could crown you."

"No one will be crowned until the war is won and the land is reclaimed," Citric said firmly. "And even then, it won't be me."

Everyone watched, their expressions a mixture of surprise, curiosity and confusion, as Citric walked over to Eve. She went rigid as he approached, as if suspended in time by what was about to happen. Standing before her, Citric unsheathed his sword.

Jameson's brow creased. "The Sword of Peace," he said, puzzled.

"So named by our enemies." Citric's voice was cold and lifeless. "After the great army laid waste to our homeland, they stole this sword from the temple of Alkhiem. They used it as a symbol of their victory and to evidence the alliance between the newly formed kingdoms, North and South. The leaders of both sides swore on it that they would never raise arms against the other. That North and South would be allies, but never united through conquest or marriage. And so, the Old Treaty was written."

Citric moved his hand along the length of the blade reverently. "But the sword that they reduced to a symbol and imprisoned beneath a pane of glass was more powerful than they knew. It was forged with the blood of hunnas in order to infuse the magic of this land into its steel. Since its creation, every hunna has added her blood to this sword. When restored to its place of birth, the sword will help us heal this land."

Citric held the pommel of the sword out to Eve. "You are hunna. The first in generations. Mother to our people. This sword belongs to you. You are the leader of our people now."

Eve's eyes widened, stunned, as she stared up at him. Her leg fell to the floor, but otherwise she could hardly bring herself to move. To speak. To think. To breathe. At his insistence, her hands reluctantly reached for the blade. She allowed herself to really look at it for the first time, this sword she had only ever heard stories about. It was not the most beautiful weapon she had ever seen, but the moment her fingers touched it, she could feel the power thrumming through it like vibrations over sand. The essence of its soul was calling to her blood, electrifying it beneath her skin, coaxing it from her veins.

She gasped, the air stolen from her lungs. "It didn't feel like this when I touched it before."

"Your blood has been awakened. You know who you are now. What your destiny is."

"I take it back," Brielle said, alarm seeping into her voice. "The soldiers will be more terrified of being led by a sixteen-year-old girl than entering the Red Wood."

"Then they are free to leave," Citric returned coolly, his eyes never leaving Eve.

"They just might," Brielle muttered under her breath.

Eve's eyes snapped to her. "I am the true leader of Sirasinda."

"Apparently. But it doesn't matter how legitimate your claim is, you have the wrong ... body parts."

"That never stopped you from trying to be queen and lead your people."

"Yes and look how well that turned out for me."

"I am not you." The words cut between them, deadlier than any blade.

Brielle looked away and resumed pacing.

"There is something else." Citric's gaze lifted to settle on Brielle. "Last night I felt Henri in pain. Significant pain. It hasn't stopped. I believe King Heroux is torturing him."

Everyone's attention shot to Brielle, whose face had completely drained of color.

"W-what do you mean?" Brielle stammered.

"Something must have happened. King Heroux must have a reason to doubt Henri's loyalty to him. Or he simply got what he wanted from him."

"But he's still alive?" Jameson pressed.

Citric nodded.

"That means King Heroux still needs him for something, or else he would have killed him already," Eve deduced.

Or perhaps King Heroux was simply having fun torturing a former prince of the North. His reputation for bloodlust was well known. He made the Butcher look merciful. Eve observed Brielle as she struggled to contain her emotions. She looked like she might collapse, but somehow she remained upright.

Brielle's voice wavered as she said, "We must rescue him. Now. We can't let him die."

"We have a war to fight," Eve interjected before anyone else could suggest false hope.

It sounded heartless, but it was true. As much as Eve felt for Henri, there was nothing they could do for him. King Heroux's army would begin marching on Alkhiem any day now and they needed to get there first. She would not risk everything they had worked years for in order to save the life of one man. Not even if that man had been kind to her.

And saved her life.

And protected her from being defiled by those bastards.

Steeling herself against the discomfort niggling at her insides, Eve directed her next words to Brielle. "This was your plan. Henri knew the risks."

Brielle shook her head as if she wanted to deny it. As if she refused to comprehend the reality of the situation. She looked to Citric for help, but he said nothing. Even his expression was inscrutable because he knew as well as Eve that they could not risk it.

Brielle's features hardened in sudden determination. "I will save him myself if I have to."

"How?" Eve rolled her eyes derisively. She had little patience for emotional outbursts and false bravado. They were useless to her. "There is no way to get into the castle and you will be hunted the moment you set foot in the Northern Kingdom. That's assuming you even make it that far, which you won't. Not by yourself."

"Eve." Citric's tone warned her she had gone too far, but Eve threw her hands up in reply.

"Fine. Then I'm coming with you to Alkhiem," Brielle announced.

Eve met Brielle's stare which challenged her to say otherwise. She opened her mouth to say no, but for some reason the words hesitated on her tongue. If Brielle wanted to join the army against King Heroux and get herself killed in battle, it was her choice. It made no difference to Eve.

"By all means," Eve replied.

The moment the meeting was over, Eve watched Brielle storm out of the cave. A second later, to her surprise, Jameson followed. Sienna did not. Instead, she eyed Eve from across the distance between them. Then she awkwardly forced herself to her feet before waddling over to her, a hand resting protectively against her growing belly.

Eve couldn't help but feel a little apprehensive at her approach. Sienna had not spoken to her since she returned to the castle. She had not sought her out at all. Eve had resigned herself to the fact that her loyalty to Citric had likely cost her her friendship with Sienna. It hurt, more than she wanted to admit, but it was a price she was willing to pay. Just like Henri's life. Sacrifices had to be made for the greater good. Reclaiming Sirasinda was more important than anything else in the world.

"If you want an apology, I won't give you one." Eve stood and lifted her chin defiantly.

Despite her words, she avoided Sienna's gaze by keeping her hands busy tying the sword to her belt. She would need to get used to the weight of it against her hip, its presence against her thigh. She would need to practice fighting with it, become familiar with how it moved in her hands.

"That is your choice," Sienna replied diplomatically. "But you need to be careful about your choices, especially now. You are the leader of a great army, soon to be queen of this whole country. You need to start thinking and behaving like a queen. Not a spy or a rebel or a young woman. You can't afford to make decisions based on your pride or your emotions anymore."

Eve's narrowed her eyes in annoyance. "What are you talking about?"

"Brielle," she replied simply, and Eve released a frustrated sigh. "You don't like her because you still see her as the princess she used to be. And because ... " Sienna trailed off before looking over her shoulder in Citric's direction.

He was standing by the cave's entrance, arms folded in front of his chest, watching Brielle and Jameson talk by the horses. Eve felt a flame of anger surge inside her at the fact that he was staring at Brielle so blatantly. He didn't look jealous that she was talking to Jameson, but she still had his attention and that was enough to antagonize her. Why did he have to feel anything for her at all? It was as if last night never even happened. Like it had meant nothing to him.

Her eyes caught on Sienna, who was looking at her pointedly, the absent words clear in her expression. Eve averted her gaze and tried to compose herself.

"It was Brielle's plan to reclaim her kingdom that brought you victory that day. It is Brielle's plan that has brought us to this point, this pending battle. Do not discount her worth just because you don't like her or who she used to be. Or because you wish someone would notice you instead of her."

Eve tried to laugh derisively, but it came out more like a choking sound. "You don't know what you're talking about."

"You are right. I don't know what it feels like to be in love with someone and not have them love me in return. It looks like agony."

Eve's eyes cut to hers and they held each other's as the moment passed between them, vulnerable and raw and honest. Something inside Eve cracked. She hoped it wasn't her heart.

As if she heard it, Sienna softened her tone. "I want you to know that despite what you did, I am still your friend. You can talk to me, about anything. I will listen."

Eve's wounded heart stumbled in relief despite herself. Part of her thought she shouldn't be so weak as to desire the approval of others, to crave their friendship. But perhaps that was not weakness. Perhaps it was strength. To surround herself with people she admired, friendships she could rely on, advice she trusted.

"Thank you, Sienna."

Sienna tilted her head slightly. "Take care of my friend. You are both strong women, born to a great destiny: to lead your people. United, there is not a king on this earth who could stand against such power."

Brielle marched out of the cave to her white mare, which was grazing beside the other horses. She felt sick to her stomach and light-headed with fear. Every nerve in her body was on edge, her limbs itching to get up into the saddle and ride until the Northern castle loomed in front of her.

Henri.

Tortured.

She couldn't bear the thought of it. Not knowing what they were doing to him. Not being able to help him. He was alone and in pain and it was all her fault. It was her plan. They had all known the risks, but knowing them and having them come to pass were two very different things.

"Brielle," Jameson called out as he followed behind her.

She forced herself to stand by her horse and wait for him to catch up. Before he could get a word in, though, she turned around and said, "I'm not going to let King Heroux kill him."

Her voice was firm with conviction but inside she was churning with uncertainty.

Jameson nodded as if he actually believed her. "What's your plan?"

Brielle considered for a moment. Eve was right, though she hated to admit it. With no army at her back, she was only one person. With a price on her head. She wasn't a trained fighter or a skilled spy. She didn't know the North well enough to safely navigate it, and the Northern castle was all but impenetrable. She couldn't do this by herself.

"I will follow the army to the Northern border. Then I'll find someone who knows how to get inside that castle. Someone who will want to save Henri just as much as I do."

"Let me come with you."

"No. Citric has given you an order to stay here."

"Damn his orders! I won't let you do this alone."

"I won't be alone. Besides, Citric will feel it if you betray him. I can't have anyone knowing what I'm about to do. Anyway, it's too dangerous."

"Too dangerous!" Jameson balked.

"You have a wife and child to care for. They can't afford to lose you. I have no one depending on me, except Henri. Besides, you have the harder task. You have to deal with the consequences of a dead council. An arrest of nobility is no small thing."

Jameson's features twisted in concern, as if he felt torn in two different directions.

"I swear to you, I will bring him back to us."

"I know you will do everything you can. But if it is not enough, if King Heroux kills him, just know that Henri would be glad to have died protecting you."

Brielle stilled at his words. She didn't want to hear them, but they buried themselves deep inside her soul, carving their mark on her heart.

"You must know that he is in love with you."

She pinched her lips together to keep the tears from falling. She tried not to think about the kiss they had shared or the words he had said. The moments of tenderness between them, or the nights they had lain beside each other beneath the canopy of the Red Wood, watching the stars until they fell asleep.

"Love is such a precious and fragile thing," Brielle forced the words out around the lump in her throat. "I know things are strained between you and Sienna, but they will come right again. She loves you and you love her. And you did nothing wrong by swearing the oath to Citric and going to her. I have told her as much."

Jameson's face crumpled in gratitude. Brielle flung her arms around him and he grasped her tightly in return. When they pulled away, they turned to find Sienna waddling over to them.

"I assume you have a plan?" she asked.

"I do." Brielle turned her attention back to Jameson. "Jameson, I charge you with the safety of my friend, your wife. May you always put her safety and wellbeing above all others."

The corner of Jameson's mouth tugged up into a faint grin as he bowed to her in courtly fashion. "Yes, my queen."

A knowing smile spread across Sienna's lips and she slid her hand into his. Jameson looked at his wife with all the love in the world shining in his eyes.

Turning back to Brielle, Sienna said, "Now, go save your prince."

Brielle sat straight-backed in her saddle as her eyes drank in the sight before her. The army, made up of Southern soldiers and men from various camps within the Red Wood, stood in regimented lines just beyond the city gates. Some soldiers were on horses, most were on foot. The Southern soldiers were armed to the teeth, wearing polished chain mail and armor that had been battle-tested over the years. They stood in perfect formation, a well-trained legion, a slick fighting force. Citric and his men, on the other hand, did not wear any armor. They were dressed in their usual leathers, and even though they stood in the lines next to the Southern soldiers, they were clearly forged from a different fire. Despite the lack of armor, sitting atop his dun mare at the head of the army, Citric looked every inch the commander of a great force.

"Men of the South," he called out to them, his booming voice carrying across the land. "Men of Sirasinda. Today, we march as one army to defend our homeland from the invasion of a tyrant. We march to reclaim the land of the North as our own and to free its people from oppression. We march to restore this country to what it used to be: a land of peace and prosperity."

Brielle felt a chill wash over her, raising the hair on her arms. He was captivating when he spoke, a natural born leader. She tore her eyes away from him to cast her gaze out among the men. The faces of the Southern soldiers were stoic, battle hardened, but she recognized the fierce resolve there. Many of them had fought alongside her father to defend the Southern Kingdom against its enemies over the years. Many of them were there at the battle where her father had been betrayed and murdered, and King Heroux had pronounced himself king. This was their chance for revenge and she could see it in their eyes. The men from the Red Wood were even more resolute, their expressions leaving no room for doubt or fear; they would reclaim their homeland or die fighting like their ancestors.

"History will remember this day for generations. Not only as the day when the war began, or when two people became one, but as the day when a queen came to her throne."

The men's steady expressions suddenly faltered, their eyes shifting amongst each other in uncertainty. Brielle licked her lips nervously. Even her horse stirred beneath her, as if sensing the change in the air.

"I hereby renounce myself as your king."

Shocked murmurs broke out among the men and their perfect lines began to dissolve. Their gazes collectively turned to Brielle, and it took all the strength she had to remain poised beneath their scrutiny.

"I give you your queen: Evelyn." Citric swept his arm out behind him, and Eve drove her horse forward to stand alongside his.

The Southern soldiers visibly recoiled. Their trepidations only intensified at the sight of her youth. Eve did not look like any queen they had ever known. Her expression was too harsh, too confident, and she dressed like a man, in leathers and pants. Brielle winced at the sight. The soldiers exchanged disapproving looks, some outright swore, whilst a few dared to spit on the ground. To her credit, Eve did not flinch.

"If you do not respect my decision, you should leave now. But you will die a deserter's death."

The men from the Red Wood clutched their weapons tighter and looked around as if waiting to cut down anyone who dared to desert. With Citric's words hanging heavy in the air, Eve gave the command for the army to move out. Brielle sucked a breath in between her teeth and turned her horse to join a line. To her surprise, the rest of the army followed.

The first few days traveling across the Southern lands to the Northern border were tense, to say the least. Citric, Leif and the men from Alkhiem ensured that the soldiers knew Eve had their full support and they were quick to snuff out any disrespect or talk of dissent. It was clear that if the soldiers chose to desert the army, they would be hunted down and executed as traitors to the Crown. Hence, they had little choice but to accept Eve as their rightful queen.

Worse than serving a young queen, though, was when the soldiers were ordered to enter the Red Wood. For as long as she lived, Brielle would never forget the looks on their battle-seasoned faces. Grown men who had seen the horrors of war countless times over and whose bravery knew no bounds, turned into an army of frightened children, ready to retreat to the safety behind their mothers' skirts at the prospect of entering the infamous wood. It was understandable, given the stories they had heard about it their whole lives. Rumors of vengeful spirits and lost souls. Now Brielle knew those rumors held a lot of truth to them. The woodland floor had been soaked in the blood of Citric's ancestors. If she ever met such a fate, she would probably become a vengeful spirit too.

Then there were the rumors of blood magic. Brielle wondered if the soldiers believed in those too. If they were curious about the blood oaths they had sworn to Citric. If they questioned whether the act was simply a pagan ritual or something more. No doubt they would flee in a heartbeat if they knew they had unwittingly given themselves over through a blood bond and would forever be tied to a pagan.

The soldiers had entered the Red Wood slowly, fearfully. For the first few days, every sound had them drawing their weapons, checking their blind side, and praying to God for protection. They could feel it, a strange presence in the air surrounding them. There was an awareness amongst the trees. An ancient knowing buried deep beneath the soil. The rumors were true; there was something not right about this wood. After a few days, though, the soldiers began to relax a little. They no longer startled at every noise they heard. And though they could still feel the strangeness of the wood around them, they had grown somewhat used to it. A tentative trust had grown between them and the land they walked on. Perhaps the Red Wood knew that the soldiers posed no threat and were, in fact, here to defend it, to reunite it with the rest of who it used to be.

For her part, Brielle couldn't help but become lost in thought as they marched through the Red Wood. It brought back not so distant memories of the last time she had traveled through this wood with an army, intent on reclaiming her kingdom. Despite the campaign being hers, Citric had led that army, an army of no more than thirty men, with Eve at his side. Now Eve led the army, a great and vast army made up of Sirasindan and Southern combined, with Citric at her side. Henri and Jameson had ridden beside her for the entire journey to the Southern court, keeping their vow to Sienna to safeguard their queen. But now she was no longer a queen, and she rode alone.

How everyone's fates had changed.

Brielle's heart twinged in pain, feeling the absence of her friends. She was not afraid. She was barely aware of the fact that she was one of only two women traveling with an army of men. It was simply that she missed the company of her friends and the comfort of knowing that they would face the enemy together. Instead, Jameson remained behind at the Southern castle to ensure civil unrest didn't break out, and Henri was trying to survive unspeakable torture in the North.

Pinching her eyes closed, Brielle tried to rid her mind of the relentless worrying thoughts that circled like vultures preying on her fears. When she opened them again, she kept her focus on the horizon and pretended not to notice that Citric was looking back at her from the front of the company. Again. He had been watching her closely ever since they left the Southern court. Even when she laid her bedroll out at night, Citric always ensured his was no more than a foot away. Perhaps he was simply being protective, knowing the base nature of some men. But it felt like more than that. It felt like he was waiting for her to do something.

Citric casually turned his mare around and waited until her horse naturally came up alongside his. Eve cast her eyes back at them and scowled. Brielle pretended not to notice that either.

"We will be arriving in Alkhiem today," Citric informed her.

Brielle nodded but didn't take her eyes off the horizon. A moment of heavy silence passed between them.

"Have you missed my woodland?" His tone was playful, as if he wanted to coax her from her dark thoughts.

"I was just thinking about the last time we traveled through here with an army."

His impish smile faded. "You were a brave queen, determined to save your people. And you were victorious."

"Victorious," Brielle scoffed and gave him a dry look. "I was betrayed by my allies and lost my kingdom."

"But you did free your people."

Brielle pursed her lips in annoyance. Of course he would try to twist the narrative to suit his own purposes and assuage his guilt. If he even had any to begin with. She doubted it.

"Brielle, I don't think you realize what your actions have achieved. Look behind you."

She reluctantly cast her eyes over her shoulder to take in the sight of the great army traveling behind them.

"A queen leads this army. After this battle, a queen will rule this entire country. Isn't that part of the reason why you fought so hard? To prove that a queen could rule these lands in her own right? You have done that."

She turned back to him and their eyes caught. The raw earnestness in his face dissolved her defenses. He was right. In a way, her lifelong ambition had come true. Just not for her. Not in the way she had envisioned it.

"What about you? It must have been difficult for you to give up being king."

His expression shifted into a rogue grin, as if the situation amused him. "I never had any desire to be king."

"No, but you have been a leader to your people for years. You cannot tell me that you are happy to give that up and hand it all over to someone else. A young queen, no less."

"She is my hunna," he said simply.

Brielle watched him carefully, but there were no traces of dishonesty in his features, no hint of resentment in his tone, no ghost of regret in his words. She blinked, perplexed. He had handed it over as if it meant nothing to him. She had never met a man like him before. In that moment, she wasn't even sure he was real.

"How did you come to be the leader of your people?" she asked, curious.

All amusement faded from his features, replaced by a solemness that was almost haunted. "I was born and raised in Alkhiem. From the moment babes are put to their mother's breast, the old ones tell us stories about the history of our people and what was taken from us. Trauma is passed down from generation to generation, like eye color or skin tone. When I was a boy, barely old enough to hold a weapon, my grandfather was convinced that I would be the one to reclaim the land for our people. My family's bloodline is the purest among the descendants of Sirasinda and I had been born with the strongest connection to the sensorium of all my people. My father and grandfather started to train me in the use of weapons and I discovered I had a particular skill for the bow. My mother did not approve of them training me so young, putting the weight of my people's hopes on my shoulders, but even she looked at me and wondered. It didn't matter anyway. They all died soon after that."

"What?" Brielle spluttered. "How?"

"They were murdered by the King's Guard." At her look of shock, he inhaled a deep breath. When he spoke again his words sounded strained, as if he were forcing himself to say them out loud. "My people rarely leave the Red Wood. There is no need. The wood provides what we need because we care for it. But that day, my mother took me to a nearby village. She somehow knew there was a fair that day and she wanted me to see it. Looking back now, I think she wanted to give me some reprieve from the relentless training. My mother was very beautiful and was a stranger to the village. A woman alone with a young child is easy prey. I tried to defend her but—" The words died on his lips.

Brielle felt her stomach turn to acid.

"That's how I got this." His fingers tapped at the prominent white scar that ran down his left cheek. "From the blade of a King's Guard, to convince my mother to stay quiet. My father felt all of it through the blood bond and came to our aid with Grandfather, but they were too late and they were outnumbered. I don't know why the King's Guards let me live. I think it entertained them in the moment."

Digging her fingernails into the palms of her hands, Brielle tried to keep the tears from spilling onto her cheeks. The horror of it all was just so overwhelming.

"After that day, I returned to Alkhiem and trained myself with whatever weapons I could. Then, when I was ready, I left the Red

Wood and joined the Northern army. My plan was to become the best bowman in the army, to gain a reputation for myself, and eventually come to the attention of the king. It was my only way into court."

Brielle's eyes narrowed as her mind raced with the implications. "You planned to take the Northern Kingdom first."

The corner of his lips tugged into a sly smile before it faded like a memory. "But then Rowan was killed in battle and I deserted the Northern army. There was no going back after that."

"And then you met Eve."

Citric nodded, his gaze landing on the young queen riding ahead of them, leading her army. "She was so strong and smart and determined. She reminded me of Rowan. I decided to trust her with my secrets and introduce her to my world. It was never my intention to involve her in any of this, but she wanted to fight for it. I think something inside her recognized the Red Wood as her home and the people of Alkhiem as her people. She saw the cause as her own."

"So you sent her to court as a spy to learn information to help you take the Southern Kingdom."

He cocked his head in acquiescence. "By that time, I had already carved out a reputation for myself as the notorious Vogel. I knew one day I would need money to fund a war, so I became an outlaw. My people haven't had a leader in generations. They began to believe what my grandfather believed: that I would be the one to reclaim the land for our people. They swore blood oaths to me, like they would a hunna."

Brielle pressed her lips into a thoughtful line. "But before you could bring war to our door, war came in the form of King Heroux. Did you know about the commander's plot to betray the king?"

"No."

"Then how did you know that Nathaniel spared Henri's life that day on the battlefield?"

"I didn't. But I suspected it. As a young man, Henri would train with the soldiers of the Northern army. He was paired with Nathaniel most of the time, but they shared a training ground with the rest of us. I observed Nathaniel carefully over the years, and I saw his feelings toward his friend change. I knew that Nathaniel would do anything to protect him."

"Like surrendering the King's Guard if Henri's life was threatened," she murmured, deep in thought. When her head cleared, she said, "And then I entered your woodland."

"And then you entered my woodland."

"How fortunate for you."

"Very."

His expression held something she couldn't quite interpret. She frowned, equal parts aggravated and curious.

"From that first night you entered my woodland, I watched you. It didn't take long to figure out who you were. I followed you to the Sodisce and when I saw Henri, I suspected you were both planning to reclaim what had been taken from you. It was fate that sent you both back into my woodland."

Fate. Destiny. She was not sure she believed in such things anymore. History had robbed her of her destiny. All she had left now were her choices.

"And now here we are, marching to battle to reclaim the rest of your ancestral lands. Your grandfather was right about you."

Brielle looked at him sidelong and he smiled at her. "In a way, yes. When we reclaim our homeland, I will be at the front of the battle lines. But I know that when we win this war, it won't be because of me. It will be because of you."

CHAPTER TEN

Henri was not dead yet. It was a miracle and a bitter disappointment, but also a relief. After days of being strung up naked in a dark cell, being beaten, brutalized, and starved, his body felt broken. Certainly several of his bones were. His skin was split open in various places and his body was a patchwork of colored bruising. But his mind was the part of him that had been tortured the most.

Devoid of any stimulus but the pain, Henri tried to send his mind elsewhere, to happier times and comforting thoughts, but it lingered stubbornly in the dark, deep waters of guilt and shame. He couldn't save them, the three innocents. But at least he had fought for them. He hadn't fought for his mother. He hadn't fought for Fleur. He hadn't fought for his kingdom or his Crown or his people. Every blow inflicted, every broken bone, every piercing crack—he deserved it. This was his penance for giving away his power so easily, for abandoning his people, for failing to protect them. They had been suffering this pain, and worse, every day since King Heroux had conquered the North. It was high time that he suffered as well.

King Heroux had been personally overseeing his interrogation. He only ever asked one question: where was Alkhiem? And Henri would answer him. Eventually. But not yet. He needed Citric to know, through the blood bond, that he no longer had King Heroux's trust and that they could not rely on him for more information. They would have to fortify Alkhiem as best they could and prepare for war, not knowing King Heroux's numbers or battle plans. Henri also needed to buy them time. If he gave up the location of Alkhiem now, King Heroux would march on it within the hour and Citric's army would never make it in time to defend his home. It would be a slaughter.

So Henri held out against King Heroux's ministrations. He would not kill him, Henri knew that. Not until he got what he wanted. And the moment he did, Henri would die. Strangely, it did not bother him. His only regret was that he did not get more time with her. Wading in the murky waters of guilt and shame, there were moments of light when he called Brielle's face to his mind. The sweeping slope of her lips when she smiled her secret smile. The brightness in her eyes, the scent of her skin.

If he had his time again, he would do things so differently. He would have fled the battlefield that day only to raise an army. He would have acted like a king, coming to aid his queen. He would have led her armies, followed her into any battle, fought alongside her. He wouldn't have let precious moments with her slip through his fingers like smoke. He would have touched her. Kissed her. Claimed her over and over again. No doubt Citric would have one day rose up against them, but who knew how that story would have ended? It didn't matter because he would have been by her side. A king worthy of his queen.

"You surprise me, prince."

King Heroux's words brought Henri's attention back to the pain and the cold stone walls of a damp, dark cell. The only light was the flicker of a single oil lamp King Heroux brought with him every day. There was nothing else in the cell, save for the both of them.

"You have held out longer than most men."

Henri's wrists were shackled to chains suspended from the ceiling and his feet were shackled to the floor. He tried to lift his head which was slumped against his shoulder, but he didn't have the energy. It was pointless anyway. His left eye was swollen shut and his right eye was so bloodshot he could barely see out of it.

"But you will tell me what I want to know. If you don't, I will find every person you have ever cared about and you can watch me kill them. Slowly. Painfully. Taking them apart piece by piece."

Henri felt his bloodstained skin prickle with unease. Brielle was safe, he reminded himself. Safe in the Southern Kingdom. Safe surrounded by guards. He had no one else left to lose.

"Very well, then." King Heroux's voice held the foreboding threat of a blade held over hot coals. "I will bring the first one to you."

222 TO REFORGE A DESTINY

Eve felt her heart surge with joy and relief as she led the army into Alkhiem. She had been terrified they would not make it in time, or that Henri would betray them and she would be forced to feel King Heroux's army entering the Red Wood while they were still miles away, unable to do anything to stop them. She saw it in her nightmares; arriving to find her people slaughtered. The city of tents burned to ashes and the ground scorched with fire. Instead, they had arrived to find the people gathered to greet them, overjoyed to see their loved ones again. The men ran to their wives and families, who engulfed them in their arms. Children squealed with delight at seeing their fathers and brothers return home. It was a mercy that no lives had been lost in their quest to reclaim the Southern lands. Of course, if she was honest, that was largely due to Brielle's plan. She owed her that much recognition.

She glanced back at Brielle to see her and Citric dismounting, their horses standing side by side. The sight of them together inflamed her insides, but she tried to ignore it and remember Sienna's words. She was no longer just a girl in love with a man, waiting for him to notice her. She was a queen. A hunna. Leader of her people and this great army. She had a war to win.

Eve turned her attention to the Southern soldiers, who remained in formation. Their eyes wandered around the camp in awe, as if they could not believe that people actually lived in the Red Wood. Swinging herself down from her horse, Eve greeted her people as they approached to welcome her home. It soured her joy to think that such a happy day of reunification would swiftly be followed by a bloody war.

Casting her eyes around the camp, she noted the defenses the people had already put in place. Alkhiem was a city of tents, not walls. It had no moats or forts or fortification of any kind. There were no doors to defend, no hidden escape passageways. It was all open ground. Weeks ago, Citric had sent a raven instructing the people to dig deep trenches around the outskirts of the city, covered over with leaves and branches to hide the sharp spears they had placed beneath. Footholds had been struck into the trees surrounding the camp, providing people with the ability to quickly climb them to take up vantage points. She had also noticed strong vines gathered at different locations further afield of the camp. She suspected they also formed part of the defense strategy, but she wasn't sure how. No doubt tomorrow would be spent implementing more defenses and ensuring the people were ready for what was to come.

Her attention caught on Citric as the people crowded around him, professing their gratitude for the return of their loved ones, but also the return of their ancestral lands. He accepted their thanks, clearly humbled by them, and she couldn't help but smile as she watched him. Through the blood bond she felt all the emotions that swelled inside his chest, his love for his people. He would die for them. Every single one of them. She knew for a fact that his men would die for him too. Citric had been their leader for years. Anyone who looked at him would say he was born to lead these people. But now things had changed. She was their hunna. How was she ever supposed to live up to Citric? She had spent less than three years with these people, and although they had accepted her as one of their own, she was not him.

Eve suddenly remembered the Southern soldiers were still standing in formation, waiting patiently for her orders. She began to delegate tasks to her people to ensure enough accommodations and food were provided to the soldiers. It was a daunting prospect, housing and feeding an army this size, but they would do it. It wouldn't be for long. The Southern soldiers followed her commands and accepted the hospitality offered to them, but they remained wary. She observed them sniff at the strange food, their eyes roaming suspiciously over the domed tents and the scarred ruins of the temple. It was a different way of life here, different from anything they would have ever seen before. She would describe it as simple. They would describe it as pagan.

The soldiers sat amongst each other and murmured between themselves, clearly unsettled. It was as if they were waiting for the pagans to lure them into a trap. Perhaps demand that they offer up one of their own as a human sacrifice. It was absurd, of course, but ignorance always was. Still, the soldiers kept their weapons sheathed and their fears leashed.

In fairness, the soldiers were not the only ones who were wary. Despite their warm welcome and kind hospitality, her people were clearly uneasy. It felt unnatural, almost disrespectful to the spirits, to have the soldiers sleeping on the very ground that their ancestors had soaked with the blood of her people generations ago. For centuries these soldiers had been occupying their homeland, claiming it as their own, while her people were forced to live in secret. Now they were eating their harvest and breathing the same air. Her people had every right to resent these soldiers, but now they were under her command and they would fight to set right the wrongs of history. Or she would kill them all herself.

It was dusk by the time everyone was taken care of. Eve considered going to her tent and passing out from exhaustion, but instead her feet wandered into the ruins. A cold silence greeted her as she stepped inside. The walls were washed with faded murals that had once been bright with color. Vines snaked over the archways and crawled up cracked pillars that reached for the open sky above. A light breeze wafted in through exposed windows, sending brown leaves scattering across cracked tiles. Eve had explored the remains of this temple many times before, but this time felt different. It felt as if she belonged here. No, more than belonged. Like she was a part of the walls, the tiles, the foundation stone. She swore she could hear the echo of memories from her ancestor who had walked across this very floor. Her ancestor had led the people of Alkhiem generations ago as their hunna. She had worshiped the natural world here, survived the attack on her people and found a way to ensure their bloodline continued.

Eve wandered mindlessly until she found herself standing in the ceremonial room. It was the largest room in the ruins and the most beautiful. Though it was dark, she could still make out the faint lines of the mosaic patterns on the floor, made up of thousands of tiny tiles. She walked to the center of the room, her hand resting lightly on the sword strapped to her side. Beneath a canopy of stars, she released the sword from its sheath. It warmed to her touch and hummed in the moonlight, as if sensing that it had finally come home.

The blood of hunnas had forged this sword, her ancestors' blood. Soon, she would also bleed, as would many of her people. Her heart suddenly seized, as if the traumas of history had grasped it in warning. Eve gripped the hilt of the sword in determination. She would not let history repeat itself. This time they knew what was coming for them and they were prepared. The woodland itself was wiser to the world and ready to defend itself. She could feel it changing around her, the ground pulsing with the desire for revenge, the air growing thick with violent energy. She would lead her people to victory and restore this land.

Sensing movement behind her, Eve whirled around to find her people silently pouring into the room. Each one of them held a candle, the light illuminating their faces as they assembled before her. The expression on every face was the same no matter where she looked: reverence. To her, she realized with wonder. Citric must have told them.

Sensing him in the crowd, her eyes caught on Citric as he slowly moved from the back to break through to the front. Standing before her, he held a candle in his hands, the flame flickering in the slight breeze. He offered her an unlit candle and she immediately understood the symbology of it. Feeling the weight of this moment, she accepted the candle with trembling fingers. He used his flame to light hers and then his eyes rested on her face, saying everything that words could not. That he believed in her. That he would be by her side every day until the last. That these people were hers to lead now.

Eve's gaze drifted over his shoulder to the crowd assembled in front of her, her people. Her eyes took note of each and every one of them. Together they would fight to reclaim their ancestral land. As hundreds of candles burned brightly in the night, the earth beneath their feet trembled like the drums of war.

Brielle had considered waiting another night, allowing herself a chance to properly rest, but then she had seen the people of Alkhiem gathering in the temple. She knew she would not get a better opportunity than this to slip away from the camp undetected. Still, she allowed herself a moment to peer around the corner of the doorway into the ceremonial room, curious to see what or who could draw such a crowd. What she saw was absolutely mesmerizing.

The entire camp had silently gathered inside the room, each person holding a single candle in their hands. Eve stood before them, holding a candle in one hand and the Sword of Peace in the other. The people did not bow to her or call out blessings of long life or throw flowers at her feet, but there was no doubt in Brielle's mind that Eve was their queen now. Their hunna. Something consecrated was forging between them in that moment. Brielle shivered as she witnessed it, felt the power of it in the room. Eve had always been one of them, but now she was sacred among them. There was a time not too long ago when Brielle would have felt envious of Eve being treated like a long-lost queen, leading her great army into battle against her enemies, being worshiped like a goddess. But not now. Now her only thought was Henri.

Quieter than a shadow, Brielle slipped away from the ruin. The Southern soldiers paid her no mind as she hurried past them and with the rest of the camp gathered inside the temple, there was no one to stop her from fleeing. Earlier, she had asked Citric about the defenses already put in place around Alkhiem so she was well aware of the hidden traps around the camp. Still, she couldn't help the flicker of anxiety every time she placed her foot down in front of her. The last thing she needed was to be impaled. Once she was certain she was clear of any danger, she began to run, racing through the trees and over rocks as if she knew this path by heart. She could have sworn the woodland was guiding her as the fireflies raced ahead, lighting the way.

Hours later, Brielle released a breath of relief as she entered the town. Pulling her hood closer to conceal her face, she made her way across the familiar dusty road. It was late in the evening, but Clontarf showed no signs of going to sleep. The buildings were overflowing with patrons. The noise of music, laughter, and drunken escapades exploded out of open windows and flowed onto the streets below. It gave the night a certain reckless feeling, as if one could get into trouble very quickly, but would enjoy every moment of it. It was certainly a different atmosphere from the tense mood of Alkhiem.

Brielle hesitated as she stood in front of a derelict wooden door in a back alleyway. Last time she had entered this building through the front door and it had not gone well. This time, she was determined to go unnoticed. Summoning all her courage, she rapped her knuckles against the rough wood. A heartbeat later, it was yanked open by a large man with arms the size of small logs. His beady eyes swept over her from head to toe, though there wasn't much to see with her cloak masking her body and her hood covering her face.

"We have no need of more girls tonight," he said gruffly and moved to close the door.

Brielle stuck her boot in the door jamb. "I need to speak to the *Petit Maitre*."

The man narrowed his eyes at her. "You don't have an appointment."

"Nevertheless, I need to speak to him."

"No one speaks to the *Petit Maitre* without an appointment."

"Tell him that the man he serves is in trouble and needs his help."

Brielle barely had time to rescind her boot before the man slammed the door shut in her face. She exhaled a nervous breath and glanced around. She was alone, which on the one hand was a relief, but on the other hand, she knew how dangerous it was for a woman to be alone. Especially in this part of town. Her daggers were well hidden on her body, and she would be able to defend herself if she needed to, but still, she preferred not to have to use them.

The door opened abruptly to reveal a boy standing beside the brute of a man. The boy looked different to how Brielle remembered him. He was wearing fine clothes, the clothes of a businessman tailored to the size of a child, and his previously boyish mop of curls was slicked down. Brielle knew the boy couldn't be more than ten years old, but somehow he looked older. His expression was serious as he scrutinized her. That, at least, had not changed. Brielle lowered her hood so he could see her better.

"You." The word was an accusation. Regardless of his fine clothes and mature demeanor, his voice still had the tone of a child.

Brielle mentally kicked herself for being unable to recall his name. It hadn't seemed important at the time, but now this child might be her only chance to save Henri.

"Please," she said, the single word holding all of her fragile, desperate hope.

The boy considered her for a moment before he jerked his chin to the man beside him in silent permission to let her pass. Brielle eagerly stepped inside, grateful to be somewhere safe. She almost couldn't believe that she had made it. She had snuck out of Alkhiem undetected, made her way alone through the Red Wood, and entered Clontarf without anyone noticing her. A flush of pride kindled inside her.

Brielle quickly scanned her surroundings. To her surprise, she realized they were standing backstage. Through the sides of the heavy burgundy curtain, she could see scantily dressed women dancing provocatively on stage. Beyond them, the room was full of men drinking, gambling, groping, and enjoying the performance.

Women rushed past them, causing Brielle to stumble a little in their wake as they fixed their hair and makeup and changed into extravagant, brightly colored costumes that left little to the imagination. It was confronting to see so much naked flesh up close. Brielle was not sure where to look, but she also couldn't tear her eyes away. For their part, the women seemed completely oblivious to her staring and entirely comfortable putting their bodies on display for all to see. They almost seemed proud of it.

"You have information for me."

The boy's commanding tone jerked her attention back to him. She cleared her throat self-consciously.

"Henri went to the Northern court as an emissary for King Citric with the mission of convincing King Heroux that he was willing to betray his king in exchange for a position at court. In truth, he was our spy. We have reason to believe King Heroux discovered this and Henri is now a prisoner and being ... questioned."

She couldn't bring herself to say the word *tortured*. It hurt too much. But the grave expression on the boy's face told her he knew exactly what she could not say. His features had turned stark and fearful, as if he could picture his master in the dungeon of the Northern castle. Perhaps he had even been there himself. Brielle did not know anything of the boy's background or how he came to be in service to Henri. All she knew was that the boy was loyal to him.

"I came here because I need a way to get inside the castle. I'm going to rescue him."

The boy pinned her with an assessing look, clearly doubting her abilities to do so. "You would risk your life for him?"

Brielle squared her shoulders. "I would die for him."

After a moment, he returned a curt nod. "So would I."

"You will help me, then?" Brielle's heart soared in hope.

"Just you? Where are your friends?"

He meant Jameson and Sienna.

"It's just me."

He blew out an anxious, slow breath. "This will not be easy."

The boy paced a few steps away from her, rubbing his chin in thought. The gesture was incredibly adultlike.

"The Northern castle is like a locked strongbox. Fortunately, I have never met a lock I could not open." He tossed a crafty grin over his shoulder. "I think I know how we could get inside."

Before Brielle could open her mouth to speak, the brute of a doorman appeared again. She hadn't even noticed he'd disappeared until he returned to place himself between her and the boy.

"*Maitre*, the King's Guard are here. At both doors."

The boy's eyes shot to Brielle in accusation.

"What? I ... no! I was careful not to be seen. I made sure I wasn't followed."

"They say they are looking for someone and wish to speak to you," the brute directed to the boy.

Brielle shook her head, unable to comprehend how this could be happening again. She had been so careful! Hadn't she? The boy's gaze quickly traveled her body as if he were a man fully grown. She shifted uncomfortably before he called out to a beautiful woman standing by the stage, waiting to go on and perform. As she approached, the woman eyed Brielle curiously, as if she were appraising new competition. Clearly, the only women who ever came backstage were those willing to perform on it.

"Ameena, this is Brielle. She's a friend of Henri's. She's come to us for help, but the King's Guard are here and they are looking for her. We have to hide her. Get her dressed and looking the part."

Brielle's eyes widened in horror. "What?!"

"The best way to hide you is to make sure you blend in," the boy insisted.

"No one looks twice at whores," Ameena agreed.

Brielle's mouth gaped in protest. "Can't you hide me in the hidden wall in Henri's study?"

The doorman swiftly cut in, his tone urgent. "The guards are already searching the floor. There's no time. You'll be seen."

"Come with me." Ameena grabbed her hand and pulled her over to a rack of clothes.

Brielle glanced back at the boy to see him speaking hastily to the brute before straightening the lapels of his jacket and disappearing to the front of house, presumably to speak to the King's Guard. Ameena began tearing furiously at the laces of Brielle's dress and within minutes she was stripped naked. It was mortifying. She had been naked in front of other women before, but they had been her servants and it was in the context of being bathed and dressed. This was different. She didn't know these women and even though they barely noticed her, probably assuming she was a new girl the *Petit Maitre* had brought on, she still felt incredibly exposed.

The dress Ameena tossed at her did nothing to help matters. The black lace corset was far too small and pushed her breasts up so far they were almost spilling over the top of it. It had no sleeves so her shoulders and arms were completely bare, and the ruby red skirts, though full, were hitched up at the sides to reveal the entire length of her legs all the way up to her thighs. Ameena wasted no time pulling her hair free of its neat braid and letting it fall around her shoulders in soft waves.

"That will have to do. We have no time for anything else. Now, you won't be able to make it past the King's Guard at the front door, so don't even try. My advice? Go out on the floor and blend in. Find a punter and stick to him. Better yet, get a room. The guards will still search it, but I doubt they'll look too close, if you know what I mean. Or maybe they will, but it won't be because they recognize you."

Brielle stood frozen, in shock and alarm.

"Go!"

Her body jolted from the urgency in Ameena's voice and she stiffly walked to the side of the stage. She couldn't believe this was happening. She couldn't believe she was about to go out into a room full of drunken leering men looking like ... well, this. Her heart slammed against her chest and her knees threatened to buckle beneath her. But when her eyes caught on the King's Guard moving swiftly through the crowd in her direction, her feet instinctively propelled her forward.

Stepping out onto the floor, Brielle's senses were immediately assaulted by the overwhelming smell of stale liquor, sweet smoke, heady perfume, and ... sex. She stumbled awkwardly as her mind scrambled to come up with a plan. Ameena was right; from what she could see, the King's Guard surrounded the front door. There was no chance of her slipping past them unnoticed. Guards were searching every inch of the Sodisce, pulling back the burgundy-colored curtains to each of the private spaces, and heading upstairs to search the bedrooms. There was no avoiding them.

To her surprise, the patrons were not alarmed by the presence of the King's Guard. In fact, they hardly spared them any attention at all. They were too busy drinking, playing cards, or simply enjoying the company of the beautiful women on offer for the night. The women draped themselves over plush lounges, or leaned suggestively against the wall. She could do that, she thought, and perhaps with any luck no one would bother her. Ignoring the eyes that ogled her body as she passed them, Brielle forced herself to move between the tables as she searched for a place where she could stand but would likely go unnoticed. A shadow perhaps, or a corner. It took less than a minute to realize there were none.

Just then a pair of hands yanked her down onto a lap and she shrieked in panic.

"Don't push me away." The voice commanded as a muscular arm slid firmly around her waist, holding her down.

She knew that voice.

Brielle pushed back against his broad chest so she could see his face. "What are you doing here?"

Citric hissed at her to lower her voice, and she glanced around. Thankfully no one seemed to be paying any attention to them.

"I could ask you the same question."

As realization dawned on her, she scowled. Of course he would have felt her fleeing through the Red Wood. He felt everything that happened in that wood. Citric lifted his hand and softly brushed a knuckle against her cheekbone as if he were admiring the softness of her skin. Then he plunged his fingers into her chestnut hair, running them tantalizingly through the strands. Before she could object, she realized what he was doing; arranging her hair like a curtain across her face so she would not be recognized.

"I'm trying to find a way to save Henri," she whispered.

Citric dragged his eyes over her body inch by inch and she couldn't help but watch, mesmerized, as they smoldered with desire. Leaning forward, he pressed a light kiss to her bare shoulder. The act was shockingly intimate.

"What are you doing?" She had meant it to sound chastising, but it came out like a breathless plea.

"Playing the part." He continued to place soft, leisurely kisses on her shoulder that left a burning trail on her skin. "And have you?"

"Have I what?"

He pulled back, a smug smile spreading slowly across his lips. "Found a way to save him."

Brielle scowled. "The *Petit Maitre* said he knows a way to get inside the castle."

Citric's eyes flashed at something behind her and his grip on her hips tightened, pulling her body flush against his. Brielle opened her mouth to protest, but his expression warned her to remain silent and play along. Gritting her teeth, she did her best to seductively wrap her arms around his neck. Rogue amusement tugged at the corner of his lips as he watched her trying to tempt him. The bastard was enjoying this. Brielle unfolded a sickly sweet smile before lowering her mouth to hover just below his ear, as if she were kissing his neck. Then she ever so slightly shifted her hips to line her sex up with his. Citric's body went rigid beneath hers, his muscles pulled tight as a bowstring.

"How did you know I was here?" Her warm breath caressed his ear as she whispered sensuously. To her delight, she felt the evidence of his growing arousal hardening beneath her.

"I followed you."

His body relaxed a little beneath hers, as if he was forcing it to loosen. The next thing she felt was his fingers lazily stroking the skin of her exposed calf. The touch sent a hot flood of desire through her. Her mind screamed in warning at the dangerous ground she was currently walking on, but her body screamed for *more, more, more*.

"So did the King's Guard, apparently. They are searching for me."

"I know." Citric slowly dragged his fingers up along the split of her skirt. Her heart hammered against her ribcage as every nerve in her body focused on the singular sensation of those fingertips traveling the length of her leg, rising higher and higher, until they suddenly splayed possessively across her thigh. Panic and pleasure ignited in her core, a combustible combination.

"Straddle me."

"What?"

"We need to move, now. Straddle me."

Brielle shifted her legs to sit astride him and he stood, lifting her with him in one powerful, swift motion. Instinctively she wrapped her legs around his waist and he held her firmly against his thighs with both hands on her—

She glared at him, her expression murderous, as his hands gripped her ass. His features held no remorse as he strode over to the nearest wall and slammed her against it. Her breath caught in her throat, surprised by the thrill that jolted through her body. But she would be damned if she let him know that.

Brielle pushed back against him, seemingly incensed by the indignity of it all. "Put me down."

Citric relented by giving her just enough space to unwrap her legs from his waist. The moment her feet hit the floor, he pressed his hips into hers, hard, effectively pinning her body against the wall. Before she could blink, his lips were kissing her neck, his tongue devouring the salt from her skin. Her eyes went wide in alarm, but her body electrified as it instantly melted against him. Her sex pulsed in urgency, desperate to seek more friction, more touch, more of him. His manhood pressed against her, firm, demanding, dominating.

Somewhere in the back of her mind she knew that she should push him away, that she shouldn't want this, but the rest of her mind could hardly form a coherent thought. All she knew was that his hands were on her body, her breasts were flush against his muscled chest, his cock was pressed hard against her sex, and his wicked mouth ... Brielle closed her eyes, allowing herself a moment to savor the sensation. Her insides hammered like a heartbeat, craving him. His teeth grazed her earlobe and she might have released a small moan. Unable to help herself, Brielle hitched a leg up to wrap it around his waist, locking him firmly against her. Citric pulled back an inch to look at her, surprised, and their eyes fastened onto each other with feverish desire. Brielle could see he was barely restraining himself. If he wanted to take her right here in front of everyone, she didn't know that she would have the strength to say no.

"Can you still see them?" His eyes examined her mouth as if he wanted to conquer it.

She forced herself to look over his shoulder and her body stiffened.

"What?" he demanded.

"They're taking him."

Citric glanced back at the door. "Fuck."

Brielle watched in horror as several King's Guard wrestled the struggling *Petit Maitre* out of the Sodisce.

She gripped Citric's muscled arms in urgency. "We can't let them take him. He's the only one who knows a way inside the Northern castle."

"There's nothing we can do."

Brielle tried to free herself, but Citric pinned her firmly against the wall.

"Let me go!"

"There are dozens of them and only two of us. Henri would not want you to get yourself killed trying to save him."

"I can't just do nothing! I can't just let him die!"

Citric raised his hands to cup her cheeks, but offered no words of comfort. No promises he couldn't keep. She wouldn't have believed them anyway. His expression told her he understood her panic, her pain, her helplessness. He knew what it felt like to know someone you loved was about to die.

CHAPTER ELEVEN

They rode back to Alkhiem in silence, Brielle's arms wrapped loosely around Citric's waist. She didn't notice that his hand rested against her clasped fingers, his thumb making steady, comforting strokes against her skin. She didn't marvel at how eerily quiet the woodland was tonight, as if every living thing within it sensed her grief and devastation and the only comfort they could offer her was the compassion of silence. It was all Brielle could do to hold the fractured pieces of herself together and not pierce the silence with a scream born from the depths of frustration and despair.

She had failed.

She had sworn that she would bring Henri back and she had failed.

The weight of that knowledge crushed against her chest and stole the breath from her lungs as bitter tears spilled down onto her cheeks. The *Petit Maitre* was her only hope of finding a way into the Northern castle. Without him she had nothing. And Henri ... she pinched her wet eyelashes closed as the thought stabbed her in the heart.

He would die.

Broken. Alone.

A martyr for one of her stupid schemes.

Jameson had said that Henri would be glad to die protecting her, but she did not want him to die for her. She wanted him to live for her. That was all she had ever wanted. For him to fight for himself, fight for his people, fight for her, and now that he had, that fight would cost him his life. She couldn't bear it. Knowing that each moment could be the last that he drew breath. She couldn't imagine this world without him.

And it was all her fault.

Brielle was barely aware that they had stopped until Citric dismounted. She looked around and vaguely registered that they were at the stables in Alkhiem. Swinging her leg over the side, Citric helped her to the ground. She was still wearing the ridiculous dress, but she hardly cared anymore. With no energy left for words and absolutely no desire to talk, Brielle began making her way back to the ruin.

Her mind, on the other hand, was manic. Her thoughts obsessively replayed the events of the night over and over again. It just didn't make any sense. Why would the King's Guard want the *Petit Maitre*? It was possible that King Heroux was seeking revenge against the people who had dared to harbor a fugitive to the Crown, but that seemed unlikely. If he wanted that, he could have slaughtered everyone ages ago and burned the Sodisce to the ground. No, he wanted the *Petit Maitre* specifically. Perhaps King Heroux had learned that Henri cared for the boy and he intended to use that against him.

In one way, it was a relief to know that she had not been the target of the King's Guard. That she hadn't been followed by them and unwittingly placed everyone in danger. Again. But in another way, she almost wished she had been their target. She feared what they would do to the boy. She feared for his life.

Brielle wandered through the shadows of the ruins until she stepped inside her old room. Though it was dark, her gaze traveled over the three crumbling walls before rising to the night sky, which formed a ceiling overhead, bursting with the light of a thousand stars. Her heart pinched in pain. The room looked exactly as she had left it. It almost felt like coming home. Almost. She didn't know the hour, but she guessed it wouldn't be long until dawn. She could try to get a few hours' sleep, but she knew that it would probably be pointless.

A faint sound had her turning around to find Citric entering the room, silently carrying an armful of logs to the fireplace. She watched him, dimly surprised, as he arranged them in the hearth before kindling a flame. It reminded her of how he had mocked her for not being more useful and learning how to build her own fire. Sienna had taught her. The thought of her friend fractured something inside her. She missed her so much. The memory reminded her of the way Henri had looked at her, shocked but impressed, when she built her own fire the night they had slept in this room together, side by side. He had defended her that day and paid the price of Citric's rage. She had cleaned his wounds and he had told her that he would always defend her. Brielle swallowed a rising lump in her throat as she recalled how Henri had asked her to leave this place and start a new life with him. It had been unthinkable at the time, but now it didn't seem like such a horrible idea. If she had, how different things might have turned out.

"You love him, don't you?"

Brielle blinked to find Citric standing in front of her. She had almost forgotten he was there.

Hastily wiping a tear from her cheek, she replied, "Of course I do."

Something flickered across his features. Something she couldn't quite decipher. Maybe it was understanding, but it almost looked like hurt.

"He was the king you had been looking for." The words were a statement, not a question. They sounded resigned. As if he wished they weren't true.

Brielle allowed herself to really look at him for a moment. His demeanor, normally serious and calculating, had softened. She had never seen Citric quite like this before. She was used to him always being so confident, so direct, but now he looked unsure. Nearly vulnerable.

"But I am not in love with him."

Brielle did not know the truth of those words until she uttered them. Henri was everything to her—except that. There had been times when she had thought there might be something between them. Hoped for it even. But though his kiss had surprised her, it had not haunted her. Henri was her friend and she loved him desperately, just not passionately.

Citric's eyes latched onto hers. "He is in love with you," he said carefully.

"I know."

She did. Though she wondered how deeply Henri's love truly went. He had lived his whole life in search of purpose. A purpose that was not given to him by default of his birth, but rather a purpose he could choose for himself, a purpose he could earn. Something that would prove he was worthy, if only to himself. He had found it first in the Sodisce, in running a business and protecting those under his employ. When he lost that, he had found it in her. By pledging himself to her campaign, he could protect her and atone for his past failings. Just like losing himself in drink or lust, he had lost himself in her. In her cause. It was easy to confuse such a thing with love.

It would not have lasted, of course. If she had succeeded in reclaiming her kingdom and becoming queen, Henri would have lost his purpose. He had no desire to become the king she needed and even if he had married her out of some misguided sense of loyalty or duty, he would not have been happy. He would have grown to resent her and everything about the life they shared to-gether. Henri needed the freedom to discover who he was and what he was prepared to fight for without the expectations of others influencing him, especially her. He needed the freedom to forge his own destiny. Not that he would ever get that opportunity now.

"You did everything you could," Citric said firmly, as if he could read her thoughts.

"I failed him." She choked on the words through sobs.

"You didn't. You went in there alone, prepared to do whatever it took to save him. Just like you were prepared to do whatever it took to reclaim your kingdom. You are a force of nature, Brielle."

She tipped her head back to look up at the sky, trying to drain the tears from her eyes and hold back the storm of grief threatening to break within her. Out of the corner of her eye, she saw Citric take a careful step toward her, as if he didn't want to frighten her.

"I am sorry I betrayed you. You need to know that if things were different, I would have supported your claim to the throne. I would have fought beside you, fought for you, as my queen."

Her chin came down as her eyes fell on him and the world around her stilled. She searched his face, but all she saw was raw sincerity. His words were so unexpected, she didn't know what to say.

Trying to compose herself, Brielle forced a small, mocking smile. "I can't imagine you bowing before anyone."

The smile slipped from her mouth as Citric immediately lowered himself before her.

"You do not have to be my queen for me to go to my knees for you."

Her lips parted, speechless. The sight of this man, strong and unyielding, down on his knees in supplication before her, was hedonistic. It made her feel slightly lightheaded. But also incredibly powerful.

"I swear on my ancestors and everything that I am, I will never betray you again. I pledge to you that whenever you need me, you will have the strength of my sword, the truth of my words, and my undying loyalty, all the days of my life."

Brielle's throat flexed as she swallowed his words. It felt like her rapid heart was trying to take flight. "I thought Sirasindans only swore two oaths in their life; when they chose to follow a leader and when they chose to spend their life with someone."

"I have sworn my oath to my hunna. This oath I swear to you."

The air between them electrified.

Trying to break the unbearable tension pulsing between them, Brielle teased, "Is this the part where we exchange blood?"

"If that's what it takes for you to believe me."

"It wouldn't work, though, would it? I don't have blood magic."

"You don't need blood magic to know how I feel about you."

Indeed, he was laying himself bare at her feet. Literally. His words seized her heart, holding it captive. In truth, it was a willing prisoner. Without even realizing it, she had surrendered her heart to him long ago. Citric placed his hands tentatively around her calves and her pulse quickened at his touch. He watched her for any signs of resistance before he slowly moved them up the back of her legs, sliding his fingers beneath the splits of her skirt, as he rose to stand a breath away from her. His hands rested torturously on her thighs and her body trembled at the sheer proximity of him. As she stared up into those intense eyes, which never left hers for even a fraction of a second, she knew that she had utterly and irrevocably fallen for this man. She no longer cared whether it was right or wrong or made any sense at all. He had declared himself hers, but she was the one under his spell, and she no longer cared to fight it.

"If you tell me to go, I will," he murmured.

He would. She knew that it would take all his willpower to do it, but he would.

"I order you to stay." At her command, he returned a slow, dangerous smile. "I thought I was looking for a king. Turns out I was looking for an outlaw."

His strong hands gripped her face as his lips claimed hers. Her hands encircled his wrists, holding on to him as her body ignited. She opened her mouth to him and he deepened the kiss as his hands moved to encircle her body, pulling her hard against him as if he could not stand to have any distance between them. She arched into his embrace, meeting his impatient desire with her own. Citric's fingers stripped the laces from her corset until it fell to the ground between them. He tore his lips away from her mouth and bent down to devour her nipple between his teeth and tongue, while his hands cupped her breasts possessively. Brielle threaded her fingers into his copper hair and closed her eyes, lost in the sensation of his hot mouth consuming every sensitive inch of her skin. His hands moved to her skirt and released it from her body, leaving her standing there completely naked. Citric pulled back to survey her and Brielle waited for her cheeks to blush in embarrassment or her hands to instinctively move to cover herself, but she felt no shame at all. She was beautiful and strong and she owned this body. She would never be ashamed of it or what it desired.

His eyes drank her in as he said, "You are so beautiful it hurts."

Brielle reached for him in silent order and his mouth found hers as his body maneuvered them both to the ground in front of the fire. He laid her down before sitting up to undo his leather straps and lift his shirt over his head. Even in the darkness, his broad chest rippled with muscles and she smiled faintly at the scars that marked his skin. It amazed her that she knew this beautiful body. Every scar, every powerful line, every trail of dark hair. The story of him. He removed his pants and heat flooded her insides in anticipation. His length was impressive but intimidating. Even so, she welcomed it desperately.

Citric lowered himself over her, but to her disappointment he did not enter her. He dragged his lips tormentingly down her skin, starting from her neck down to her chest, where he sampled her breasts before moving to her abdomen and even lower. It felt amazing but it was not what she wanted, what she needed. He seemed to notice because he let out a low laugh that almost sounded like a growl.

"Patience. There has been something I have wanted to do since the moment you swore the oath to me."

His tongue suddenly flicked across her apex and she bucked, shocked at the unexpected invasion, but he wrapped his arms around her thighs and yanked her down, holding her firm.

"Let me worship you, Brielle."

Brielle was stunned as his tongue swept inside her sex in a way that mimicked what his cock could do between her legs. Her body immediately unraveled and Citric groaned in satisfaction at the wetness he found waiting for him. His tongue luxuriously licked the roof of her center before plunging in and out, slow and hard. Brielle's lips parted in a moan at the intense ripples of pleasure the movement wrought through her body. While his tongue conquered her, the stubble on his jaw provided additional friction that sparked her insides to fire. Citric feasted on her, licking, sucking, and kissing her epicenter until the need built inside her like a crescendo, finally exploding and shattering her walls into a million pieces.

Brielle hardly had a moment to breathe or recover before he was on her, like a predator pouncing on immobilized prey. His mouth crashed into hers as his manhood plunged deep inside her. His kiss swallowed her gasp as the sensation of him filling her prolonged the pleasure of her climax. It was as if his thrusts could send her over the edge again so easily. Brielle's hands found his buttocks and gripped him tight, feeling the strong muscles contract every time he sunk himself into her. Citric growled in approval as he increased the pace—faster, deeper. She could feel the ache growing again, her breasts tightening beneath him. He seemed to notice because he moved in a way that drew out her pleasure exquisitely and when she cried out in release again, he slammed into the hilt and came with her.

Eve curled her body tighter into a ball and gripped the bedroll in her fists. Angry tears stained her cheeks and hands and soaked the bedding beneath her. She had been lost in a deep sleep, dragged under by exhaustion, but the brutal force of it woke her. At first, she had been confused by it, like smelling smoke on a seemingly clear night. But then she realized; she was feeling him.

Citric's desire was overwhelming, like a brush fire spreading quickly with the aid of a swift wind. He craved her like a desert craved water, like the trees craved sunlight. Eve felt every excruciating second as he consumed her, satiating himself with her. It was unbearable. As all her hopes withered to ash and her heart bled out beneath her, all she could do was cry. Because love was the loneliest place to fall alone.

Henri wasn't sure how much time had passed. After King Heroux released him from the shackles that had suspended him from the ceiling, he had lain on the stone floor like a crumpled piece of paper, drifting in and out of consciousness. When he was lucid, he simply stared across the room, waiting. He was too weak to move and there was no point in trying to get up.

He hardly felt human anymore. His own body was foreign to him, wrecked and useless. His mind equally destroyed. Death would come for him soon, either from his infected wounds or from King Heroux's blade. He welcomed it, but before he died, he needed to tell King Heroux the location of Alkhiem. Surely enough days had passed now that Citric had arrived and the people would be ready to defend themselves in battle. His duty was almost done. Soon he would be able to let go.

Perhaps this was what it had been like for Nathaniel in his last days. His arrow wound would have been enough to kill most men, but he had held on through the pain, determined to live three more days. He had held on for Henri. Because that was all he could do for his friend. Now Henri would hold on as well. Because that was all he could do to atone for all the wrong choices he had made in his life.

He was about to drift off into blissful unconsciousness again when the rattling sound of keys caught his attention. He didn't have the strength to lift his head from the floor, but he raised his eyes just a little to see King Heroux standing in the doorway to his cell with a boy standing beside him. A flicker of something sparked through his muddled mind until recognition slammed into him with alarm.

Ele.

The word sounded like a moan as it escaped through his dry, cracked lips. His body spasmed as if he had tried to move it involuntarily. How had King Heroux found out about the boy? No one knew about him and his relationship to Henri, except for the staff at the Sodisce and they never would have sold him out. But then again, things had changed since he'd left the Sodisce. Ele had taken over running the business and, by Jameson's account, had built quite a reputation for himself as the *Petit Maitre*. It was difficult to hide secrets when one commanded such public attention. Someone must have made the connection that it was possible the boy meant something to him. It was an assumption, a long shot, but in this instance, it had paid off.

Ele looked ashen white and terrified, as if he might wet himself on the spot. Henri could only imagine the thoughts racing through the boy's head. That this was the fate that awaited him. Lying naked and broken on the bloodstained floor of a stinking cell, waiting for death to release him from the horror of unspeakable pain. Henri wanted to comfort him, to protect him, but he couldn't. He knew what King Heroux was capable of and he knew that his ministrations knew no bounds. He would have no hesitation inflicting them on a child.

"Get him up."

At King Heroux's command, a guard appeared from the shadows outside the cell door. He took Henri by the armpits and dragged his limp, reeking body over to a wall before propping him up against it. Henri's head lolled to the side, but he tried to keep it upright, tried to focus on Ele. Just then, a bucket of icy water hit him and he startled painfully at the shock of it. If it was meant to clean away his stench, it would take more than water to do so.

"I warned you, prince, that if you didn't tell me what I wanted to know, I would find every person you care about and tear them apart piece by piece. This boy is the first."

Henri began to shiver uncontrollably, from the cold or the threat he didn't know. His teeth rattled so hard he thought he might bite his own tongue. Ele squealed as King Heroux grabbed him in a choke hold and bent his head painfully to the side as a blade pressed just above his ear.

"Shall I take his ears first?"

Henri gritted his trembling teeth and gathered all his strength. "No."

The word exhausted him. It felt strange to speak at all after endless days of silence.

"Then tell me what I want to know, prince."

He would kill the boy anyway, that was implied. But at least he would not cut him up into tiny pieces before doing so. Henri tried to force the words up his raw throat, but they came out too thin.

"Get him some water," King Heroux demanded impatiently.

The guard appeared in front of him again and forced a waterskin to his mouth. The liquid rushed down his throat, making him choke, but he managed to swallow a bit of it. Water dribbled down his chin and chest, and the guard pulled it away. It felt foreign to consume something after days of surviving on barely anything.

Henri's eyes sharpened on King Heroux as he croaked, "I'll take you there."

He had hoped to simply tell King Heroux where Alkhiem was and then find blessed relief at the edge of the blade that cut his throat, but if he did that Ele would die too. He would need to hold on a little longer. All his life he had been powerless to save the ones he cared about, either because someone held more power than him or because he had given his power away. He had agreed to this reckless plan to make sure it would never happen again, that no one else would die because of his failure to act. Now here he was, too weak to even move. But he would, he would find the strength, because he would be damned if he let Ele die.

King Heroux's mouth tightened in anger and Henri thought he might take the boy's ear off just to spite him. Instead, he released the boy and turned to the guard.

"Get him fed and cleaned up. I want him ready to ride within the hour."

Citric watched Brielle as she slept beside the fire. Her features were smooth and peaceful, mercifully free of worry and grief, her mind at ease for a few precious hours. It tore his heart out to see her in so much pain, knowing that this was only the beginning of her suffering. There was nothing they could do for Henri now. It was only a matter of time before Citric would feel the blood bond snap and know that the prince was dead. He dreaded the thought of telling Brielle and watching her fierce heart break into a million shards in front of him.

Citric had learned long ago that the world was filled with senseless cruelty. Life sometimes felt like an endless string of hard choices. Having lived a charmed, privileged life behind high castle walls, Brielle was only now starting to learn this harsh reality. He wished he could shield her from it so that she wouldn't bear the scars that he did. She had already lost so much: her father, her kingdom, her future. And now she stood to lose even more.

Her naked body lay curled against his. Warm. Satiated. Safe. It was a sight he wanted to sear into his memory. A moment in time he wanted to hold on to for eternity. Because while the world was filled with senseless cruelty and soul-destroying grief, moments like these were pure. Rare but beautiful. More powerful than hate or ambition or even revenge. The way he felt about this woman was unlike anything he had ever felt before or even knew he was capable of feeling. Loving her was almost a religious experience. It scared the fuck out of him. To think what he would be capable of doing to protect her. To know that he would not survive the pain if he ever lost her. Up until now, every breath he had drawn into his lungs, every choice he had ever made had been with the singular focus of reclaiming his ancestral lands and ensuring his people's survival. It was the only dream he had ever known, his destiny. But all of that had changed the moment a princess had fled into his woodland.

Citric cast his gaze over the clothes scattered on the ground around them. Dawn was fast approaching. He could smell the change in the air and hear the camp stirring to life outside. He was acutely aware that Brielle only had the dress she wore last night. The memory of her in that dress made his cock immediately thicken with desire. The way her delicate shoulders and collarbone were exposed, her breasts plumped up over the seams of the corset, her legs and thighs scandalously on display. The moment he saw her in the Sodisce he had wanted to gouge out the eyes of every man in that room. They did not deserve to breathe the same air as her, let alone look at her. He had wanted to pull her away from their prying eyes, to escape into a private room or a secluded corner. To protect her modesty and her innocence. But fuck, he had also wanted to shred that innocence to ribbons, to claim her so thoroughly that no one would ever question who she belonged to.

Citric slid his gaze to her, renewed desire vaulting from the hilt of his manhood to the pome. The urge to claim her again was primal, his need animalistic. But he would resist. She needed the sleep and he would not deprive her of it. Nor the few hours of peace before the battle that awaited them. The truth remained, though; she could hardly wear that dress in public. He would need to fetch her something before she woke. Inching himself carefully away from her warm, supple body, he silently pulled on his clothes and ran a hand through his hair before walking out of the ruin.

As he walked through the camp, he noted that some of the soldiers had already woken and the women had begun preparing food. The army was sizable, but he didn't know if it matched or exceeded King Heroux's forces. Henri hadn't managed to get any information to them. Citric could only hope that their numbers would be enough. Then there was the tension and mistrust he felt rippling from the Southern soldiers. It roiled in his gut and bubbled away in his veins, simmering just below the surface of his skin. He would feel it if any of the soldiers made a move to desert or betray them. Returning to the woodland, immersing himself in the womb of his people, had restored his connection to the land and thereby to the blood magic. The number of tethers he held was still taxing, but he was stronger than he was before, more capable of discerning who and what he was experiencing.

Citric approached a table where the women were working, laying out a breakfast of fruits and bread.

"Willow." When she looked up, he inclined his head, silently requesting her to speak to him in private. He grabbed an apple and she followed him until they were outside of hearing range. "Brielle needs some clothes to wear. She hasn't got anything appropriate."

"The princess doesn't own a set of leathers?" Willow teased, wiping her hands on her apron. "I'll find her something."

"Thank you. Where is Eve?"

"She was up before sun's rise, checking the defenses around the camp I think."

Citric nodded and focused on the tether that connected him to her. He could feel her and—something was wrong. His senses immediately locked onto her location and quick strides took him to the outskirts of the camp. He found her gathering sticks to make more arrows.

"Eve."

She froze at his words, as if she had been too distracted to notice him approaching. Inside, she was a hurricane of emotion. Pain. Fury. Desperation. Determination. They hardened her like an iron fortress, yet she felt as fragile as thin ice. And twice as dangerous.

"What's wrong?"

Last night the people had accepted her as their hunna, their hearts overjoyed at the unexpected blessing. It was no small thing to hold the expectations of her people on her shoulders, let alone the hopes of past generations. The spirits were watching her closely now. He could feel them. He knew she could feel them too. The spirits knew better than anyone the carnage they would soon be facing and the leader that she needed to be.

When Eve lifted her face to him, her expression was equally devastated and devastating. Her skin was flushed in a way that told him she had been crying. Suddenly he knew that this was not about the pending battle or the weight of everyone's expectations. His stomach plummeted in realization.

"Tell me," he urged.

Her eyes shifted back and forth as if her mind was racing with a thousand things she wanted to say, but she was holding the words back.

"Say it. All of it." He needed to hear it and she needed to purge it.

Eve met his words with a razor-sharp look that cut deeper than any blade ever could. "Why?"

He braced himself and waited.

"I have stood by your side for years. I have done everything you have ever asked me to. All of this," she gestured wildly to the camp, "I did for you. I have been waiting for you my whole life. To notice me. To really *see* me. Why don't you want me?" Her voice cracked in anguish. "Why am I not enough for you? Why don't you even want to try with us?"

"Eve—" He stepped toward her, but she backed away.

"You used me."

"I did not." His tone was a warning.

"I have loved you this entire time and all I ever wanted was a small part of what I gave you back. I gave you everything, all of me, but you chose her. I am your hunna. I am going to achieve what you could not and restore this land to our people but still that's not enough for you, is it?"

"You are my hunna," he said gently. "I have sworn a blood oath to you and I will not break that oath. The way I feel about Brielle does not change the promise I made to you."

Or the promise he had made to Rowan. Though he didn't say those words out loud, it was clear Eve heard them.

"But she gets your heart, right? She gets to love you."

Citric flexed his fingers, unsure what to do. He hadn't had much experience in dealing with matters of the heart. Dedicating his existence to the survival of his people had left little room for anything else in his life. But that didn't mean he didn't know what it felt like to be in love with someone and to face the prospect of having them not love him back.

"Evelyn, I never meant to hurt you. You are important to me. Even before you were my hunna. You know what you mean to me. But I don't feel *that* way about you. I can't."

"Because of her."

"Because of me."

He didn't know what else to say, how else to explain it. Words seemed pointless. They wouldn't take away her pain. They couldn't stitch her broken heart back together again. Not even time could do that. Time simply left a scab over the wound and every now and then something would rip it back open again to bleed fresh blood.

"So that's it, then." Eve shrugged bitterly as she sniffed. "I get to go back to watching you watching her watching me."

Citric stood there, powerless against the spite of her words and the onslaught of her emotions as they battered his defenses. He tried to hold the line, keeping his emotions separate from hers. It was the only way he wouldn't drown in them. Eve had always been so strong, so confident and self-assured about who she was and the decisions she made that the sight of her unraveling was unsettling. Sometimes he forgot that she was only sixteen years old, a young woman, falling in love for the first time. Falling alone. Of course it felt all consuming to her, like it was the end of days.

"No. You get to lead this great army into battle and win victory for our people. You get to be the first hunna in generations. The hunna that will bring our people out of hiding and give us a future. You get to heal this land and restore it. I am nothing compared to that. I am just a man. But for what it's worth, and as long as you will have me, I will be by your side for every moment of it. Because that is all I can offer you."

Her stare clung to him, raw torment glistening in her eyes. The sounds of the woodland filled the silence between them, the breeze wrapping around them as if the wood felt their pain.

"Then I will have you. Because I would rather have that small part of you than nothing at all."

Citric felt the weight of her words as he tried to weather the monsoon of her emotions. He wished he knew how to—

The knowledge seized his senses at the same moment it snatched at Eve's. Without a word they began moving swiftly back to the camp, all else forgotten, because war had just entered the wood.

CHAPTER TWELVE

B rielle awoke to the sounds of the camp outside. A blanket had been draped over her naked body and the fire in the hearth had burned down to embers. She was alone, but that was not surprising. Citric would have been up at dawn, perhaps earlier, readying Alkhiem for battle. The events of last night caressed her memory, the images bringing a satisfied smile to her face. She couldn't remember falling asleep, but she remembered everything else in delicious, vivid detail. It still didn't feel real to her that Citric had declared himself hers. That she had surrendered herself to him. It felt like the start of something new. Something precious and fragile.

Henri.

The rest of the night came back to her in flashes that caused her heart to pound. Citric had said there was nothing more she could do for Henri, but she refused to accept that. She needed to do *something*. There had to be a way to get inside the Northern castle.

Her attention caught on a pile of clothes folded neatly beside her. Brielle pulled herself up into a seated position and cautiously reached for them; a dark cotton shirt, a brown leather vest fashioned like a breastplate, and—pants. Men's clothes, except cut for a woman's figure, like what Eve wore. Brielle hesitated. She had never worn pants before, but she had little other options and these did seem practical.

Brielle pulled the pants on. It felt strange to have material clinging to her legs, hugging her backside. The dark cotton shirt was comfortably loose, but by the time she had done up the leather straps she felt indeed like she was putting on armor. It was thick and a little stiff and it smelled like oak. She walked around the room, feeling the way her body moved in these new clothes. They felt light. Certainly less restrictive than her corset and skirts. Perhaps she could get used to them.

Walking out from the ruins, she found that the camp was a hive of activity. The soldiers were either being put to task in building defenses or they were training. It was easy to tell the Southern soldiers from the Sirasindans. The Southern soldiers were polished and precise as they ran their group drills. The Sirasindans, on the other hand, were coarse and brutal as they engaged in one-on-one combat with each other. The rest of the people were scattered around the camp preparing for battle: whittling long, sharp spikes, sharpening the blades of swords and daggers, assembling dozens upon dozens of arrows. The sight made her stomach twist in anxious knots.

Hundreds of years ago, Alkhiem had been filled with people just like these, living ordinary lives, raising their children and growing old. It had all been destroyed in an instant by man's ambition, man's greed, man's ruthless entitlement. Almost. Brielle couldn't fathom it looking at the scene before her now. This city had been burned to smoke and ash. The ground beneath her feet soaked with blood. This proud woodland violated, scarred and captured. The thought that it could happen again made her feel dizzy and nauseated.

Dazed, she wandered over to a table where some remnants of food remained on offer.

"You've got to get up earlier if you want porridge."

Brielle glanced up to find Aelis smirking at her. The old woman had not changed. She was still large and loud, the skin on her face weathered and the crinkles around her eyes pronounced. Brielle could hear the snickers of the other woman standing behind Aelis, but she didn't bristle. They weren't mocking her. Or perhaps they were, but it no longer felt as though it was being done at her expense. It felt like they were including her in the joke.

She couldn't help but smile back. "I can't say I've missed your porridge, Aelis."

Aelis chortled with laughter, before tossing a look over her shoulder at the women behind her whilst jerking her thumb in Brielle's direction. "Used to finer foods, this one."

That's when Brielle looked past Aelis and her smile slipped. The table the women were gathered around, usually reserved for preparing food, was piled high with weapons. All the women, except Aelis, were dressed in leathers and pants. Swords were fixed to their belts, daggers strapped to their lithe bodies, their hair wound back from their faces. They looked fierce. Like a small, formidable female army.

Brielle instinctively approached them as if she were being drawn to them, her eyes scanning the weapons they had prepared before lifting to take in the sight of them again. "You're all going to fight?"

"Why wouldn't we?" Willow returned, her expression perplexed.

"I just—I didn't realize. I never saw any of you in the training ground or out on patrol."

"Every Sirasindan is taught how to fight. Being able to defend yourself and your home is a basic human right, don't you think?"

Brielle nodded, but she was still a little surprised.

Willow offered an indulgent smile. "A long time ago, when our people lived safe and free in this land, we looked to our hunnas to lead us. Their connection to the land, their knowledge of the art of healing, ensured our people's survival. They were our lifeblood. Even though we lived in peace, we still faced threats from time to time. The hunnas were protected by a small number of warriors called the gureira. The gureira have only ever been made up of female warriors chosen by the hunna."

Brielle's lips parted, astounded. Not too long ago she would have thought the notion of female warriors fanciful. Now she just stood in awe. Her gaze traveled to a few young girls sitting around the table grinding seeds and leaves into different stone pots.

"What are you making?" she asked, as she leaned over for a closer look.

One of the girls tipped up her pot to show her a fine ground powder. The girl added some water from a waterskin and the powder turned red. "Paint."

"War paint," Willow explained. "We will wear the land on our skin when we fight for it."

The pots were filled with different colors: green, brown and red.

"The leathers suit you." Aelis's lips twitched with amusement.

"Yes, they fit well. You're welcome, by the way." Willow winked at her.

So Willow had been the one to deliver them to her. Which meant she had seen her naked curled up by the fire ... and had probably put the obvious conclusion together. Before she could reply, the women's attention snapped to something behind her. She turned to find Citric and Eve striding toward the camp with urgency, their expressions dark and foreboding. The whole camp fell to silence at the sight of them.

"The Northern army has crossed into the Red Wood," Eve announced, her voice carrying across the distance of the camp. "They are coming."

Brielle's stomach hollowed out, but to her surprise no one screamed in terror or began to panic. The ominous silence simply shifted into swift, purposeful movement.

"The day has come, spirits be with us." Aelis turned back to the table to look at each of the women with grim determination. "Your children will be safe with me in the caves. You show those Northern bastards why we belong to this land."

The women nodded and Brielle watched helplessly as Aelis began to round up the children. It seemed the older children had been trained in what to expect because they did not look alarmed or frightened by the thought of an army coming to destroy their home. They helped Aelis by grabbing the little ones and soothing the infants who had started to cry.

Brielle turned back to find the women focused, despite the looming promise of bloodshed and the haunting cries of their babies as they were taken away. Their faces were stoic as they handed out weapons to people and painted their skin. Brielle's heart sank to watch the brief, somber farewells between loved ones. The silent tears, the brave last looks. Her attention caught on Citric's voice as he shouted orders to the soldiers, Southern and Sirasindan alike. They quickly donned their armor and weapons before taking up various positions around the camp. Unsure what she was meant to do, Brielle's gaze flittered around the camp helplessly.

"You're going to need this."

Brielle startled to find Eve standing beside her, holding out a crossbow, her expression severe. Despite the cold fear crawling beneath her skin, Brielle felt her insides forge in steely resolve. She took the crossbow and swung it onto her back, welcoming its familiar presence against her spine.

"These too." Eve swiped a set of daggers from the table and held them out to her.

The corner of Brielle's lips lifted into a smirk as she took the blades. "Boots, bodice, and belt, right?"

"Don't miss." Eve turned away from her and began shouting orders to her men.

Somehow, in the midst of it all, Brielle felt Citric's gaze on her. As their eyes met, her breath suspended in her lungs and every moment of last night, every touch, every kiss flooded her senses.

His expression was controlled, imperceptible to anyone else, but she recognized the ghost of emotion between his sharp features. He took measured strides to close the distance between them and with each step her heart quickened.

A small smile tugged at his lips as he placed a hand lightly against her hip, as if he couldn't stop himself from touching her. "The sight of you in those pants might just kill me before the battle."

"Don't even joke about that."

The smile faded, his features sliding into seriousness. "There is something else you should know. Henri is traveling with the Northern army. I can feel him."

Brielle's heart leaped, clinging to the thread of hope. "We have to save him."

Citric nodded and brushed an errand strand of hair from her face. Though his face was composed, a flicker of concern flashed in his eyes, there one moment and erased the next. She almost asked him about it, but Willow came around to place three small pots of paint on the table beside them. Citric gave her a curt nod of thanks before dipping his fingers into the mixture. Brielle watched, fascinated, as he coated his arms and neck in green and brown paint. It was a form of camouflage, she realized. Then he dipped his fingers in the red paint and starting at his forehead, he drew his hand down the front of his face.

"What does the red symbolize?" Brielle asked, though she was sure she already knew.

"The blood of our ancestors. The blood that was spilled long ago."

Standing before her now, Citric looked every inch like an avenging warrior. Bloodthirsty and vicious. Ready to reap lives on the killing field. His ice-blue eyes, made more intense by the red that masked them, searched her face for an answer and she nodded. She held still as he painted her arms and neck with the colors of the woodland, before coating his fingers in red and drawing them down the center of her forehead, along the ridge of her nose, across her lips and down her chin. It felt strangely powerful, this ritual. As if the paint, created from the earth, bestowed upon her the magic of the Red Wood. It warmed the blood in her system and fueled her fight. She was still afraid, but she owned her fear. It would not hold her back. She had chosen this fate. She had forged this destiny. To fight for her people, to fight for this land. She would be brave.

Time seemed to hasten around her because moments later the people of Alkhiem were armed, painted and ready for war. The Southern soldiers had taken up defensive positions around the camp, but the people of Alkhiem gathered in the center, awaiting Eve's orders. She stood in front of them, surveying them, as if taking measure of their strength. With her hair braided tight against her scalp and red paint shadowing her eyes as if they were bleeding, Eve looked like vengeance itself.

"Citric, take east. Leif, take north-east. I'll take south-east," Eve commanded.

The people intuitively split into three groups. As Citric began to lead his people away, Brielle fell in line behind him, but Eve called out to her, "You're with me."

Brielle blinked in surprise. Citric stilled, his gaze darting between Eve and Brielle. He looked as if he wanted to protest, but Eve's expression gave no quarter. Citric turned to Brielle and pressed a light kiss to her forehead, the movement so tender it stunned her.

Hovering near her ear, he whispered, "When you arrive, get to a tree and stay there. Do not take any unnecessary risks."

She nodded, though she wasn't quite sure what he was talking about. Looking up into his eyes, Brielle knew she should probably say something poignant in this moment.

Be careful seemed obvious.

I love you felt terrifying.

Please don't die sounded stupid.

His touch slipped from her as he turned to walk away, his people following behind him. She was conscious that Eve had already begun leading her people past the outskirts of the camp, but still Brielle lingered, allowing herself one last look at the muscled back of the man who had ruined her and restored her at the same time. In that moment she prayed to the spirits of the wood, the ancestors of this people, the ancient magic of the land, and anything else that would listen, that they would both survive this day.

Forcing herself to turn away, Brielle sprinted to catch up to the group. She spotted Willow amongst them and fell in step beside her. They moved stealthily through the woods, Eve leading the way, until she stopped abruptly. They were a short distance outside the camp, but far enough away that the camp was not visible. No one moved or spoke. Everyone's attention remained fixed on Eve's back, waiting for her next command. She would be able to feel the army through her connection to the Red Wood. She would know exactly how far away they were. So would Leif and Citric, which was presumably why Eve had chosen them to lead the other two groups.

It was unnerving, standing out in the open, silently waiting for the war to appear through the trees in front of them. Brielle was very aware of the sound of her own heart pumping in her ears. She began to feel a bitter cold seeping through her skin, penetrating deep into her bones. Her senses pricked and the hair on the back of her neck lifted, alerting her to—something. Something was happening. She cast her eyes around her. The woodland was changing. The leaves on the trees were altering shape from soft smooth surfaces to prickly exteriors. The bark on the tree trunks split into thousands of tiny needles, perched like thorns ready to penetrate flesh. The fungi on the ground shifted color and a strange floral odor leaked into the air.

"What is happening?" Brielle whispered to Willow.

Willow's lips stretched into a slow, satisfied smile. "The wood is preparing to fight."

⁂

Henri's body swayed precariously from side to side as the horse beneath him moved cautiously through the Red Wood. Every muscle in his body screamed in pain as he struggled to remain upright in the saddle, but eventually he couldn't hold it any longer. He let himself slump forward, leaning heavily against Ele's body. The boy's small frame was all that was keeping him from falling forward or sliding off the horse entirely.

The guards had given him water and food, a hasty scrub with soap and clean clothes to wear, before binding his hands with rope and shoving him and Ele up onto a horse. A guard rode beside them, holding on to the other end of that rope, ensuring they wouldn't be able to escape without Henri falling from the horse. King Heroux rode on the other side of them and together they led the Northern army deep into the Red Wood.

The Northern army was a formidable size, larger than Henri expected it to be. King Heroux had clearly recruited men from his other conquered lands to reinforce his numbers. It was satisfying to know that he felt threatened enough to bother calling in reinforcements, but it also crippled Henri's hope of victory. The Southern army would not be able to match the Northern army in strength. Perhaps combined with the Sirasindans they would stand a fighting chance, but Henri was acutely aware that the Sirasindans had no experience in waging war. They were skilled fighters, but they did not know how to work together as an army. A fractured army was worse than a small one. Their only advantage was that they had chosen the battleground and they had the element of surprise. King Heroux was not expecting to face the Southern army until they reached the border of Nistan. The destruction of Alkhiem was mere foreplay to the main event.

As they rode deeper into the wood, the horses became skittish. The men equally so as they noticed the woodland growing strange around them. The trees were becoming narrow and malformed, their bases stretching out along the ground like snakes. The trunks were twisted into abnormal shapes and the foliage above them grew thick and dense, almost blocking out all natural light from the sky.

"How much further, prince?" King Heroux's voice was gruff with impatience.

Henri forced his head up to better take in his surroundings. He had memorized the route to Alkhiem in his mind before he left the Southern Kingdom and now he could see they were drawing dangerously close. The moment the camp came into view King Heroux would order their deaths.

No. Ele would not die today.

Henri refused to let it happen. At the right moment, he would urge the horse into a swift gallop, giving Ele a chance to break free while he was inevitably yanked to the ground by the rope. It didn't matter if he died, trampled beneath horses hooves or cut down by a blade, as long as Ele lived.

"Not much further," Henri replied.

Suddenly, Ele jabbed him in the ribs and he released a hiss of pain. The boy was silent, but the message was clear; he had seen something. Or heard something. Henri forced himself to sit a little straighter in the saddle, his ears straining for sound, his eyes scanning the tree line.

A thin fog began to seep out from behind the trees, the swirls of mist crawling toward them, carpeting the woodland floor. The army halted at the sight of it, the soldiers struggling to control their horses which jerked and whinnied in fear. Then a mournful cry pierced the air around them. Henri recognized that sound. His gaze snapped to the treetops, where he saw flickers of movement between branches, like the shadows of ghosts. Henri's attention caught on a familiar form as it slowly emerged on a high branch, stretching the string of his longbow and aiming an arrow in Henri's direction. Henri nodded once in understanding and lifted his arms over Ele's head to clutch the boy's body tight to his chest. The moment the arrow flew into the soldier beside them, Henri kicked his heels into the horse and they bolted.

Citric released his arrows rapidly, picking off the soldiers one by one. His men, perched high in the trees surrounding the army, joined him in raining their arrows down onto the enemy below. The soldiers raised their shields, but at least two dozen had already fallen. King Heroux staggered for a moment in the face of the ambush, but his recovery was swift as he ordered his soldiers to advance. On Citric's command, his men released several arrows which shot thorny vines between trees, effectively blocking off escape routes. The soldiers scrambled in confusion before they were forced to disperse in three different directions. A wolfish smile unfurled on Citric's lips at the sight of the army splitting. He let the soldiers flee, knowing that Leif and Eve would be ready for them. He waited the few heartbeats it took for the army to thin out and then he and his men released a roar that ripped through the woodland as they leaped down onto the killing field.

His blade sliced through skin and organ and bone indiscriminately. The smell of warm blood assaulted his nostrils and the screams of dying men filled his ears like a familiar song. His body moved with an awareness born from years spent fighting in battles. His movements were based on pure instinct, not thought. There was no logic in killing, only a primal desire to obliterate. He reveled in it. Never was his mind more at peace than when he unleashed that part of himself that he kept caged. The savagery. His primitive urges. They reduced him to little more than a wild beast.

The battle was a combustion of violence. The Northern soldiers moved like a well-trained unit, their actions calculated and controlled. Citric and his men fought with feral, frenzied rage. He saw the fear in the eyes of the soldiers' seconds before he ripped their entrails from their bodies. They were used to fighting armies driven by greed and power and entitlement. They had never fought an enemy fueled by retribution. They had never fought men like him before.

This was vengeance. For the generations his people had suffered, hidden and patient. For his ancestors who had not lived to see this day and whose bones were buried deep beneath the soil they now fought on. For the woodland who had endured unspeakable trauma and yet somehow found a way to survive and bloom. For a princess who'd had everything ripped away from her and who still chose to fight for what she lost. This was revenge.

The ground was slick with blood and littered with broken bodies before Citric forced himself out of the haze of bloodlust long enough to assess the situation. His men were making short work of the Northern soldiers, but he was aware that a good number had managed to push forward to Alkhiem, led by King Heroux. He knew that was where he needed to be, but the urge to go to Brielle was almost overpowering. He couldn't stand not knowing if she was safe or not. He was not used to this kind of uncertainty. The blood bond afforded him connection to those he cared about most, lives he was responsible for, and yet he shared no such connection with her. His need to be at her side, to protect her, was primal.

But his people also needed him.

Fuck.

Releasing a wild roar of fury and frustration, Citric led the charge back to Alkhiem. Brielle was smart, he assured himself. She would stay safe in the trees like he told her to. The others would watch out for her. But the memory of Eve calling Brielle back to join her set his senses on edge. In that moment he had slammed down the blood bond, searching her for any evidence to confirm what his instincts suspected. Her motivations felt harmless, though, strategic even. Still, Citric couldn't ignore the fear crawling in the back of his mind.

War was chaos.

Accidents happened.

Tragedies could easily go unnoticed.

The echo of a roar in the distance was the only warning Brielle had that the army was coming.

"Get to the trees!" Eve yelled.

"This way." Willow tugged on her arm and Brielle followed as she sprinted toward a tree.

She watched in awe as Willow, Eve, and the others scaled the trees within minutes, their bodies flinging themselves with ease from one hold to the next. Setting her jaw in determination, she pulled herself up. The first few holds were easy enough, but then her pace slowed. The muscles in her arms, shoulders, and back began to strain from holding her entire body up. Her fingers felt stiff from gripping the narrow holds so tightly. She glanced up at the treetop where Willow waited for her with an anxious look on her face. It still looked so far away. She didn't dare look down. She knew that if she did it would paralyze her with fear.

Brielle forced herself to keep going, her movements slow and deliberate. Her heart was racing, but it almost atrophied when her legs began to shake. She clung to the tree trunk for dear life and allowed herself a moment to try to calm down.

"Come on!" Willow urged from above.

Gripping the holds and gritting her teeth, Brielle pulled herself up. She tried not to think about the approaching army or her fear or her pain. She just focused on the next hold, the next step. It was a series of problems to be solved, nothing more. She could do that. She *would* do it. If she had learned anything from the past few months, it was that she was capable of more than she knew.

Not too long ago, she would have balked at the idea of climbing a tree, let alone with a crossbow strapped to her back and wearing men's pants. The thought almost made her laugh out loud, but she swallowed it down, afraid it would throw her off balance. She had endured so much and she was still alive, holding on tight, pushing forward. There had been moments when she felt like she was about to break, but she was not broken. She was unfolding. Reforging. Born a princess, forced to live as a fugitive, held prisoner in her own castle, and now choosing to be a renegade, fighting in a war to protect everything she had ever cared about, even though it was no longer hers.

Brielle blinked as Willow thrust her hand beneath her nose. She had climbed the distance without even realizing it. Grateful, Brielle gripped it and let Willow haul her up to the safety of the branches. Her body screamed in agony and relief, but she couldn't help the grin that beamed across her face. Willow mirrored it before crouching down low on the branch. Brielle joined her and they both looked to Eve, who was squatting in a tree across from them, waiting for the army to appear in the distance.

Swinging her crossbow from her back, Brielle silently loaded a bolt. She heard the army before she saw them. They spilled through the tree line like an infestation, like rats running from a fire instead of an invading army of a thousand soldiers strong. When they came within range, the archers released several arrows, which triggered spiked gates to shoot up from the ground, entrapping the soldiers.

As the others jumped or used ropes to swing down into the fray, Brielle remained in the tree and lifted her crossbow before selecting a target and releasing the bolt. Her hands shook slightly as the adrenaline pumped in her veins, but she tried to steady her breathing and remain focused. These were not men she was killing, with families and hopes and fears. They were the enemy and they would kill her or her friends without a second thought. At least that's what she told herself each time her arrows speared flesh.

While she kept her eye trained on each new target, she was keenly aware of Eve's movements on the battlefield. Honestly, the girl was hard to miss. She tore through the soldiers like a reckoning, the Sword of Peace reaping lives. Blood already covered her face, blending with the red paint around her eyes. Anyone who saw her fight, ferociously tearing apart men twice her size, would know that she was a true warrior queen. This was her battle. These were her people. She would either lead them to victory or die on the ground that she was bound to protect.

Brielle reached for another bolt, only to find that she was out. Alarm flooded her veins as the carnage continued below her. Citric's warning echoed in her mind, but she couldn't just sit here, safe, and do nothing while others fought around her. Perhaps once she was content for others to fight for her, but not anymore. She was well aware she was no soldier, she had barely any training in how to fight or defend herself, but that didn't mean she wasn't deadly.

Eve's arm sang with the reverberations of impact as steel repeatedly met steel. She dodged, parried and struck with brutal efficiency. The soldiers of the Northern army were well equipped, their bodies protected by expensive armor, but it weighed them down and slowed their movements. Wearing only cotton and thick leather, she was small and light and fast. She knew where the gaps were between their metal plates, the weak spots of their scales. Her blows were short and sharp and targeted. If this was only a third of the Northern army, she knew she could not afford to be wasteful with her efforts.

She was aware of the tree roots and fungal networks conversing through their electromagnetic fields, apprising each other of the state of battle. She had never realized that trees were such social beings, but now their chatter was like a constant white noise in her head. The woodland was hungry for blood and retribution. It had armed itself well. Where she could, Eve maneuvered the soldiers toward the trees, slamming their bodies up against the trunks so that the woodland could claim its share. The leaves of the trees were now spiky and pumped full of noxious toxins. The bark on the trees had split into thousands of tiny needles filled with poison. The soldiers that brushed up against them with their hands or other exposed parts of their bodies would not live. Those that were fortunate enough to avoid contact with their skin would not be immune to the burst of gas that the trees released upon impact. The scent was attractive, light and floral, but it was also lethal.

Eve slashed through the enemy like she was scything wheat in a field. With every strike she grew more carless and impatient. She needed to get this done and return to Alkhiem, where the real battle would be fought. Through the blood bond, she could feel that Citric was already making his way there, but the soldiers needed her too, as their hunna and queen, to lead them. She needed to—

CRACK.

Eve's head whipped to the side as she was thrown off balance by a devastating blow. Her vision swam and the copper tang of blood filled her mouth. She stumbled back a few steps before recovering her footing, positioning her body to the defensive. Her sword was already raised in anticipation to deflect the blow, but it still rattled her entire body when it came. The soldier hammered her with brutal, unrelenting strikes designed to hack through her. It took all she had just to withstand them and keep her footing. There was no opportunity to slip in a quick strike of her own. She needed to get the upper hand somehow, break his momentum, but just as she thought it, the sword was knocked from her hand and a fist to the face had her flying into the dirt. Eve spit a mixture of soil and blood out onto the ground before quickly rolling onto her back, ready to defend herself with her bare hands if necessary. As the soldier loomed over her, she reached for her daggers, but before she could whip them out, a dagger had already buried itself in the soldier's throat. His eyes bulged as blood spluttered from his wound before he slammed down to the ground.

Eve pushed herself up on her elbows and glanced behind her to find Brielle breathing heavily, a vicious, satisfied smile on her face.

"I didn't miss," she called out, triumphant.

A little dazed, Eve got to her feet and retrieved her sword before casting another mystified look in Brielle's direction. She had somehow acquired the sword of a Northern soldier and was trying to engage in combat, but she lacked any upper body strength and her footing was all wrong. Eve raced to her side and sliced open the back of the soldier's torso beneath his breastplate. A cry of anguish tore from his lips before he crumpled to the earth.

"What do you think you're doing? You are going to get yourself killed." Her eyes blazed as she gripped the bloody sword in her hand. She had no time to deal with amateur heroics. "Stay behind me."

"Fight beside me," Brielle countered. "Fight with me."

Eve held her stare for a moment, assessing her weak body, her awkward fighting stance, and her unbreakable spirit. After a heartbeat of silence, she dipped her head in acknowledgement, took up position at her right flank and together they went to war.

CHAPTER THIRTEEN

T he horse bolted. Spooked by the arrow that whizzed past its head and spurred on by a kick of Henri's boots to its ribs, it ran like it was being chased by the devil himself. Which wasn't too far from the truth. The sounds of war erupted behind him: the scream of metal against metal, the roar of battle lusting, blood-thirsty men. Henri seized Ele tightly to his chest and clenched his thighs, keeping them fastened to the horse as best he could. If they fell at this speed, they would die instantly. He tried to wrestle back control by yanking on the reins, but the horse was too agitated. As Alkhiem came into view ahead, something about the scene did not look quite right.

The ground.

On the outskirts of the camp, the ground looked too neat, too perfect. It was almost too late before Henri realized why. He had no time to try to guide the horse around it, so he braced himself by leaning forward and lifting them both out of the saddle, their legs the only points of contact with the animal. The horse must have sensed the trap too because it fully extended its back and legs, building speed in the gallop right up to the last second before it jumped. Henri did his best to make them stay with the horse and match its center of gravity, aware that if they didn't, they would either fall forward or fall down into the lethal pit below.

The horse landed hard, gravity knocking Henri back into the saddle with a bruising thud. Relief washed over him as he pulled the animal to a halt. It must have been exhausted because it obeyed without protest. Looking behind them, Henri could see it clearly now. The outline of the trenches were covered over with leaves and branches, but beneath them lurked certain death, probably in the form of spears.

At the thundering sound of hooves, Henri glanced up to see that King Heroux and the Northern army were barreling toward them. Ele immediately slipped out from beneath his arms, jumped to the ground and ran. Henri couldn't blame him. His hands were still bound with rope, but he slid to the ground, his eyes darting frantically around the city of tents. It was silent. Abandoned. Perhaps all of Citric's men were already in the woods fighting the Northern army. If that was the case, the battle would be swift and decisive and they would not be the victors.

Standing in the open ground, the city of tents behind him, Henri watched as the army hurtled toward him. He knew he should run. He was in no condition to fight, not that he had a weapon. Instead, he stood firm and watched them come. If they focused on him, perhaps they would not see the trap that was waiting for them.

"Master."

Henri turned to find Ele running toward him, breathless, carrying an axe.

"What are you doing?" Henri scolded him. He had thought the boy had run to safety.

Ele used the head of the axe to cut through the ropes of Henri's bound hands and then he handed him the weapon.

"It was all I could find."

Henri nodded in understanding before placing a hand on the boy's shoulder. "Now get to safety."

"No, master." Ele shook his head frantically. "I want to stay and fight with you."

The Northern army was almost upon them. The boy's features hardened in firm resolve as if he had decided that he was prepared to die on this battlefield beside his master. The moment felt eerily familiar. Months ago, Ele had seen an army of thousands marching for his sovereign and he had not fled. He had risked his life to warn Henri, even when the odds of survival seemed impossible. Henri owed the boy his life. Several times over, it seemed. But he refused to let the boy's bravery and loyalty cost him his life.

"I can't protect you like this, now go!" Henri shoved him, just enough for him to stumble backwards a few steps, but the boy recovered to stand his ground.

"I will not leave you."

"You will! That is an order. Serve me by living."

The boy's face crumpled at the command, not in fear but in torn regret and sadness. "Yes, my prince."

Henri blinked at the word as he watched the boy flee. He turned his attention back to the army just in time to see the first line of horses spill into the trenches. They released screams of agony as beast and rider were impaled on the sharp spears. It only took a moment for the rest of the army to realize what had befallen their comrades. They halted and held back, scanning their surroundings for traps.

They didn't need to look far. The deafening crescendo of a thousand soldiers ripped through the woodland as the Southern army descended upon them. They appeared to come out of nowhere, hiding from within Alkhiem and the woodland surrounding it. Both sides met in a thundering clash of steel and blood and bone. Henri watched in awe as the battle exploded around him. He lifted his axe to defend himself, but that was all he could manage. He barely had the energy to stand.

The butchery raged around him. He had seen war before, fought in large battles, but he had never seen anything like this. It was a brutal scene of mad carnage. In the distance he spotted more Sirasindans racing toward them from two different directions. He recognized Citric and Leif leading the charge, their paths eventually crossing to merge as one. They ran side by side as they rushed into the bowels of death. He had witnessed it before, the bond that formed between soldiers, a bond forged through death. It was still a sight to behold, though.

In the midst of the slaughter and devastation, Henri's thoughts turned to Brielle. He hoped she was still safe in the Southern Kingdom. But for her to remain safe, they would need to be victorious today. If they weren't, King Heroux would march on to the Southern Kingdom and execute everyone who had defied him. Brielle would be high on that list. He couldn't let that happen.

No, this fight ended here. Now.

Across the battlefield, Henri saw King Heroux tearing a path through the bodies of men. His brutality was impressive. Henri could see how he had become the famed conqueror king. His endless war campaigns had taught him much and now he fought with the skill of a seasoned warlord, certain of his victory and insatiable in his lust for more. As if sensing his gaze upon him, King Heroux turned to spear him across the distance with a ruthless stare. It promised revenge for his betrayal and a punishing death for his stubborn determination to outlast the King's ministrations.

King Heroux stalked toward him, cutting down everyone who dared to cross his path. Henri gripped the throat of his axe in both hands and took up a defensive stance. If he was going to die today, he was sure as hell going to take this bastard with him. King Heroux lunged as he swung his sword at him and Henri blocked the blow with the shoulder of the axe. The King's assault was relentless. Henri was at a disadvantage fighting with an axe instead of a sword. He was not used to the weapon and had to think how to best wield it before he parried and blocked each blow. But one advantage the axe did have over a sword was that it delivered a blow with greater force. Henri deflected another strike before smashing the butt of the axe up into the King's face. He took that split second where the King was off balance and slashed the blade of the axe low across his thighs.

The King roared even as he struck back, the gaping bloody wounds not seeming to slow him down at all. In fact, they only fueled his rage. His repetitive strikes hacked dents into the shaft of Henri's axe, sending chips of wood flying. Henri knew that the moment his weapon splintered, he would be dead. He almost collapsed beneath the battering, but then a dagger flew past and sliced the edge off the King's ear, making him stumble backwards in surprise. Henri pounced and swung his axe in an overhead arc that the King barely had time to block. The King pushed him backward and they broke apart, Henri conceding ground. His chest heaved rapidly as he tried to take in as much air as he could. He could feel his body was about to disintegrate. There wasn't much more he could withstand.

"Looks like you aren't very useful after all, prince. You're a weak heir and an even more pathetic soldier."

The King cocked his head as he circled Henri, studying him with a critical eye. He knew that Henri was on the verge of collapsing. He knew every wound, every bruise on Henri's body because he had inflicted all of them. He was an alpha predator, circling injured prey, savoring the seconds before the kill.

"I promised if you betrayed me, I'd carve out your heart. I intend to do it very slowly, so you can feel every second of it."

Henri gripped the axe tighter, the skin of his knuckles splitting with effort. When the King dove forward he swerved, narrowly missing the edge of the blade. He threw his elbow back into the King's face and heard a satisfying crack before he delivered a swift kick to the King's right thigh. King Heroux released a frustrated grunt of pain. His pants were soaked with blood from the wounds, adrenaline clearly the only thing keeping him moving. This time when the King swung his sword, Henri locked the head of his axe around the blade and yanked. The sword wrenched out of his hands and flew across the ground. In a split second that actually felt like it lasted longer, Henri pivoted, bringing the axe around to hack into the King's neck. The blade lodged itself firmly in skin and muscle and tissue. Henri stalled at the sight of it, his mind catching up to his body. The King fumbled as if he was trying to reach for a weapon he didn't have, but then he folded to his knees, a look of shock and confusion on his face.

Of course, he had expected to win. He had expected to live through this battle, claim victory and move on to his next campaign. To be cut down by such an unworthy adversary was unthinkable. The world belonged to men like him. Rage kindled in Henri's body, building like heavy storm clouds on the horizon. This man had killed his father. Stolen his kingdom and robbed Brielle of hers. Turned his best friend into a monster. Tortured him for days and threatened to kill everyone he cared about. Leaving the axe buried in his neck, Henri walked over to a nearby fallen soldier and retrieved a knife from his belt. He returned to the King, gripped his long beard in one hand and sliced it off.

Brielle stood paralyzed in horror and astonishment as she watched Henri jerk the axe free from King Heroux's neck only to swing it again, dismembering his head from his shoulders in one swift cut. Her mouth fell open and her stomach roiled, threatening to spill its contents on the ground, as Henri gripped the long, blonde hair of the head in his fist.

The moment Brielle and Eve had arrived with the others, the battle was already gory chaos. She scanned the faces of the soldiers searching for Citric but somehow her eyes immediately locked onto Henri. He was engaged in a brutal fight with King Heroux, a fight that he looked like he was losing. She had taken out one of her daggers and waited for the opportune time to strike, but she had missed, only managing to graze the King's ear. When she reached for another dagger, she realized with panic that she had none left. Gripping her sword, she ran to his aid, but before she could reach him, Henri had lodged his axe into King Heroux's neck. It was so incredible she had halted in her tracks, her eyes refusing to believe it. The man who had taken everything from her, who had conquered nation after nation and murdered hundreds of thousands of innocent people, was on his knees about to die.

It didn't seem possible.

It didn't feel real.

Brielle stumbled forward to Henri, her thoughts hazy. The moment he looked up and saw her, his eyes widened in shock. Her expression mirrored his as she took in the sight of his battered face. His left eye was heavily swollen, his right eye was bloodshot, and his skin was a patchwork of bruising. Citric had said that he believed King Heroux was torturing him, but to see the evidence of it was shocking. Sickening. She wanted to touch him, wrap her arms around him, but if this was what his face looked like, his body was probably worse.

"Henri—" Her voice cracked.

"What are you doing here? You're not meant to be here."

"My people are here, fighting. Where else would I be?"

His lips parted as if he was going to answer, but the words didn't come. Instead, his gaze roamed over her, taking in the leather armor and men's pants she wore, the sword in her hand and the flecks of blood on her skin.

"You're right. Let's end this."

They looked around at the butchered bodies littering the ground, the soldiers still engaging in ruthless combat, and the general devastation of war. Henri picked something up off the ground before walking over to a nearby wooden cart and jumping up on it. Brielle followed to stand beside the cart as Henri lifted the King's head in the air.

His voice bellowed across the battlefield. "King Heroux is dead! The king who invaded and conquered your lands is dead! The battle is over!"

It took several repeated cries before the soldiers began to take notice and the sounds of war died down. Everyone turned to Henri, their eyes feasting on the dead king's severed head. Brielle forgot to breathe as she waited to see what would happen next. Would they care? Perhaps the soldiers recruited from conquered lands would throw down their weapons, but King Heroux's men would surely keep fighting. After all, there was land to be claimed and reputation to be gained. But the Northern soldiers didn't move, they simply stared in disbelief. Or perhaps they were weighing up their options.

Then Henri held up what looked like a severed beard, with two long blood-stained plaits. King Heroux's beard, she realized in revulsion.

"I have cut off the long-bearded hair of a Merovian king. I have removed his claim to kingship, and I claim his lands for myself."

Brielle's head whipped up to Henri in shock. He was claiming King Heroux's lands, his entire empire.

Including his armies.

"Stand down," he ordered, his tone fatally low. It promised death to anyone who disobeyed.

Brielle almost dissolved in relief to watch the soldiers sheath their swords, patiently awaiting the orders of their new king. The Sirasindans and Southern soldiers remained armed and wary, but they did not take the opportunity to strike. Through the mass of soldiers, Brielle saw Eve making her way toward them, Leif not far behind her.

And then she saw him.

Brielle's heart staggered in relief as she watched Citric move through the crowd. He looked menacing, covered in blood and smeared in paint, his muscles rippling with adrenaline and glistening with sweat. Eve came to stand in front of the cart, flanked either side by Citric and Leif. Brielle tore her eyes away from Citric to notice Henri looking down at them, his expression hard.

"I will withdraw my men from Sirasinda as soon as I am able," he promised, his tone formal. Turning his voice on everyone else, he shouted, "All lands seized by King Heroux shall be restored to their rightful people. All men recruited from conquered lands will be free to return home."

Hundreds of soldiers cried out in gratitude, banging their swords against their breastplates, while hundreds of their Merovian comrades looked around in bewilderment.

"But for now, we will take our dead and return to the Northern Kingdom."

Henri jumped down from the wagon and strolled over to Citric. "The head of your enemy," he said as he presented it to him. "Do with it what you wish."

"Eve leads our people now," Citric said and deferred to her.

If Henri was surprised, he didn't show it.

Eve took the head from him, satisfaction edging her mouth. "What happened to starting a new life away from all of this?"

"I intend to. Except I intend to do it from a position of power, where I can protect the ones I care about." His words had an iron edge. His gaze was sharp as it returned to Citric. "Seems like I owe you my life."

"Does this make us even for the times I almost killed you?" Citric's lips curved in a provocative smile.

"Almost," Henri returned, but it sounded like a warning.

Brielle had been hovering nearby, but now she stepped forward, sensing the tension between them. Before she could try to diffuse it, Ele came barreling toward them. Henri turned just in time to catch the boy as he threw his arms around Henri's waist and buried his head against his chest. Henri held the boy close, his hand clutching the back of his head.

Eve's gaze cut to hers and an imperceptible look crossed her face before she turned to give orders to her men to help the Northern soldiers gather their dead. Leif walked away but Citric lingered, his stare fastened on Brielle's face as if he never wanted to look away. She could see everything in those intense eyes because she felt it too. Relief that he had survived, that he was unharmed, along with an overwhelming urgency to find a private corner to relish in their mutual survival. She desperately wanted to tear at his clothes, capture his vicious mouth with hers, and fill herself with him until the world around them ceased to exist. A hot flood of desire pulsed through her, demanding satisfaction. The sex would be rough and hard and ecstasy.

"We will return you to the Sodisce on our way back to the castle."

Henri's words snapped her back to her senses, though her cheeks were still flushed. The boy pulled away from him, his expression confused.

"No, my king, I wish to come with you."

"It's too dangerous. The Merovians are not going to take kindly to a foreign ruler and they'll seek revenge for me murdering one of them. Claiming his empire was the easy part. Keeping it will be more difficult. Besides, the Sodisce needs the *Petit Maitre*."

"You need me more. You will need brave friends you can trust."

A string of emotions pulled at his features: sadness, regret. As if those words held particular meaning for him. She could see him struggling to remain composed, like his heart was being wrung out. Henri cupped the boy's cheek in his hand and then nodded in acceptance.

"Then you will be the first on my council of trusted advisers."

El's face lit up with wonder and excitement.

"Now, go help the Northern soldiers gather their dead. I need to speak to Brielle for a moment."

"Yes, my king."

The boy ran off and Henri walked over to her, taking her hand in his to lead her away. Brielle glanced over her shoulder at Citric to find him watching them. He looked sad, uncertain. She frowned, confused, but he turned away to join the other men and Brielle turned back to Henri. They were now a short distance away from everyone, affording them some semblance of privacy. Henri took her other hand in his and looked down at them as if they were a puzzle he was trying to solve.

"What is it? What's wrong?" she asked, worry seeping into her voice. His trepidation was making her nervous.

"I want you to come with me." The words came out in a sudden rush and Brielle's brows shot up in surprise. "Be my queen. Rule beside me. We will return the conquered lands to their rightful people, but King Heroux's empire is vast, we will still have a sizeable kingdom to rule over. You could be queen of all of it."

Brielle stilled, stunned. She didn't know the details of King Heroux's lands or his wealth, but she knew it was extensive. A year ago, she would have coveted such a proposal. A king with considerable land and wealth and power was asking her to rule beside him as an equal. It was everything she had ever wanted. Suddenly Citric's expression made sense. He must have suspected what Henri was going to offer her and he was worried she would accept. Now Henri was looking at her with a similar pained expression, as if he was worried she was going to turn him down.

"Are you sure you want this?" she asked, delaying her answer a little longer. "To be king, I mean. You never wanted to be king. What's changed?"

"I lost my kingdom. I abandoned my people to a tyrant. I let down a queen when she needed me the most."

Brielle squeezed his hands as tears welled in her eyes. She hated seeing him like this. She wondered if he had been torturing himself just as much as King Heroux had been torturing him.

"I was forced to watch the people I loved die right in front of me, powerless to stop it. I refuse to be powerless again. If I need to become a king to protect the ones I love, then I will become a king. But I will need a queen by my side. You are still the most powerful queen I know."

She choked out a laugh and he forced a strained smile.

"Where were you a year ago?" she teased.

He chuckled. "Waiting for you."

Their eyes met and her heart broke to see the way he was looking at her. With hope. With love.

"I can't." Part of her couldn't believe the words coming out of her mouth, that she was turning down a chance to have everything she ever thought she wanted. And yet a larger part of her recognized the truth in those two words. "These are my people. This is my kingdom, even though I'm no longer its queen. I belong here."

Henri's expression softened in sadness, as if he had already known that would be her answer.

"You choose him," he concluded, as if he had finally solved the puzzle.

"I'm not sure it was ever a choice."

Henri lifted his chin as if biting back words he wished he could say. He let her hands slip from his.

"Henri, I'm sorry," Brielle pleaded.

"Don't be. As long as he makes you happy and keeps you safe, that is all I ask. But if you ever change your mind or need a powerful ally across the sea, I will always answer your call."

Brielle nodded, pride gleaming in her eyes, before a playful smile curved onto her lips. "Then we shall be friends."

"The best." He winked.

"I may even visit your court one day."

"I'll be waiting."

Brielle's features shifted into seriousness. "You are going to be a great king."

Henri stepped forward to place a light kiss on her cheek. "Thank you."

⚜

Citric led a group of soldiers, a mix of Southern, Northern, and Sirasindan, through the woodland so that each could collect their dead. The men pushed the wagons along in silence, hauling bodies up into the carts as they went, packing each of them neatly on top of each other like sacks of grain.

Nobody ever spoke about the aftershock of war. Nobody acknowledged the clean-up that took place after all the killing was done. The fact that the ground was littered with vacant bodies that hours ago had been living, breathing men. The fact that the air was putrid with the stench of their blood, spilled organs, and rotting flesh. In the alehouses, soldiers would boast of their kills, their bravery, their battle scars. Young men were easily excited by talk of war and old men were given to exaggeration. But Citric had seen enough of war to know the truth. There was no dignity in a violent death. These men being loaded into the cart, their limbs sprawling over each other, had all fought bravely. Though most were the enemy, he could give them that much respect. Death, after all, was a great equalizer.

There were times when Citric had stood on a battlefield in the aftermath, surrounded by death and decay, and contemplated the waste of war. It enraged him and left him feeling hollow at the same time. He had not expected to feel that way today. He had expected to feel overwhelming joy and relief and liberation. Perhaps his emotions had less to do with the war and more to do with how it had been won. It was a moment that had played out a thousand different ways in his dreams every night since he was a boy. But even he could not have seen this coming. After generations, his ancestral lands had finally been returned to his people. History had been righted. And yet the sweetness of that victory was dulled by the thought that she might not be a part of his future.

Henri's claim on King Heroux's empire had appeared to be an impulsive move, a desperate but clever way to end the war without further bloodshed. But it only took Citric a second to realize that it had been his strategy all along. Henri could not reclaim his father's kingdom, he recognized the land was not rightfully his, but he could overthrow a tyrant king and take his kingdom. Citric had to give him credit. In one bold move, he had not only made himself a king but one of the wealthiest, powerful kings in the lands. He could offer Brielle everything she had ever wanted, the life she was born to live. Citric could offer her nothing that would compare. A city of tents. A broken, fractured land in need of healing.

His heart.

It would not be enough.

He would let her go. She didn't owe him anything and he wouldn't beg her to stay. He had declared himself hers, but that did not make her his. She deserved everything she wanted, everything Henri could give her and more.

The woodland pricked at his senses and Citric turned around. Brielle was standing a short distance away, her approach hesitant, her expression curious. He hadn't realized it, but he had wandered away from the soldiers collecting their dead, instinctively seeking out a moment of solitude in the woods. He would have asked her how she had managed to find him, were it not for the trail of small white wildflowers blooming behind her and pooling at her feet.

Noticing his gaze, she looked down at them and shrugged, somewhat perplexed. "The wood. It somehow knew I was looking for you and led me here."

"It has always been fond of you. I think it recognized from that first night that you would be the one to restore it."

Brielle walked over to a tree and rested her palm against it, as if she were trying to communicate with it. Citric felt her touch, as did the wood.

"I didn't do it alone."

He kept his expression neutral, leashing every last emotion that was threatening to burst through him. But she was just so fucking beautiful, the sight of her threatened to ruin him.

"Henri asked you to be his queen." His tone was even, as if he was stating a fact not asking a question.

"Yes."

Citric averted his gaze so she wouldn't see the hurt and fury in his eyes. It was a bitter irony that on the day he achieved everything he had dedicated his whole life to, he would lose the one thing he desired for himself.

"You told me once that history is written by the victors and you doubted my name would be recorded."

He winced at the memory and shook his head. "I was a fucking idiot."

He couldn't believe that he had not seen the force of nature standing right in front of him.

"I don't care if history remembers my name, just as long as you never forget me."

Citric closed the distance between them in a heartbeat, unable to resist the magnetic pull of her. She was gravity and he had fallen hard. Fuck, he had thrown himself down willingly. Her back pressed against the tree as his body crowded hers, but he stopped short of touching her, despite his desperate longing to. He couldn't stop his eyes from staring at her mouth, though. Her lips parted in anticipation, begging to be devoured. If he could not have her, surely she would allow him to take one last kiss from those intoxicating lips. He didn't know if he would be able to walk away otherwise.

Their breath blended as he inhaled her scent. "I could never forget you."

She was trembling now. He could feel her eyes on his face, but he couldn't bring himself to meet her gaze. He was afraid of what she might see there.

"I told him I belonged here," Brielle whispered, the breath of her words caressing his lips. "With you."

His eyes cut to hers and an endless moment passed between them. Days spent in a flourishing woodland, years passed in peace and prosperity, a lifetime of memories, magic, and love. Citric kissed her viciously and she opened herself to him, her tongue slipping in to provoke his. Desire vaulted through him and his length strained, hard. He pushed himself into her hips and she released a moan against his mouth. The sound unleashed him. It was the most seductive sound in the world. This woman. She would be his ruination and his salvation, and he would willingly submit to her for the rest of his days.

By dusk, the dead had been collected and the Northern army had left the woodland. Eve had ordered Leif to go with them to over-see their eventual withdrawal from Sirasinda. She believed Henri when he gave her his word that they would leave, but she was also not taking any chances.

Eve wasn't surprised at Henri's brisk demeanor toward her or his cold departure. They had both played the game and done what was necessary to win. She would not hold it against him, even if he seemed to hold it against her. Though she didn't say it to his face, she genuinely wished him well and hoped he found happiness. He was a complicated man, but a good one at his core. She didn't yet know what kind of king he would make. Only time would tell.

At Alkhiem, the scent of smoke and ash laced the air. The Southern soldiers had built pyres to burn their dead, while the Sirasindans had dug a long trench and buried their people deep beneath the soil. The woodland welcomed them. Over time their bodies would disintegrate into the earth, feeding the insects and the worms, providing sustenance for new life to grow in its place. Their souls had already left their bodies to join the spirit world. She felt the ancestors receiving them, enveloping them in love and peace beyond mortal understanding.

Eve swore she could feel her own ancestor walking beside her, along with all the other hunnas who had lived before her, as she led her people into the ceremonial room within the ruins. The collective strength of the hunnas had fortified her on the battle-field today, of that there was no question. Her body had never moved that way before, with such other worldly power, agility, and endurance. She hoped today's victory provided them with some long-awaited justice and that they could finally now find peace. Her thoughts fell to Rowan and the beaming grin he had tossed over his shoulder at her before he rode away to battle, never to see her or his home again. Eve had been just a girl then, confused about the world and her place in it. Now she was a woman and she knew exactly who she was meant to be.

Mother to her people.

The first hunna in generations.

Her people, reunited with their loved ones again, assembled around her as she stood in the middle of the ceremonial room. Even some of the Southern soldiers were curious enough to step inside, though they hovered by the door, wary of what pagan ritual they might witness.

"Today," she began, her voice ringing loud and clear among the ruins, "we have reclaimed what was taken from us. This land is no longer divided into Northern or Southern Kingdoms, but united and restored as Sirasinda."

The people stirred as a mix of emotion filled the room. Generations of longing, anguish, anger, and hope had culminated in this historical day of deliverance. Eve saw it in their faces as she looked around. From the old ones who could not believe they had lived to see this blessed day, to the young ones who were wise enough to know that they were witnessing something worth remembering. Her gaze caught on Citric and Brielle, who stood together at the front of the crowd, their hands intertwined. Citric dipped his head in encouragement, a flicker of pride behind his cool features.

Eve felt the familiar bite of jealousy and the dull ache of her broken heart, but she returned her focus to her people. "It is our privilege to care for this land, to defend it, and preserve it so that generations to come may also thrive. As your hunna, and with the help of the spirits, I promise to do everything in my power to lead us all into a new age of peace."

Eve unsheathed her sword, still crusted with the blood of the enemies it had cut down. She held it out in front of her, horizontal, so that all could bear witness. Running her hand across the outer edge of the blade, she clenched her fingers into a fist and held it above the steel. Her blood ran down in rivulets and hissed as it hit the surface. The sword consumed her blood ravenously, as if it had been starved for thousands of years. The blade shimmered in the evening twilight and the color shifted like glass beneath the sun's rays, bursting into a million different shades, a rainbow of light.

A wave of power suddenly detonated from it and the earth itself began to move beneath their feet. Eve felt every molecule of it, like vibrations in her soul, as the land healed and regenerated itself. It siphoned strength from her ancestors and lured the blood from her veins until it built and recharged like clouds forming lightning in the sky. The land had been reborn. The ground pulsed with new life like a steady heartbeat.

The ground settled and the room fell to silence, but she could still feel the residual echoes of power thrumming inside her. The people turned to each other in astonishment and embraced one another with cries of joy and tears staining their faces. There would be celebrations tonight unlike any they had ever had before.

It was strange witnessing the dawn of a new future, being a part of history as it unfolded before her eyes. This day would live on in infamy. The stories would be passed down for generations, told to babes from the moment they entered this world. Hopefully in time, the scars and trauma of history would fade and life would simply be that—life.

"That's an impressive sword you have there."

Eve turned to find Brielle standing in front of her, Citric by her side.

She schooled her features and tried to force a smile. "You fought well today."

"You fought?" Citric's expression turned serious as he looked down at Brielle.

"Of course she fought," Eve intercepted. "She's not useless. You will need more training, though, your footwork is terrible."

Brielle's lips twitched in amusement. "I heard that a long time ago, hunnas would choose warriors to protect them. Maybe if I train hard enough, I could be your gureira."

Eve's brows shot up in surprise as she fumbled for a reply. "Maybe."

"I did save your life," Brielle pointed out.

"Perhaps until then you could be my adviser." The words left her mouth before she could call them back. She hadn't meant to say them out loud, but the thought had crossed her mind and though she was loath to accept it, it remained true. Eve cleared her throat and tried to recover. "I have little experience ruling or leading people, so I would appreciate any advice you could give me."

Brielle returned a knowing smile. "I can do that."

EPILOGUE

B rielle tucked the blanket in, making sure it was snug around the babe's body as it lay in the shade on the picnic rug. Her little face was smooth and squishy, slightly pink, but perfect in every way. Sienna smiled wistfully as she watched her daughter sleep. Brielle couldn't help but mirror the joy on her face. She loved seeing her friend so happy.

"It's peaceful here," Sienna remarked, her gaze drifting up to take in the sprawling white oak tree under which they sat, just outside of Alkhiem. She leaned back to rest against Jameson's chest as he sat behind her. He wrapped his arms around her waist and kissed the top of her head.

"It is." Brielle drew in a deep breath, basking in the peppery scent of the woodland.

This particular spot was one of Brielle's favorite places to come when she needed a moment of quiet reflection. Much had changed in the months since the battle. Across the entire breadth of the country, the land was growing more fertile every day. Farmers had since returned to their abandoned fields to plant crops in the hopes of a good harvest. The refugees in the western camp near the Southern castle had also returned to their homes, grateful to resume their lives in peace. With the wealth of the Northern and Southern Kingdoms combined, Citric had been able to maintain favorable trade deals that would comfortably see the people fed until the farmlands were ready to sustain them.

It still felt strange to Brielle, knowing that the Northern and Southern Kingdoms no longer existed. The castles mostly sat empty, except for when Eve used the halls to host large gatherings where anyone could attend, regardless of their class, wealth, or lineage. During such events, Eve would move freely among her people as their queen, but also as one of them. Because she listened to them and understood them, they adored her. It was astounding to watch. In the past few months, Brielle had observed society change before her eyes. The common folk had embraced the change, grateful for equality, but also just happy to have food in their bellies and peace on their doorstep. The nobility, on the other hand, had not adjusted so willingly. Jameson and Citric had had to swiftly deal with a few disorganized uprisings by disgruntled nobles, but it had been easily done.

"What does he write?" Sienna inclined her head to the letter in Brielle's hands.

Brielle's smile faltered as she looked down at the parchment. "That he is well and establishing himself as king in his new kingdom. He sends his love and congratulations to you both."

Sienna beamed and returned her attention to her daughter, but Jameson's features tightened in concern. A knowing look passed between them, along with a heavy silence. Henri had kept his word and left Sirasinda with the remains of King Heroux's men, bound by ship for their homeland. He wrote to her occasionally, each letter brief, with cursory statements and polite updates. Brielle knew he had to be going through an immensely difficult, perhaps even dangerous, transition. She wished he would be honest with her about what he was experiencing, share his problems and his fears, but she also understood why he wanted to keep things short and formal. He was keeping her at arm's length in order to guard his heart, a heart she had tenderly bruised if not broken. Even so, she couldn't stop her own heart from springing in a strange mix of hope, joy, and relief whenever she received a letter from him. She wrote back often, informing him of the smallest pieces of news, and including anything she thought he might find humorous to lighten his spirit. That included her progress in becoming a gureira.

Soon after embracing her role as hunna, Eve had chosen Willow and a few of the other women to become her gureira. At Brielle's request, they had agreed to train her so that one day Eve might ask her to join them. She didn't know if Eve ever would, but their relationship was slowly improving. Eve always asked Brielle to travel with her whenever she organized gatherings with the people, and she made a point to consult with her on how best to approach delicate matters with the nobles. Brielle hoped that in time the wounds would not be so raw between Eve and Citric and they might all find a new normal. Her heart twinged every time she saw how hard Citric was trying to manage their relationship. He wanted to give Eve the space she needed, while also fiercely protecting her and supporting her as his hunna. It was complicated. Brielle could only imagine how difficult it was for them, to be intimately aware of one another's emotions through the blood bond, and yet trying to salvage what they could from their relationship to maintain a foundation of friendship. It sounded painful and it looked excruciating.

Citric's voice disturbed her thoughts. "Is this where you all gather now to plot and scheme?"

Brielle grinned as she watched him stride toward them. The sight of him still made butterflies take flight in her stomach. To know that he was hers, only hers, still took her breath away. He took a seat beside her, his eyes lingering on her in a way that told her they had been parted for far too long. She felt her pulse quicken and she averted her gaze to try to cool the heat rising in her core.

"So." Sienna drew out the word slowly. "It has been several months now, should we be expecting a wedding ceremony anytime soon? As I recall, Brie, you were quite insistent on such things once."

Jameson's expression grew serious as he turned his focus on Citric. "Yes, do I need to challenge you to a fight to defend Brielle's honor?"

"Do you think you would win?" Citric shot back, amusement tugging at the corner of his lips.

Brielle laughed. "I appreciate the concern, and the threat of violence, but I can defend my own honor. With everything that has happened and so much still going on, Citric and I are just happy to take our time and enjoy what we have right now."

"It's the blood oath, right?" Jameson pressed. "You don't want to have him crawling around inside your emotions for the rest of your life. I understand, it's unpleasant."

Brielle snickered but Citric said, "She doesn't have to swear a blood oath if she doesn't want to."

Brielle's eyes latched on to Citric's, alight with the promise of forever. "But we both know I will."

Thank you so much for reading this book! I hope you enjoyed it. It would mean the world to me if you could leave a review on Amazon, Goodreads, or BookBub. One of the most important keys to an indie author's success is book reviews. Book reviews give social proof to potential readers that it is highly likely they will enjoy the book. With so many options for books out there, book reviews are a must! Especially at launch time. By leaving a review, you are helping other like-minded readers to find my book and thereby are greatly assisting me in building my career as an indie author. So thank you!

If you enjoyed this series, you'll love the FREE bonus scene from Citric's point of view which you can get by signing up to my mailing list. It's easy, just go to my website at www.clairebutlerauthor.com and sign up!

https://www.instagram.com/clairebutlerauthor/

Clairebutlerauthor | Facebook

Clairebutlerauthor (@clairebutlerauthor) | TikTok

ALSO BY CLAIRE BUTLER

To Reclaim A Kingdom

ABOUT THE AUTHOR

Claire wrote her first book before she knew how to write the alphabet. It consisted of scribbling on a page and having her sister illustrate the page next to it. She has since refined her books to include actual words. Claire has a background in Psychology. She loves writing young adult and new adult books because it allows her to explore coming of age themes, intense emotions, the formation and shifting of identities, the power of first love, and the enduring bonds of friendship. Claire lives in Australia with her husband and two children. She is obsessed with beaches, picnics, and sunshine. Often in combination with a good book. Her favorite authors include Sarah J Maas, Carissa Broadbent, Raven Kennedy, and Tahereh Mafi.

If you enjoyed this book, you'll love the FREE bonus scene from Citric's point of view which you can get by signing up to my mailing list. It's easy, just go to my website at www.clairebutlerau thor.com and sign up!
https://www.instagram.com/clairebutlerauthor/
Clairebutlerauthor | Facebook
Clairebutlerauthor (@clairebutlerauthor) | TikTok

Claire Butler Books - BookBub

ACKNOWLEDGEMENTS

I would like to thank Page Turner Publishing for your continued support and dedication. A huge thank you to my editor, Emily Marquart, for your valuable edits and feedback. Thanks as always to my literary soul sister for being my cheerleader and ideas woman. And lastly, but most importantly, I would like to thank you dear reader. I hope we meet again!

www.ingramcontent.com/pod-product-compliance
Lightning Source LLC
Chambersburg PA
CBHW030526120726
47904CB00005B/1649